CHANGED
by YOU

An Exposed Hearts Novel

KRISTIN MAYER

Changed by You (An Exposed Hearts Novel) / Kristin Mayer – 1st ed.
Library of Congress Cataloging-in-Publication Data
ISBN-13: 978-1-942910-33-6

VISIT MY WEBSITE AT
http://www.authorkristinmayer.com

This book is dedicated to the real husky, Mariah.
I know Sarah and Ben miss you every single day.
Thanks for being the inspiration for Kane's best friend.

Note to the Reader

Changed by You is written as a stand-alone novel. However, for the full reading experience, I would suggest starting with Drake and Alexa's story in *Intoxicated by You* and then reading Hayden and Kory's story in *Wrecked for You.*

CHAPTER
One

Kane

"Fuck, it's too cold for this shit." I slammed the door of my truck before clomping up the snow-covered stairs. Skagway was having one of the coldest winters in history. We were getting so much damn snow, and no one could keep up with it.

I glared at the door of the cabin my friend Butch had rented out. He'd asked if I could help the tenant with any problems while he was away. Of course, there would be problems with some stupid city slicker renting it out. Butch owed me big.

I'd gotten twenty text messages that the heater wasn't working. *Twenty* damn text messages. *Who sends that many?* I had just as many voicemails but hadn't listened to one. I'd gotten the picture from one text. No need for twenty.

Shit.

And it was some guy named Teske. *What kind of name is that?* I would have bet this guy wore some shiny-ass loafers with his fancy-ass business suit.

It was the middle of January. Normally, this was my chance to get away from all these jokers and recharge for the hunting season. Instead, I was here, dealing with a heating issue. Teske probably couldn't find the pilot light to save his life.

I have too much shit to do.

The FBI was on my ass to find a potential serial killer. There had been a wave of unsolved murders all throughout Alaska. The last one had been in Juneau, which was too fucking close for comfort. In exchange for my help, the FBI agreed to leave Kory and Hayden alone. No more questions about all the shit that had happened. No more bothering them, period. They weren't supposed to even look Kory and Hayden's direction.

So far, the feds had been true to their word.

But now they wanted me to pull a rabbit out of my ass and make a murderer appear out of thin air.

News flash—rabbits aren't found in people's asses. At least not in mine.

I needed a fresh crime scene to track. The ones I'd been brought to so far were already tainted. In some cases, it had been four months since the murder. The Juneau incident was four weeks previous. By the time they brought me on board, the crime scene had been ruined. Even worse, the pictures they'd taken were shit. The whole case was a disaster. And they had no idea who was behind it.

The agents had nicknamed him "Lumberjack Killer." Talk about being original and unique. It was hard to even say the name with a straight face.

What the fuck ever.

I pounded on the door of Butch's cabin. In the next second, it shot open.

"Oh, thank goodness you're here! I'm about to become a Popsicle."

For a second, I was frozen in shock. I hadn't been expecting a woman to answer the door. Butch had said there was only one occupant, and I'd assumed it was a guy. She had on so much fur it was hard to see anything else. Whatever was on her head looked like what Hollis, our local town doctor who'd relocated from New York, considered a Paul Bunyan hat on steroids. Time and time again, I'd tried to tell Hollis that Paul Bunyan wore a beanie, but Hollis was Hollis, and he stuck to his beliefs.

"I'm looking for Teske," I said.

"Who?"

"Teske." I took a deep breath; my patience was growing thin. "That's what the text said."

She laughed. "No, that was supposed to say Teale. But my hands were so cold my fingers probably slipped. And I can't see much with all this fur. I'm freezing."

I stepped inside the cabin and was disappointed to find it just as cold inside as it was outside. That wasn't good. "Why didn't you start a fire?"

The poor girl was shivering. "Umm... I couldn't find the remote."

The what? "Remote?"

"Uhh... yeah. At home, I push a button and *voilà*... let there be fire. There wasn't a remote or button to push."

Well, shit.

I wanted to laugh, but I kept a straight face. *A remote? Is she serious?* Even Hollis would have been able to figure out the fireplace needed wood and matches.

"Let me check out the heater."

"Okay."

I walked to the back of the cabin and found the furnace tucked away in a closet.

Double shit.

The thing was old as dirt. It looked like a rusted tin bucket. *What the hell?* Butch should have known better than to rent out his cabin without a properly working heater. I screwed around with it for a few minutes, but the damn thing was completely shot. We needed to come up with a Plan B.

I walked into the living room where Teale sat with another blanket wrapped around her. There was a hell of a lot of luggage stacked at the door. Maybe she hadn't had time to unpack. I thought she'd been here for a week or two already. *Oh well.* I couldn't concern myself with that.

"Well, the heater is shot. Let me see if I can find some space heaters. Then we can get a fire going. You should be good to go until I can get the parts to fix it."

"Okay... sure."

I went to search the different closets, and I heard the front door open and close. When I walked back into the living room, Teale was gone. From the window, I saw her heaving one of her suitcases into the bed of my truck.

No. No. No. This isn't going to happen.

I opened the door and yelled, "What are you doing?"

She folded her arms over her chest. The damn fur obscured her face even more. "I'm going anywhere but here. I'll freeze to death here. You do not want my death on your conscience. I'll come back to haunt you. I can be very scary."

For the second time that day, I'd wanted to laugh, but I

refused to allow it. Me laughing out loud in front of strangers never happened. She wasn't coming with me. *No way.* "No, we'll start a fire and get you a space heater."

She opened the passenger door. "Hey, puppy. Don't bite me. I just don't want to freeze to death." Mariah looked at me, her big blue husky eyes asking what was going on. I closed my fist to my side to let her know it was okay. I'd trained Mariah personally, and she was the best damn dog I'd ever had.

"Teale, be reasonable."

"Nope. I'm going with you."

This was getting us nowhere. I just had to get her back in the cabin and show her how warm I could make it. Calmly, I walked toward the truck. As I reached the door, the locks engaged.

Motherfucker.

She yelled through the window, "I need you to get the rest of my luggage first. Then I'll let you in the truck."

"Teale, get out of my truck." This was ridiculous, and I was tired of playing games.

"Nope. Sorry. Luggage first. I'm coming with you."

"Teale, I will get the cabin warm again."

She cocked her head to the side and smiled at me. "Will you please get my luggage, Mr. Foster? Then you can take me into town. The one thing I do know is that I'm not staying in this cabin a second longer."

I'd known her for five minutes, but this woman was going to be the death of me. *Fine.* I'd take her to the hotel and be done with this shit. The roads out to my cabin and Butch's were still terrible. It had taken me nearly ninety minutes to make it out there. Normally it was only about a twenty-five-minute drive. I gritted my teeth and hoped the main road into

5

town had been cleared enough for me to manage it. However, I knew I would be stuck in town for a minimum of a few days. From my cabin, it was still a thirty-minute drive to my parents' on a good day. If I had to, I could stay with Mom and Dad. *Butch, you owe me.*

I pulled out my phone and texted Dad. My parents' house was only about ten minutes or so from town.

Me: *Heard anything about the roads in town?*

Dad: *If you're thinking about coming into town, I wouldn't. They're still bad. One of the plow trucks broke down and the other needs a new blade.*

Just my luck. Skagway had two plows and both were out of commission.

Me: *Okay, thanks.*

Dad: *Everything okay?*

Me: *Yep. Just had a few errands to run.*

If my brothers got wind of this... well, it wouldn't be good. I had to talk sense into this woman. "Teale, let's talk."

She shook her head and pointed at the cabin. This woman was so damn stubborn. I grabbed all fifty million suitcases and threw them into the back of my truck.

Who the hell packs this much?

When the last bag was loaded, the locks disengaged, and I climbed in.

Teale pulled back her fur hat and looked at me. I was

stunned momentarily in the deep dark pools of her eyes. They were gorgeous.

Well, fuck me.

I was in way over my head.

CHAPTER
Two

Teale

I squared my shoulders and raised an eyebrow. "You can take me to the nearest hotel. I'll pay you for your time."

I held firm and refused to look away from the Alaskan brute who expected me to stay in that icebox. It might as well be a death trap. His eyes narrowed, but I kept my face stern. I'd dealt with more jackasses in my life than I cared to count. The man I'd rented the cabin from said Kane Foster was a good guy and would help if I needed it. Butch hadn't mentioned his less-than-friendly demeanor.

He shook his head and took a deep breath. "The roads aren't passable."

I waited, but he said nothing more. "What do you mean?"

"Exactly what I said. They aren't passable."

Again, I waited for him to elaborate. Nothing. Of course, I understood "not passable," but where would we go if the roads weren't drivable?

Why in the world did I think Alaska would be a good place to clear my head?

I cocked my head. "So, we're stuck here in your truck?"

"No, I can get to my cabin. But I can't get to the hotel. Even with chains, the snow is too deep." Kane peered out the window. "Fuck, it's starting to snow again. So unless you want to stay here, we best be heading that way."

It was clear he wasn't a fan of me going to his cabin. But staying here without heat wasn't an option. *What if I lose power?* Flustered, I blurted out the first thing that came to mind. "Are you a serial killer? Are you going to chop me up into itty-bitty bits? Not that you would tell me if you are. But I need you to be honest with me. And just know that I know kung fu."

The man actually cracked a smile. "Hell, woman, take a breath."

I folded my arms over my chest. "I'm serious. You don't seem like the serial killer type. But I'm sure people said the same thing about Ted Bundy, too. Just know I can karate chop and *hi-yah* with the best of them." I positioned myself in what I figured was an intimidating martial arts stance.

We were locked in a face-off. I swore this man was the grumpiest person I'd ever met. His face was unreadable. As a thank-you gift, I would definitely be ordering him a Mr. Grumpy Pants T-shirt. Maybe not, though. I needed to take a break from the online ordering.

"I'm not a serial killer."

I pointed to the road. "Then sally forth to your cabin as long as it has heat." I stopped to think for a moment. The cabin here had been a little rougher than I'd thought. "It does have heat, doesn't it?"

"It has heat." He lifted an eyebrow at me. "Sally forth?"

"I saw it in a movie one time—it's fun to say."

He scrubbed a hand down his face before putting the truck into gear. The snow crunched under his tires, and an awkward silence fell over the truck. The husky put her head on my headrest, and I froze. "Is she friendly? What's her name?"

"As long as you don't give her a reason to be mean, she's friendly enough. Her name is Mariah."

I reached my hand back on my shoulder and let her sniff me. "Hey, sweet girl. Don't bite me. I'm super sweet unlike your grumpy-pants dad."

"Grumpy pants?"

I shrugged. "You're a little rough around the edges."

"Do you always talk this much?"

"Pretty much."

When Kane turned out of the driveway, I gripped the door handle a little closer. The roads were worse than I'd expected. The truck seemed steady enough, but the ditch that had been visible on my drive up was no longer there, obscured by all the snow.

Talk about something to get your mind off it.

"So, maybe we should learn a little about each other since we'll be roomies while the weather is crap. I'll start. I'm Teale Delaney. I'm a figure skater. I love to order things online. My favorite food is Nutella on crepes with bananas. I'm allergic to coconut. And I'm a huge animal lover."

I stared at Kane, waiting for him to respond. Nothing. So I prompted him. "It's your turn."

"Kane. Guide. Food."

I hid my face in my hands and groaned. "Do you spend much time in civilization, or are you one of those hermit types who's forgotten how to communicate?"

His fingers gripped the steering wheel a little tighter. He seemed agitated. But he said nothing.

"Man, this is going to be fun."

No response.

When I felt Mariah's muzzle nudge my shoulder, I reached up to pet her. *Poor thing. She probably never gets any conversation besides, "Sit. Food. Stay."*

The snow was picking up, and our progress was slow. The entire time, though, Kane seemed completely in control. *Am I stupid for taking off with a person I don't know?* I pulled out my phone to text my mom.

Me: *Hey, I'm going to share my location with you. The snow is getting bad.*

Mom: *Did the guy come and fix the heat?*

Me: *The heater is shot. He's letting me come to his cabin until the roads clear and we can make it into town.*

Mom: *Are you sure that's wise?*

Me: *He seems legit. I have my mace in my purse. Don't worry, Mom.*

Mom: *That's what us moms do. I got the location. Check in often.*

Me: *I will. Promise. This town is like Mayberry. Everyone knows everyone. I think this guy's brother runs the local pub, The Red Onion. His name was Drake Foster. The guy I'm with is Kane Foster.*

Typically, I could remember names after only one introduction. It was something I'd had to learn to do in figure skating. Between all the judges and skaters, the amount of people I met over a weekend of skating seemed endless.

Mom: *I'm writing all this down. Does Kane have a number?*

Me: *I'll ask.*

"Do you have a number I can share with my mom?"
"Why?"
I rolled my eyes. "In case you're a serial killer. Duh! She wants your contact information since I'm going off with a strange man in the middle of a snowstorm."
Kane rattled off his number, and I texted it to my mom.

Mom: *Thanks, sweetheart. By the way, Mason called again.*

I groaned internally. Mason was the reason I'd left in the first place. I'd needed to clear my head after I'd ended things with him. It was time for me to figure out my next step in life. And I wanted to just be in the moment for a bit.

Me: *Don't tell him where I am.*

Mom: *I won't. Let me know when you get to Kane's place.*

Me: *I will. Love you, Mom.*

Mom: *Love you, too.*

My parents had always been supportive of me. Though they'd hoped things would work out between Mason and me, they'd never questioned me when I'd told them things were over. It still hurt too much to think about. His betrayal cut deep. At some point, I would share with them what had happened. Probably after I had a chance to clear my head in Alaska.

We turned onto another road that I assumed was a driveway because of the mailbox. After about five more minutes, we stopped in front of a cabin that nearly took my breath away. It was a little smaller than Butch's cabin, but it was gorgeous. I imagined when it wasn't buried in feet of snow, it was spectacular. The sight of it reminded me of a Kincaid painting. The world faded away. It was exactly what I was looking for to escape all my worries. Large windows provided the perfect view of the mountains all around us. This was a fairy tale. "Wow, your place is beautiful."

"Teale."

I blinked and turned around to face him. "Yes?"

"I swear to you you're completely safe. I can be an asshole, but you have nothing to worry about."

I hadn't realized how handsome Kane Foster was until that moment. With his short, dark hair and chiseled jaw, he was exactly what I'd pictured rugged Alaskan men to be like. I imagined he was muscular from long days of chopping wood. Well, I realized he probably wasn't a lumberjack, but still. This man was fit. And I was mesmerized.

Kane continued, "So, you're safe."

It seemed like a big thing for Kane to give me this kind of reassurance after all the one-word answers I'd received. I kept it light. "Thank you. I'll hold you to that." I stepped toward the back of the truck. "This time, I'll help you carry my luggage inside."

One side of his mouth turned up as he unlatched the gate. Maybe there was more to Kane Foster than I realized.

CHAPTER
Three

Lumberjack

I see her.
    I want her.
    I will make her mine.
    Foster is no match for me. I'm going to fuck up his shit so bad he won't know what hit him.
    By the time I'm finished with him, he'll have lost everything. Including her.

CHAPTER
Four

Kane

"I'm going to get the last of your shit," I called as I headed to the front door. It had only been five minutes since we arrived, and I needed the space.

"Do you need any help? I feel bad you're doing it all." She seemed sincere, but it was cold as hell. Maybe this would make up for being a complete dick earlier. That woman talked a million miles a minute. Even when the ride had been quiet, I swore her thoughts filled the air. But when she asked for my number to give to her mother, I knew I'd crossed the line and had acted like an asshole.

People weren't my thing. The only people I enjoyed being around were members of my family. It was easier that way.

The hairs on the back of my neck prickled, and I narrowed my eyes as I searched the tree line. I couldn't see anything out of the ordinary, but I'd take Mariah out later just to make sure. With the amount of snow we'd had, animals could venture closer to the homestead in search of food. Teale probably wouldn't enjoy running into a bear on the front porch.

My phone vibrated.

Unknown number: *This is Teale's mother, Hope Delaney. I really hope you're not a serial killer. But if you are, just know I will stop at nothing to find you.*

What is it with this damn family thinking I'm a serial killer? Fuckin' A.

I took a deep breath before responding. If it was a member of my family, I wouldn't appreciate an asshole answer in a situation like this.

Me: *I can assure you I'm not a serial killer. Check out Foster Unlimited online. It's my business. I will deliver your daughter to the hotel as soon as the roads clear.*

Hope: *Thank you. Teale sent me a picture of you so I have that as well. You're quite the rugged Alaskan.*

What the fuck?
Another text came through.

Hope: *I am happily married. Sometimes us Delaneys have a problem with word vomit.*

How the hell am I supposed to respond to that? Perhaps her entire family was certifiably insane.

Me: *Good to know.*

I shoved the phone back in my pocket. If it wasn't so cold, I'd camp outside to avoid this entire situation. My place was on the smaller side—an open floor plan with just two bedrooms and an office. There was no need for a huge place with lots of rooms. I liked it simple—just like my life.

I walked inside with the last of her bags. Teale jumped at the sound of the door closing, and she placed her hand over her heart.

"My word, you about gave me a heart attack."

"Sorry."

We stared at each other for a second; I had no idea what to say. Teale was still wearing her big, furry-ass jacket, and her dark eyes seemed to see right through me. I held her gaze when all I wanted to do was look away and go back outside. The last thing I needed was her to know she was getting to me.

She looked away, breaking eye contact first. "Your place is nice. And it's warm. The builder did an amazing job."

I took my gloves off and shoved them in my pocket before hanging my coat up on the rack. "Thanks, I built it."

Her eyes widened. "Like you *built it*, built it? With wood, a hammer, saws? That kind of build? Or you pointed to plans on a sheet of paper and said, 'Build me this'?"

Shit, she sounded just like Hollis. "I *built it*, built it."

Teale tilted her head to the side, her voice filled with sass. "Why are you so gruff?"

What the hell kind of question is that? This woman was feisty, and I liked that more than I should have. I shrugged.

Her mouth dropped open as if she had all of a sudden thought of something. "I see."

"What does that mean?"

"Nothing." She smiled, holding up her hands. "Relax.

We're just conversing."

"What does 'I see' mean?" Bullshit, we were just conversing. She was baiting me, and it was working. *Fuck.*

She winked. "Your secret is safe with me. But now I get why you're grumpy."

Is this woman on something? I felt like I was talking to a crazy person, but I was curious what she was getting at. Normally I'd never let this kind of thing bother me. "And why am I grumpy?"

"It's okay... I get it." She giggled. "You're probably just making up for not being ... you know... blessed. You stay grumpy to keep the girls away."

I stared at her, dumbfounded. A woman I barely knew—a woman I'd just met—had just accused me of having a tiny dick.

"For the record, I don't have a tiny dick."

"Okay." She laughed. Yeah, she had purposely baited me to get a reaction. Probably served me right for being an ass, but man it pissed me off. And it pissed me off more that I was now being placated. I was beginning to see red, replaying her words in my head, when she reached out and patted my hand. Her touch was light, and I swore something danced along my skin. "Let's change the subject."

I took a step back, and her hand dropped away. But my skin still felt as if she was touching me. I needed to clear my head. Again. "I'm going to go make sure we're set for the snow. When it snows this bad, the animals can have a hard time finding food, so they get more daring."

Her eyes darted to the wall. "Is that how you got all these animal heads? Did they come hungry to your front door, and then, *bam*, you clubbed them and made them wall art?"

19

I chuckled, which caught me off guard. This woman made my head spin. One minute, I wanted to shake the life out of her, and the next, I was giggling and shit. *Tiny dick.* I was still pissed about that. Apparently, she had a way of doing the opposite of what I expected. "Not exactly. I got them on different hunting trips over the years."

I'd amassed quite the collection, from musk ox to elk to bear.

She held her hand up to her mouth and whispered, "It's a little creepy having all these eyes staring at me."

I whispered back, "Don't make eye contact, and they won't bother you."

Teale laughed and rolled her eyes. "I'm going to unpack while you search for your next wall victim."

I ground my teeth, wanting to correct her but refusing to give her the satisfaction. I wasn't wasteful as a hunter, and nearly every part of the animal was used in some way. Members of the local tribes took the bones and made them into trinkets to sell. The Klukwan tribe was about two hours away. On most hunting trips, I brought my clients there to spend money on souvenirs and shit to support the tribe. The hunters there had taught me a lot throughout the years.

Turning on my heel, I grabbed my coat from the rack and stalked away like a little girl. My brothers were going to need to take me to the woodshed and beat me for the way I was acting.

"Come, Mariah."

I heard Teale call from behind me. "'Please.' It sounds less grumpy if you say 'Come, Mariah, please.'"

My dog looked up at me, clearly confused. Without saying a word, I walked outside. Mariah stayed with me, sniffing around as we walked. Nothing seemed out of the ordinary. The snow was getting deeper. As we approached the tree line, the hair on Mariah's neck stood up. I paused, searching the trees. "Is something out there?"

She gave a low growl.

"Easy."

There wasn't any sound, but she definitely had the scent of something. I searched my surroundings. Cautiously, I took a few more steps just inside the tree line. As we approached, I saw some fresh bear tracks about ten to fifteen feet away. But there were still no sounds, no signs of anything nearby. The tracks were semi-fresh—the newly fallen snow hadn't filled them in yet.

From the tracks, it looked like the bear had a limp in the way it walked. There wasn't any blood in the snow, so it was likely a healed injury. I needed to warn Teale so she didn't go traipsing around out in the wilderness. Not that such a scenario was likely, but Alaska could be deceiving. It was beautiful but dangerous if you weren't aware of the environment.

I turned back to the cabin, wondering what she was doing. A shadow passed by the window, and it looked like Teale was dancing. I shook my head to clear my thoughts.

I wasn't ready to go back in yet, so Mariah and I walked the entire perimeter. Nothing else looked out of place. With the cold temperatures, I'd taken down the outside cameras and brought them back inside. The extreme cold would ruin them. While I was outside, I pulled my truck into the garage and tried to find something else to do. At some point, I'd have to go back inside and face this dark-haired, no-more-than-a-buck-twenty-soaking-wet girl who had set my quiet, well-balanced life askew.

After putting the truck in the garage, I looked around for a minute. If things got bad, I had a snowmobile we could use. But hell, that would be beyond cold in these frigid temps, and with the snowdrifts, it was only more dangerous.

After I checked the rest of the supplies, the generator, gas, and anything else I could think of, I headed back inside. I'd manage to pass two hours. Two hours down, a hundred million to go.

When we walked back in, Mariah gave a great shake, flinging all the loose snow from her coat, and I slipped off my boots and put my heavy jacket on the coat rack. I glanced to my right and stopped in my tracks. "What the fuck?"

Teale appeared at the kitchen door. "It's better, don't you think? Now instead of creepy dead things staring at us with their judging eyes, they look more cheerful and hopefully enjoying the pose they'll be stuck in forever."

"I… you…"

"I think you're trying to say *thank you*. To which I'll reply *you're welcome.*"

I was speechless as I stared at my taxidermy. My prized mounts. The results of days of hunting, in some cases. I blinked again, making sure this wasn't some kind of nightmare.

Every wall mount was dressed in some sort of scarf, hat, or sunglasses. One was even wearing a necklace. The bear that stood near the fireplace was holding a glass. I was now officially in hell, and I could feel my blood pressure rising. Maybe I should leave her outside with the lame bear. That might be safer than staying in the cabin with me.

I scowled, needing to set this shit straight. "Teale, this isn't—"

"Dinner will be ready in ten. Go wash up." She disappeared back into the kitchen.

Have I just been dismissed? In my own house?

That shit wasn't going to happen. I stomped into the kitchen after her. "Teale, we need to set some ground rules."

She turned around, placing her hands on her hips. Fuck, she was wearing a pair of those clingy pants that left nothing to the imagination. And her top was just as tight. My mouth suddenly felt dry. Underneath all that fur she'd been wearing earlier was a body made for sin.

"And what ground rules are those?" She tilted her head and gave me a smile.

Snapping out of my daze, I dug deep for the fury. I leaned in a little closer. "Do not touch my shit."

I couldn't help it—my eyes darted to her chest for the briefest of moments.

She cocked her hip to one side. "Well, you're looking at my shit, so I guess that makes us even."

"What?"

"My eyes are right here, Mr. Foster." Teale pointed to her face with a playful smile.

This woman… this woman… *Fuck.* I had been checking out her shit for one tiny second, and she called my ass on it. This wasn't good. I wanted to shake some sense into her and fuck her at the same time. I needed out of this situation. Without a word, I turned, left the kitchen, and headed to my room. Maybe if I stayed in there until I was able to get to town, that would keep me sane.

I sat on the bed and ran my fingers through my hair.

Shit.

Fuck.

Damn.

The last time I let a girl have an effect on me, she ended up dead. After that, I swore I would never get involved again. And now, not four or so hours after meeting her, I wanted this woman. Yeah, I'd had one-night stands throughout the years, but those were out of town. I'd never gotten involved with anyone in my hometown. When I hooked up I never felt a connection. And now things were spiraling out of control fast.

CHAPTER
Five

Teale

At the slamming of his bedroom door, I leaned against the counter, knowing I had crossed a line. *Why, Teale, why?* I hardly knew the man *and* he had given me a place to stay. No, I knew why I had done it. I wanted to make Kane laugh—or at least smile. There had been times in the truck I'd seen a glimmer and I enjoyed it. Obviously, playing dress-up with his dead things hadn't been a good idea. But they looked better wearing some of the clothing and accessories I'd brought. The place had color now. Kane's cabin, though beautiful with the richness of the wood, felt sterile and cold with all the mounted corpses.

When he'd stepped closer to me in the kitchen, I'd had to catch my breath. Kane was all rugged and mysterious and untouchable. And for some reason, I enjoyed pushing his buttons. There was something inexplicable that drew me to him like no man before. Even when I'd dated Mason, the spark hadn't

25

been as strong as it was with Kane—a complete stranger.

I waited for Kane to come back, but there were no sounds after the slamming of the door.

I'll give him a few minutes.

The kitchen was stocked surprisingly well. It looked like there were plenty of supplies to last for days. I glanced at the backyard that was now completely pitch back. If the snow stopped and it warmed up, I thought I might be able to make it into town in the next day or so. I sighed. If only Butch's cabin had been like this. Not that Butch's cabin was bad. It would have been fine without the whole freezing to death thing. But Kane's cabin was something else.

He still hadn't come back to the kitchen. There was no sound at all from his room.

I probably should apologize.

After I pulled the lasagna out of the oven, I walked over to the door and knocked.

No answer. *Surprise, surprise.*

I knocked again.

Silence.

"Kane, can we talk?"

More silence.

I groaned. "Seriously, why are you acting like a two-year-old? You stomp around giving two-word answers and then you give me the silent treatment."

The door swung open, and he filled the doorway. *Wow, he's huge.* I almost giggled at the situation I was in. *Naïve, I know.* Instead, I gave him a sweet smile. "There you are. I wanted to apologize for dressing up your animals. In my defense, they are a little bit creepy, and while I was cooking, I thought they might like a change of scenery. And it adds color to your place, considering it's all white and brown with more brown. And of course the walls are brown. So it's a sea of brown."

Why can't I just apologize and let it be? No, I had to keep going and working him up.

Kane took a deep breath. "Was that an apology laced with an insult about my decorating?"

I smiled again. "My apology didn't really come out right, and I got sidetracked. But I am sorry. I'll remove it all if you want it returned to a drab, brown, creepy place." I pointed to the thing with huge horns that hung over the fireplace. It looked like a moose. "See how much he loves the sunglasses? And your fox loves the flowery scarf. It adds life."

Kane closed his eyes and shook his head. "Out of all the people I could get stranded with…"

I finished his dangling sentence. "You get stranded with the most awesome person there could ever be."

I waited for him to apologize, but he just stared, struggling to keep his stoic nature. *Back to square one.* At least when his feathers were ruffled, he talked. "And are you sorry for stomping off and being a brute today?"

Finally, he laughed. I liked how husky it sounded. "Hell, woman, you are something else."

"I'll take that as a compliment and an apology. Are you hungry?"

"I could eat."

As we walked back to the kitchen, I kept rambling. "Or you could say, 'Wow, Teale, dinner smells amazing. Thanks for cooking. You are my most favorite houseguest in the entire world.'"

Kane stopped to pinch the bridge of his nose, and I suppressed a giggle. This man was totally out of his element. Having people in his space obviously wasn't Kane's thing. I slapped his shoulder. "I'm just messing with you. But it would help if you practiced stringing a minimum of five words together in a sentence."

Something danced in his eyes, and it lightened the stern expression he usually wore. In a smart-ass tone, he responded, "Thanks for cooking the food."

"Good boy. Next time we'll try seven words."

For a split second, his eyes darted down the length of my body again. If I hadn't been watching, I might have missed it. I definitely enjoyed him appreciating my body. It was dark and a little exotic. This time, I'd let it go without comment. In a different set of circumstances, I could see myself enjoying a fling with Kane. He seemed like the perfect guy to have rebound sex with.

He snapped his fingers in front of my nose. "You in there?"

"What?" *Did he say something?* I felt heat race to my cheeks. "What did you say?"

A knowing smirk flashed across his face. "Nothing. Nothing at all."

"You did so."

He shrugged, letting a little more playful side come out. "Are you ready to eat dinner now?"

Seven words. I winked. "You might be trainable yet. Go have a seat, and I'll bring the food."

I brought a bowl of broccoli to the table and set it down. "What is this?" The curl of his upper lip told me Kane wasn't a veggie eater. Good grief, the man probably only ate the meat from his latest kill.

"Broccoli. It's a vegetable, a member of the cabbage family. It's closely related to cauliflower and is high in vitamin C and carotene."

"I know what it is. Where did you get it?"

"From the garden out back." I rolled my eyes… it was plainly obvious where I'd gotten it.

"What?"

I laughed. "Your freezer. You didn't buy it?"

"No, I'm a meat and potatoes kind of guy."

Bingo. Except on the potatoes part. I rolled my eyes again. "Oh, you're one of those."

"What does *that* mean?" He looked offended, and I could feel the energy building as I riled him again.

Tucking a stray piece of hair behind my ear, I tsk-tsked. "You're a vegetable hater. If you ate your greens, your muscles would look better."

He peered down at one arm and then the other. "What's wrong with my muscles?"

"Nothing. I'm just saying you'd be buffer than you already are if you ate your veggies."

Man, oh man, Kane was already buff. Even in a longsleeved shirt, his muscles bulged. He snapped his fingers again. "Hey, my eyes are up here."

Oh, he's calling me out. I liked it. "Touché."

Mason had been dull and lacked any type of lust for life. If I said something, he simply nodded and agreed. It was boring. He'd done me a favor by forcing my hand.

Leaning back in his seat, Kane folded his arms across his chest. Mariah lay underneath his chair. "Do you always argue this much?"

"I wasn't arguing; I was informing."

Without missing a beat, he responded, "Do you always inform this much?"

"Yep. It's a talent of mine."

He cursed under his breath. I went back into the kitchen for the lasagna and put it on the table. Motioning to the pan, he said, "You first."

His manners momentarily stunned me. Somehow, I'd pictured him just diving in like a savage beast and eating. That image made me smile. "Your freezer is stocked with all sorts of vegetables. If you didn't buy them, was it your girlfriend?"

Way to be subtle. It wasn't the smoothest way to find out if there was some sort of woman in his life.

Kane looked up, horrified. It was priceless. "Hell no. No girlfriend. That's like asking for a ball and chain to be wrapped around your ankle before someone drops you into the ocean."

"Wow. Tell me how you really feel."

Kane stopped and then smiled. "I'd rather have my balls in a vice."

"Well, that sounds... terrible. So, who bought the veggies?"

"My mom."

I pressed my lips together to keep from laughing and just nodded. That was the last answer I'd expected. For some reason, I pictured Kane being brought up by wolves in the forest. But of course he had a mother.

"What?"

I shrugged. "Nothing."

"What were you just thinking?"

I deliberately answered in a way I knew would agitate him more. "No judging here. It's cute."

"*Cute*? You've said I have a tiny dick, my muscles could

be bigger... you dressed up my animals and commandeered my truck. And hell, this is just the first day."

I bit my lip. This was something I'd missed being stuck in a dead-end relationship. For the first time in forever, I felt alive. However, it was probably best to not address all my offenses. When he laid them all out together, it was clear I'd had a busy day. I shrugged. "Yeah, it's cute your mom does your grocery shopping."

He let out a long breath, ignoring the bait, and took a bite of the lasagna. "You know how to cook. I thought figure skaters ate carrots and shit."

"Well, we eat that, too." For some reason, I kept going. "Well, I might not be a figure skater for much longer. I'm thinking about retiring."

For whatever reason, that stopped Kane. "Why?"

I pushed around some of the broccoli on my plate. I hadn't really talked to anyone about this yet. My parents thought it was a temporary decision, but deep in my gut, I knew I was done. My parents would support me either way. Skating had been my life, and they just wanted to make sure I was okay and ready to make that decision. After I broke up with Mason, they'd suggested I take some time to myself over the winter and get my thoughts together.

"Ever since I was a little girl, I've spent more hours on the ice than off. And I was good with that life. Actually, I thrived on it. It never bothered me that I missed some of the simple things like building forts in my living room or having a close group of girlfriends. There just wasn't time with my skating schedule."

I stopped, and Kane watched me. He leaned forward. "There's more to it than that."

In that moment, I felt more exposed than I'd ever been in my life. I felt like an open book to him. "Yes, there is."

"What's the real reason?"

I moved more of the broccoli around on my plate. "Something happened not long before I came to Alaska, and it made me realize I want more out of my life. What used to fulfill me now leaves me feeling empty inside."

"And what do you want?"

So there was a softer side to Kane. One that wasn't gruff and grouchy. I liked this extra dimension that added to the enigma he was. "I don't know yet. I'm still searching for it, I guess. I thought I knew, but I was wrong."

Kane waited, and for whatever reason, I kept talking. "I was leaving practice, and there was the most beautiful sunrise. I stopped for the briefest of seconds to enjoy it. Then I realized I couldn't remember the last time I enjoyed a sunrise. So, I went over to the grass and just sat. I watched the sun rise and simply enjoyed a moment in my life. It occurred to me that I wanted to enjoy more sunrises and take in the sunsets, not worry about getting in my protein shake for muscle optimization within a certain amount of time. I just wanted to live."

I took a breath, the next part a little harder to retell. "I went home earlier than planned. When I left practice, I was supposed to go to my masseuse. After that, I was meeting with my accountant, and then I was going to meet with my nutritionist. I wasn't due home until that evening. But I decided I wanted to talk to Mason and canceled my appointments. Honestly, until that moment, I had never deviated from my schedule. Never. Well, my boyfriend knew this and was surprised, to put it mildly, when I showed up early. Turns out, he had been bumping uglies with my trainer for who knows how long. I dumped him, fired my trainer, and came here for a chance to get my head on straight. Thank goodness the media hasn't picked it up. And hopefully they won't. The last thing I want is a circus."

Kane looked at me like I'd grown a second head. "Why would the media give two fucks about your love life?"

This was something I hadn't really wanted anyone in Skagway to know. "Because I was a gold medalist in last year's Olympics."

"Fuck. You really can skate."

His response made me smile. Normally people were in awe of the gold medal and the Olympic title. Kane simply was impressed I really was able to skate. I chuckled. "Yeah, I really can skate."

"You want my two cents?"

I thought about that for a second. "Sure."

"You're making the right move. You've got one life to live. Live it. And that dipshit doesn't deserve you."

My heart sped up. Somehow, this complete stranger got me.

CHAPTER
Six

Kane

"Fuck," I groaned into the pillow. For the past three nights, I had tossed and turned, barely getting any sleep. There was a certain ice skater who had embedded herself under my skin. For three damn days, I'd put up with her sassy mouth and shenanigans.

Three. Days.

Never in my life had I been this out of sorts. My mind kept straying to thoughts about her body. Asshole move, I knew. But, hell, it was hard not to with all that tight shit she wore.

Not in my house. Not in my town.

My dick was as hard as a post every time I thought about Teale. But today, she was heading to the hotel. The roads had finally cleared enough for us to drive on.

Thank fuck.

I would finally have peace.

I tossed the covers aside to get up. My black sheets were a mess from not sleeping. Yesterday, Teale had made what she called a digital board of "manly looking bedrooms" that weren't done in shades of black and grays. What could I say? I liked the color. It was simple. However, my *grumpy* personality apparently came from surrounding myself with dark colors since the rest of the house was done in a "sea of brown." I gritted my teeth at the psychology report she'd shown me.

Surely, she'd still be asleep at four in the morning. The first morning, she'd gotten up at five. The second, six. I was hoping for seven today. As soon as the sun came up around nine, I would drive us to town and drop her off.

I threw on some sweatpants—just in case—before heading to the kitchen. I was able to cope better if I caffeinated before Teale bounded into the room, full of sass and defiance.

Mariah stretched and followed me to the kitchen. I peered out the window before letting her out the back door to do her thing. Everything was still covered in snow, but no more had come yesterday. There was something about the snow I always found peaceful.

Snow was a huge part of the entire hunting experience—the crunching of boots as I hunted, the random branch falling from the weight of the snow, and the animals moving stealthily against the white.. Mariah cruised the yard. It appeared nothing had come close to the house. I went to the coffee maker, poured some grounds into it, and turned it on.

The deck of cards from last night was still on the counter. Teale had talked me into playing Go Fish and War with her. And I'll be damned if I didn't have a good time. When she won, she'd danced and carried about like a loon. But I'd enjoyed it.

And that irritated me.

"Good morning!"

"*Shit!*" I nearly jumped out of my skin. I hadn't heard her, which pissed me off. People weren't able to sneak up on me—not usually. Of course, my mind had been absorbed in her.

I cracked my neck, trying to relieve some of the tension before turning around. "What are you doing up?"

As if she'd been up for a bit, she came bouncing into the kitchen, full of energy. It wasn't right. Things had a time and a place. Being this *happy* wasn't supposed to happen at four in the morning.

She stopped just near the door that led outside to the back deck. My response hadn't fazed her. Nothing I said fazed her. Typically, people kept their distance from me. Not Teale. She pushed every damn button I had.

She looked outside before focusing on me. "I typically get up around three thirty or four every morning. I thought I heard you, so I figured I'd come get some coffee. And it doesn't look like it snowed. Yay!"

Mariah barked at the back door, and Teale let her in. "Good morning, sweet girl. Was it cold? Let me dry you off."

Teale ran to her room in some itty-bitty shorts that weren't appropriate for Alaskan weather at all. I scrubbed my face as my dick hardened.

Simmer down. She's leaving today. Not in my house. Not in my town.

I pressed start on the coffeemaker while silently talking to my dick. *I swear I will spill hot coffee on you if you don't deflate.* That seemed to do the trick just in time. Teale came back with a fluffy towel and began to dry Mariah's fur. It was almost comical. My dog looked at me as though wondering what the hell was going on.

"There you go, sweet girl. You won't be cold now." Teale straightened up, and her shirt fell off her shoulder. "What's the plan today?"

Get the hell out of here as soon as possible. I took a sip of my coffee. "What time do you want to head to the hotel?"

"I'm packed, so whenever you're ready."

Have I been that big of an ass? I hoped not. I wanted my space back, but I never meant to be a total jerk. "Sun comes up a little before nine. We can head in then if you want. Or we can wait until closer to lunch. Up to you. Remember, the sun sets around three-ish."

She bounced on the balls of her feet. "Perfect. Let's go at nine. I'm so ready to head to town. I think I'm getting cabin fever. I'm not used to this much isolation. I was searching the internet last night. Seems like there's one taxi service in town. A guy named Doug?"

"Yep." Doug and his wife, Darlene, were good people. They liked to procreate. Man, it was chaos at their house with their five kids.

"Good. Once the roads get a little better, I'll have him take me to get my rental car at Butch's."

I hadn't thought about that. "I'll help you get out there. Just let me know."

Why did I just offer that? Obviously, I was a glutton for punishment.

Teale quipped back, "That's nice of you. I appreciate it. And it'll save Doug having to go through the whole 'Are you a serial killer?' and 'I know kung fu' speeches."

My lips twitched, and I took another sip of my coffee. "I'll make sure Doug buys me a beer."

"You're going to miss me, Kane Foster. Admit it. You already miss the décor." Last night after cards, Teale had undressed all my animals.

"That is not something you'll ever get me to admit."

She pinched my cheek. "You're so cute when you lie. I'm going to take a shower before I let you load up my suitcases into your monster truck."

There was no use arguing. *Just agree and let her move on.* "Sounds good."

That ass sashayed back out of the kitchen. *Damn.* Mariah followed Teale. Over the last few days, Mariah had grown close to Teale, which was unusual for her. Normally, she kept everyone at a distance like I did. She was an oddity to her breed. Most huskies were friendly and people-oriented. Mariah was protective and distant to those who weren't family. It made no sense. But it wasn't something I needed to understand. Soon the issue would take care of itself.

CHAPTER
Seven

Kane

"You've got to be kidding me. Can you check again? *Please*. A month? What? I appreciate it. Yes, please call me if anything becomes available." She hung up the phone and banged her head on the table. "This cannot be happening."

I had just come back inside from loading Teale's suitcases into the truck. This sounded bad. "What's going on?"

Turning slowly in her chair, she gave me one of those you're-not-going-to-like-this smiles. I braced myself. At least she was actually dressed appropriately in some jeans and a big sweater that swallowed her. Hardly any skin showed, which was a huge plus.

"Well, I called the hotel this morning because I wanted to see what my options were." This wasn't starting off the way I wanted. I waited for her to continue, but she just scrunched up her nose.

"And?" *Don't let it be what I think it is.*

"Can I first preface it by saying something?"

This woman was going to be the absolute death of me. I hated when people did that beat-around-the-bush thing. But, if I told her to just spit it out, it would turn into a lecture and take a hundred times longer to get to the point. I had learned my lesson the hard way... multiple times. "Yes."

"So last night I looked for cabins in the area to rent. I'm not going back to the other one. It just has bad mojo now with the heater thing."

Mojo? I wasn't touching that with a ten-foot pole. I'd gotten the impression that when Teale's mind was set, it was done. I swore she was more stubborn than I was. "Okay... and you found something?"

"No. They're all booked. I even found a party-planning place that has a cabin it rents out. It's booked through the end of February."

That would be the business my sister-in-law Kory ran with my other sister-in-law, Alexa. I tried to steer the conversation back to the topic at hand. "So the hotel is open?"

She gave me a pretty smile and cocked her head to the side like an innocent angel. The devil in disguise was a more accurate description. Teale made her voice sugary sweet. "It's booked, too. Well, it's booked for the week. Then they're closing the rooms for renovations before the tourist season begins again. So, we have two options."

We? Oh, fuck. "And those are?"

"I go back to the cabin I was staying at, where I will most likely meet my demise and end up frozen solid until spring comes and someone finds me, and it will be on your conscience for the rest of your life."

She hadn't taken a breath the entire time she spoke. I, however, remained silent. A headache lurked at the back of my skull. I knew where this was going.

"That sounds like a terrible option, right?"

I paused. "Well, what's the other option?"

"Kane! You do not want my death on your conscience. I'll come back and haunt you. Have you seen *Ghost* with Patrick Swayze?"

I grimaced. "No, I definitely have not seen that."

"What do you have against Patrick Swayze?"

"Nothing. I just don't do chick flicks."

Teale groaned, "Of course you don't." She stood, and her hands became animated as she talked a hundred miles an hour. "Okay, well he comes back as a ghost and sings 'I'm Henry the Eighth, I Am' to a psychic until she does what she wants him to do, which is help find his killer." She took a big breath. "I will do that over and over and over and over and over again. There will be no relief."

That sounded miserable. What the hell, now I was buying into this *Ghost* bullshit? I still hadn't said a word.

"Kane Foster! You would not want that. Tell me that."

I held my hands up. "Okay. Okay. Of course I don't want you to die, reincarnate as a ghost, and sing some shit to me repeatedly."

"Then that only leaves us with one option. So I take back what I said. There aren't two options."

Fuck, she'd trapped me... again. I hesitated, trying to think of a way out of this. "And that is?"

"You let me rent out your second bedroom until the renovations are done at the hotel or someone rents me a cabin that won't kill me. And because we'll have to haul all my luggage

41

back in, I'll give you frequent luggage miles. Imagine frequent flyer miles but for luggage. It's a win-win-win."

There were so many suitcases. Suitcases that would be in my house again. Stuff in those suitcases that would desecrate my trophies and drive me wild while she waltzed around the house wearing them. "Where do I win in all this?"

"You get to keep my brilliant personality around for your entertainment purposes."

I was going to be living in my own personal hell. *Maybe Hollis can give me some sedatives to make it through the winter. Or her. Maybe I can move in with my parents and let her have the cabin.* What the hell was I saying? I wasn't a pussy and refused to let a hundred-and-twenty-pound girl run me out of my own house.

"So is that a yes?" Teale sounded so hopeful.

I held up my hands, appalled that I was agreeing to this. "I have conditions."

She rolled her eyes. "Hello, party pooper." I raised my eyebrow, and she laughed. "Okay, what are the conditions?"

"No dressing up my animals."

Pointing behind me, she asked. "Can that stay?"

I turned and found my eighteen-point buck wearing dangling things from his antlers and some frou-frou pink scarf around his neck. "I thought you cleaned all that shit out last night?"

"I was leaving that as a present. Something to remember me by. Like a memento of our fun time together. I did it while you were loading my luggage."

Lord, give me patience. Please. Because the alternative isn't pretty. Shaking my head stiffly, I tried to keep my tone in check. "No. It has to go."

"Okay, spoilsport."

Is this woman really calling me a name when I'm considering letting her stay here? I stared at her, unrelenting.

"Okay, okay, fine. No dress-up with your victims."

"Second condition." I held up two fingers. "You have to refer to them as trophies."

Her lip curled in absolute disgust. "You're kidding me, right?"

"Nope. You do always have the option of becoming a ghost and haunting me. That Henry the Eighth song is sounding better by the moment. Will you sing it in multiple languages?"

She slapped my shoulder. "You're a funny guy when you want to be. You've got a deal. It's been great negotiating with you. I'm going to go get my coat so we can go into town."

She skipped off, and I realized Teale had just ended the negotiations and I'd only gotten two demands in. Outlawing those itty-bitty shorts was next, or I was turning off the heat.

CHAPTER
Eight

Teale

"Oh, we have veggies now! Aren't you excited?"

Kane put the first bag in the bed of his truck. "Ecstatic."

"You're a closet veggie lover. I knew it."

No response.

Normally, when Kane grew silent, it was because he was trying not to let me bother him. I smiled. It had been a pleasant morning. Each day, he opened up a bit and became a little more talkative, which was nice. I hated having one-sided conversations. On day two, when I'd started responding for him in a deep, gravelly voice, he finally started to exercise the vocal cords the good Lord gave him. But the moment we entered town, I saw some of the distance come back. *Ugh.* In the grocery store, he'd been like a fish out of water—especially in the vegetable section. I wondered if he'd ever entered that part of the store in his entire life. Well, I would be introducing Kane to the amazingness of the important vegetable food group. Maybe a morning spinach smoothie would be good for his disposition.

We'd loaded the last of the bags in the back of his truck when two older ladies approached us.

"Fuck my life a thousand times over."

That sounded bad. I glanced back at Kane, who had wiped all expression from his face.

"Yoo-hoo, Kane," the older lady to the left called. The two looked like sisters, but I had no idea.

Kane bit out in a low voice, "Just get in the truck. Pretend you didn't hear them."

He turned and headed to the driver's side of the vehicle.

That seemed rude. I took a few steps toward them and smiled. "Hi, I'm Teale. I'm new in town."

The one on the right pulled a notebook and pen from her coat pocket. "Oh, you're a sweet one. I'm Elvira, and this is Sylvia. We run the local town newsletter, Twiner Tellings. It's a way for the community to stay in touch with the latest happenings in Skagway. Some think of us as more of a newspaper."

Oh no, a newspaper. I glanced over at Kane, who was sitting in the truck giving me the *I-told-you-so* look.

"Oh, that sounds fun." What else was I supposed to say? Hopefully they had no clue who I was. Not that my status as an Olympian was news breaking, but if Mason wanted to know where I was, finding me on the web would lead him straight to me. I wasn't ready to deal with him yet.

I think it was Elvira who answered. "Oh, it is. Do you have an email address? We'd love to add you to our list."

"Sure." I rattled off my email, not sure what I was getting

into. These ladies seemed harmless enough, though.

The other one, Sylvia, took a step forward. I felt like I was being tag-teamed. "What are you doing in town?"

"Just came to Alaska for the winter. I rented out Butch's cabin. And Kane is giving me a hand with all the weather since Butch is out of town."

That wasn't a complete lie. But I wasn't necessarily going to tell them all that had transpired. If I said I was living with Kane, the story would spin out of control. Been there, done that, bought the T-shirt. The media were able to manipulate an innocent story with the exclusion of a few important facts just for ratings.

Both were scribbling notes at a hundred miles an hour. The windows of the truck rolled down, and Kane said, "Elvira. Sylvia. Good to see you. Teale, time to go." He was losing patience, and I was getting cold.

I waved. "See you ladies later. Can't wait to get my first Twiner Tellings."

"You bet. There should be one today," Elvira answered with a smile. I wasn't sure how to take that.

The other one, Sylvia, handed me a card. "If you ever have anything to report, this is how to get ahold of us. We keep everything anonymous."

"Perfect!" I leaned in conspiringly. "If I see anything out of sorts, I'll be sure to give you ladies a call."

Sylvia nudged her sister. "I like this one. Full of spunk."

"Me, too. I've got a good feeling about her."

I had no idea what that meant.

"Teale, time to go." Kane's patience timer had gone off.

"Got to go, ladies. He's a bit on a schedule and a little cranky."

They snickered. "Oh, that one is tough as nails on the outside, but I bet he's marshmallow fluff inside."

Elvira smacked Sylvia's arm. "Don't scare the poor girl off. They might be perfect candidates for our new program."

They weren't making any sense. Maybe they were a bit delusional.

Sylvia's eyes widened. "Oh... right. Well, hurry along, dear. We'll be in touch."

Time to leave before Mr. Grumpy Pants started honking the horn. "Well, I better be going before he leaves without me. Bye, ladies."

They waved good-bye as I hopped in the truck. "Wow, they're unique."

"What did you tell them?"

They obviously made him a little nervous. Or maybe it was me talking to them that made him uneasy. I picked at my fingernails. "Nothing much."

"Teale, I'll take you to Butch's."

I looked over to him. "You know that's an empty threat. You already made a deal, and I believe you're a man who sticks to his word. And despite your hard, crusty cracker exterior, you are marshmallow fluff inside."

"*What*?"

I giggled. "Well, Sylvia and Elvira said you were tough as nails on the outside with a marshmallow fluff center. I changed it to crusty cracker because it has more flare."

"I am not a crusty cracker."

I patted his leg. "Okay, I believe you." Sometimes that was the way to get under his skin the most.

"Finally."

I should have dropped it. I really should have. But, of

course, I pressed on. "I'm glad you realize you're marshmallow fluff. That's the first step to embracing your newfound self."

"You are infuriating."

"And amazing. Don't forget amazing."

Kane was trying to keep a straight face, but I saw his mouth quirk up ever so slightly. "What did you tell them?"

"Let's see. I told them I was your long-lost girlfriend who showed up pregnant, needing your help to have the baby."

Kane looked absolutely horrified. And I could barely keep it in before I erupted in a fit of giggles. "Gotcha."

He put the truck in gear and drove only one block when I saw the post office. "Oh, can I see if any of my boxes arrived?"

He parked right in front. "Sure, let me go check. I'll get them for you if there's any. Stay in the truck."

"Thanks."

That was definitely the marshmallow fluff coming out. Maybe Elvira and Sylvia were right. Or he just wanted to keep me from talking to more people. Who knew? I gave Mariah a pat on the head as we waited.

Kane came out carrying a huge stack of boxes, and I clapped in excitement. He loaded them in the back of the truck.

"What did you order?"

"A bunch of stuff. Remember? I love online shopping."

"Let me go get the next load."

"You're the best roomie ever!" I called.

Kane shook his head while pinching the bridge of his nose. This roomie thing was pretty fun.

CHAPTER
Nine

Teale

"I'm going to give you more luggage miles for getting the boxes."

After two more trips, Kane hopped back in the truck and stared at me, repressing a smirk the whole time. "And what do I get for these miles?"

"I'll work out a rewards chart."

Kane chuckled and checked his phone when it vibrated. I waited while he typed a few things. An older man in a thick coat walked across the street and waved. I put my hand up. Skagway was a small town. It was what had attracted me to it in the first place. The town itself was only a few blocks long.

"You ready to head back?"

I needed to stay in civilization for just a little longer. "Can we get some lunch at the Red Onion? It has fantastic burgers. Or at least the burger I got there that one time before the snowpocalypse was great."

Kane seemed a little wary. "I'm not sure that's a good idea."

I raised my eyebrow. "Because of your brothers?"

"I'm not sure how I'm going to explain *you* without getting shit from *them*."

Oh, good grief. Over the last few days I had gotten details about his two brothers and sisters-in-law. "Why would they give you shit because of me?"

"You're living with me. And they aren't going to believe nothing is going on between us. So… they'll give me shit. I've given them enough that I'm due."

That made sense. Sort of. But I wasn't going to hide out in the cabin all winter long. "I'll set them straight. Promise. No tomfoolery. And won't it be worse if they find out I've been there for an extended amount of time and you said nothing about it?"

"You're not going to stop until we go there, are you?"

"You know me so well."

Without saying another word, Kane drove to the Red Onion. We got out of the truck and walked straight in. He motioned to Mariah, and she headed toward the back. Kane nodded to the people we passed without saying anything in response to their greetings. The place was packed. Probably everyone had come out after being cooped up from the snow.

"Hey Crete, is Drake here?"

The bartender, Crete, served a beer before looking our way. He seemed to be in his earlier twenties. Probably a couple of years younger than I was.

"Yeah, he's somewhere. I think he went in the back for supplies."

"Thanks."

Kane made a beeline for the hallway off the end of the bar. Mariah waited in front of a closed door. The woodwork was exquisite there, as well. I tried to take it in since I had somehow missed it the first time, but Kane was walking fast. I wondered if his dad had helped build the bar. A large man came out of the back room carrying a box. It was the same man I'd briefly seen the first time I'd eaten there.

He asked, "You finally able to dig your way out?"

"Something like that. Care if I order some food and have it in your office?"

From the way they spoke to each other, it was obvious they were close. I loved close-knit families. I had one of my own, so I couldn't imagine it any other way.

Drake shifted the box and he asked, "What do you want?" I wasn't sure if he'd even noticed me yet.

"Beer. Burger. Fries. Teale, what do you want? We'll eat in the Drake's office."

Drake apparently noticed me then, and he stared at me as if I was a mythical creature. Then his eyes shot to Kane before returning to me.

Kane widened his eyes at me as if to say "*Told you so.*"

I held my hand out. "I'm Teale. Your brother's roomie. Long story, but after almost freezing to death in his friend's cabin and finding no vacancies in town, your nice brother was kind enough to offer me his spare room. But before we head back to nowhere land, I'm going to have a nice meal with actual human beings in the dining room of this fine restaurant."

Kane closed his eyes and pinched the bridge of his nose.

What did I say? I just wanted to set the family straight. No kidding around. And everything I'd said had been the truth.

Drake smiled. "*Nice* brother? *Roomie*?"

Oh no, the description.

Kane shook his head. "Don't go there. It's not what you think. I had the choice of letting her freeze to death or offering her a room."

I jumped in. "It's true. And he's not really that *nice*. More like a crusty cracker of a person who's gone a little stale."

Muttering a curse, Kane ran his hand over his face.

Drake looked truly intrigued. "Teale, take any open seat. I think there's a couple left. I'll be out there shortly to take your order."

"Sounds great."

I turned and headed back into the crowded dining room. I found an empty seat on the far side of the room. Kane sat across from me. "I thought you were going to eat in the office?"

"Changed my mind."

"I'm okay to eat out here by myself. I'll make new friends, and it'll show everyone there's no hanky-panky going on. Plus, you can prove me wrong when I called you *nice* and maintain the crusty cracker status you seem to love."

Kane held up three fingers. "Rule number three: no more calling me crusty cracker."

In actuality, the negotiations were over and we would be in the amendment stage, but I only nodded and agreed. It was good to let Kane win a round here and there. "Got it. But you can go eat in the office if being around living things is too much for you."

I figured it had to be a transition from his most prominent company being the victims on his wall outside of Mariah.

Kane smiled but hid it as he wiped his hand over his face. "I'm staying. My brother is going to try and get dirt on me."

"That's funny. My lips are sealed."

Kane raised an eyebrow. "I don't think you're able to help yourself."

I pantomimed zipping my mouth and throwing away the key.

"We'll see."

Man, I hope no one comes to talk to us because I will for sure talk.

CHAPTER
Ten

Teale

"Hey, Kane." A petite blond walked up to the table. She held out her hand to me. "I'm, Alexa. You just met Drake, my husband."

She was adorable. "Teale, Kane's friend. He's letting me rent out his spare room." I wanted to rattle on additional details but kept my mouth shut to show Kane I could practice some restraint.

Kane checked his watch, held up two fingers, and mouthed, *"Two minutes."*

I ignored him. Okay, so I hadn't lasted very long with the zipped lip thing.

Alexa's mouth dropped open. *What did I say?* Good grief, I'd have to resort to one-word answers like Kane if I wanted a place to stay.

"He willingly let you stay at his place?" she asked.

This would be easy to clear up. "Well, not really. I commandeered his truck when he came to look at the heater at Butch's cabin. Then, when everything in town was booked, I guilted him into letting me rent the guest room at his cabin. He had the choice between letting me stay or taking the chance that I would come back as a ghost and haunt him. And I do have conditions as part of my rental agreement. I can't dress up his *trophies*." I lowered my voice. "Personally, I call them his victims, but I'm not allowed to say that under our agreement. So, we came to get some lunch since I've only had Mr. Grumpy Pants to converse with for the last three days. Typically, his responses are four words or less, which makes for many one-sided conversations." I turned to Kane. "You cannot add Mr. Grumpy Pants to the agreement. That would have to have been added this morning."

A large, booming laugh behind me made me turn my head. "Mr. Grumpy Pants?"

Kane shook his head. "Drake, I'm warning you."

"How long are you in town for?" Alexa asked, diffusing the tension between the two brothers.

"Just for the winter. I'll head back to Montana in the spring."

A new voice interrupted Alexa. "Teale."

No.

Not that voice. The voice of the man I loathed. There was no way I'd heard that right. I had to be hearing things.

I turned my head to see Mason walking toward me. I felt the blood drain from my head. As he got within a few feet, I regained my composure and realized I was pissed. He had some balls approaching me. And if he got too close, I'd have no problem castrating him. *What is he doing here?* And what infuriated me the most was that Mason had on the navy sweater I'd given him for Christmas the year before.

"I can't believe I found you." He stepped closer, his hand outstretched, and I scooted back.

Did he forget that I caught him in bed with Vanessa? The betrayal still cut deep. I thought she had been my friend after coaching me for ten years, but not everything was as it seemed to be.

"What are you doing here, Mason?" I asked, ice clear in my tone.

From the corner of my eye, I saw Kane stiffen. He must have recognized the name and now knew this was my asshole of an ex-boyfriend.

"I came for you, of course. We need to talk. I tried to explain that it wasn't what it looked like, but you ran out before I had the chance." Mason was smooth, used to getting his way most of the time. Those baby blues of his normally had people bending over backward to fulfill his every request. I sure fell for them once upon a time.

I wasn't touching that statement. His assuming I was a stupid bimbo who would take him back only made me hate him more. *Not in a million years.* I folded my arms across my chest. "How'd you find me?"

"I logged into your online account. Checked the history and saw you were shipping stuff to Skagway, Alaska. It's a small town, so I figured I'd run into you eventually. But it seems luck is on my side since I only arrived yesterday. I walked in for some lunch and saw you."

Gah, I'd forgotten to change the password. And now he had Kane's address from the last order I placed three days ago. I wanted to slap him and kick him in the nuts. Thank goodness the restaurant was busy.

"We need to talk."

"No. No, we actually don't. I have nothing to say to you."

Mason cleared his throat and shifted his eyes left. "We need to settle our bills."

I gritted my teeth. "Is that why you came? For money? You said you weren't moving out, so I had my name taken off the lease. I paid for half of the apartment for the next three months, as per the contract. So you have two choices: move out or pay up."

In the last couple of years, Mason had quit his job to "explore other avenues," which meant he'd been living off me. Before I got my name off everything, Mason had emptied a joint account we had with about ten thousand dollars in it. The only reason he was here was to get more money. I turned back to Kane, clearly dismissing Mason. "Now, if you'll excuse us, we're going to eat our meal. And if you don't leave me alone, I'll get a restraining order against you."

"Who's this?" Mason pointed at Kane, who leveled an icy stare at him. To an outsider, Kane would seem intimidating with his huge muscles and stern expression.

The first thing that came to mind shot out of my mouth. "My boyfriend."

"Boyfriend?" Mason appeared shocked. I was shocked.

Why did I say that? Oh, dear. I was going to be in so much trouble. But I'd said it, so I'd have to set the record straight with Alexa and Drake as soon as he left.

"Yes, boyfriend. Except he doesn't cheat."

Mason's face turned red. "No way you're dating him. And like I've said, I want to clear up what you saw, but you're not leaving me a lot of options."

"No, you need money. I imagine you probably convinced

Vanessa to buy your ticket up here under false pretenses." The way Mason's throat bobbed repeatedly told me I was right. I refused to listen to anything he had to say about not cheating. Instead, I focused on his first statement. "Why wouldn't I be dating Kane? He's more of a man than you'll ever be."

"He's not your type."

Kane's chair scraped across the floor as he stood. "I'd suggest you get moving, motherfucker. I'm standing right here."

Oh no. If Kane called me out, Mason would hang around longer. Dealing with a restraining order would be a headache.

Mason looked to me. "So it's true?"

Kane narrowed his eyes. "I don't explain myself to anyone, especially cheating bastards like you. And Teale sure as hell doesn't have to explain herself, either. Get gone."

Mason obviously hadn't been expecting Kane's anger, and he took a few steps back. "I'm at the hotel for the week. I'd like to talk. Call me."

That asshole took my room. I should have kicked him in the shin.

"No thanks. I'll keep my big, beefy boyfriend, who's amazing in the sack."

The restaurant went silent. *Oh, shit.* Apparently, I said that a little too loudly. Alexa stared at me, wide-eyed. In fact, every eye was on me. I waved to the room, wanting to defuse the situation. "Hi, I'm Teale. New to town."

"Hi, Teale." A handful of people chimed back.

I'm going to be in so much trouble.

Kane grabbed my hand and yanked me down the hall to Drake's office. I went without a fight. From the set of Kane's broad shoulders, it was clear he was pissed. In the office, Mariah rose from where she'd been sleeping on the floor by the couch. Drake and Alexa came in right behind us.

The huge desk in Drake's office was another gorgeous piece of woodwork. I loved all the handmade furniture the Foster family had. I had to speak to their dad, Ike, about making me some. But bringing that up at the moment might not be the best idea.

I began to speak, but Kane cut me off. "We are not dating. She's not my girlfriend. And I'm sure as hell not some big, beefy boyfriend."

"He's right," I said. Kane shot me daggers. "Don't get your panties in a twist. I got a little riled up when I realized the asshole had followed me up here. Hello stage-five clinger." I waved my hands. "I thought of the first thing that would make him leave and maybe said that last part a little too loudly."

"But now the whole damn town thinks we're dating. This town spreads shit faster than you can stop it."

I shrugged my shoulders. "Well at least I said you were amazing in the sack. I mean, it would have been bad if I had said the opposite. So now you'll have girls dying to hook up with you when I'm gone."

The thought of Kane hooking up with anyone bothered me.

Before Kane could respond, my phone dinged.

Red Hot Twiner Tellings News! Kane Foster has a girlfriend.

Alexa looked at her phone, and our eyes met. *Uh oh.* She grinned. I began to freak out. On the inside, of course.

"What?" Kane snarled.

"Nothing," we said in unison as we shoved our phones back in our pockets.

Drake pulled out his. "Best damn day of my life—other than when I married Lex."

Lex. *That's a cute nickname.*

Kane reached for his phone. My hand shot out to stop him. "There's really no need to check it. I mean, people rely too much on technology. They say that we shouldn't just grab our phone and react every time it goes off."

"What does it say?"

I held my hands out as I thought. *Be vague.* "That there's a new person in town."

"You're lying."

Gah! "Well, I'm sure it says that somewhere in the red-hot newsletter."

Kane took out his phone. "Fuck my life."

Drake's phone rang. Things were spinning out of control. "Yeah, Hayden, I'm staring at the girlfriend right now."

"Son of a bitch. Tell him the truth." Kane took a step toward his brother.

Without missing a beat, Drake winked at me. "Yeah, we're in my office if you want to meet Teale. Sure thing." He turned to Kane. "Hayden's on his way."

I looked at Kane. "Just look at the positive. You're going to get to see both of your brothers in the same place before we head back to your cabin. And I can finally put faces to the names. Did you know you have zero family pictures in your cabin?"

Kane looked like he might be sick. It was really hard to keep a straight face.

CHAPTER
Eleven

Kane

Worst. Day. Ever.

My phone was going crazy in my back pocket. But there was no way in hell I was answering one text message.

The door to Drake's office swung open.

"Well, hello, princess." Hayden strutted in, wearing a cocky smirk I wanted to knock off his face.

If Hayden thought he was going to be able to pass that title to me so easily, he was about to be disappointed. "I do not have a girlfriend."

He waved his phone. "According to the red-hot Twiner Tellings, you do."

"Don't believe everything you read," I snarled back.

Teale stepped toward Hayden. Hell, the woman was charismatic. And every time she opened her mouth, she dug us deeper into this mess. But I was interested to see what she'd do. I didn't believe she created chaos intentionally; she just lacked the filter most sane adults possessed.

"Hi, I'm Teale. Kane's roomie."

Hayden shot a look at Kane. "Changing the title of 'girl-friend' to 'roomie' doesn't count."

Teale laughed. "If I say I'm his girlfriend, he gets dubbed 'princess'?" Teale looked at me with a mischievous look on her face while she tapped her chin. I raised my eyebrow in warning.

Alexa laughed. "It's a thing that started a few months back. Drake slept in one day, and Kane called him 'princess.' Then Hayden used the word *meaniehead,* and the title was transferred to him. Kane agreed if he ever got a girlfriend, he'd take the title forever."

"Man. And I thought some of my stories were crazy. He's really a girlfriend hater, I've found." Teale threw the raised eyebrow right back at me.

My brothers were grinning like loons. And it pissed me off that they thought they'd won. They'd see in time when she went back to Montana.

So why I was unable to just leave her comment out there was beyond me. "I'm not a girlfriend hater."

"Well, you don't want one, and the thought makes you look like you might be sick."

"Does not."

"Does so a million times infinity factorial. That's the highest number possible, so there's no beating that. Just ask a mathematician."

This was getting us nowhere. My brothers would have to see just how much she *wasn't* my girlfriend by the way we acted.

I looked at Hayden. "Do you see what I've been dealing with for the last seventy-two hours? This. This is what I have been dealing with." I pointed to the woman beside me.

Hayden's face fell. "She's really not your girlfriend."

Leaning in, Teale mock-whispered, "No, I'm really not. But I'll be forever grateful if he lets my ex keep thinking I am so the jerk goes back home and I can enjoy my winter here in Skagway." Teale gave me those puppy dog eyes, and everyone in the room looked at me. Hell, I'd be a total ass if I didn't agree at this point. What did I care what people thought of me? Never had. Never would. And Mason pissed me the hell off with his shiny loafers and his slicked-back hair. *Douchebag.*

I nodded. "But for the record, the title of 'princess' remains with Hayden."

Teale mock-whispered, "He's not man enough to handle me. And he's a bit of a Mr. Grumpy Pants."

I pointed at my brothers. "Don't even think about it, dickheads."

Alexa put her arm around Teale. "I think a girls' night is in order."

"Oh, that sounds amazing."

Nope. Nope. Nope.

There had been enough chaos done for one day to cause absolute havoc on my life. I'd be hearing about this for years. "I think it's time to go."

Teale took a step back. "But we haven't had lunch. And a girls' night sounds fun."

Not fun at all. A recipe for disaster. "I'm leaving."

"Okay. I'll call Doug and have him bring me later. No worries."

I closed my eyes for a second to rein in my temper.

Hayden said, "Man, I like her a lot. I have never seen him this riled before."

Drake laughed. "Me, neither. Pop us some popcorn."

I wasn't sure what came over me, but I picked Teale up and threw her over my shoulder.

She squealed. "Put me down!"

"No. It's time to go, and you're coming with me, roomie." Teale squirmed, but I held on tighter.

"Kane, you're being unreasonable."

"We'll talk about how unreasonable I've been, considering the turn of events of today."

She ignored me. "Seriously, a man should not manhandle his roomie. If I say pretty, pretty please with sugar on top, will you put me down?"

"No."

"Pretty, pretty, pretty please?"

I swung around to face my brothers. They were smirking. Nope, I wasn't saying anything else. The time for talking to all of them was over. I headed to the door with a firm grip on my roomie. "Come, Mariah."

"You're making me sick with all this swinging around, Kane. You'll feel bad if I puke."

I said nothing but kept moving. Behind me, my brothers laughed. Hayden called after me, "Bye, Mr. Grumpy Pants."

I shot back, "Later, asshole."

They just laughed harder. I picked up my pace. When I entered the crowded dining room carrying Teale over my left shoulder, everyone stopped to look. I didn't pause, but of course the pain in my ass on my shoulder raised her head.

"Bye, everyone. Kane's in a hurry to leave, and apparently I can't walk fast enough."

More fucking laughter.

I stomped to the truck, where I opened the door and gently dropped Teale inside. I looked up to see Mason standing outside, watching us with some asshole grin on his face. *Prick.* That motherfucking prick had caused me a lot of grief. If he thought he was going to talk to Teale, he had another think coming.

I put my hand on the back of Teale's neck, and her eyes flared with something I hadn't seen before. Not going there. *Not in my house. Not in my town.* But if I was going through with this fake boyfriend thing, I needed to act the part. "I need to go set him straight. A boyfriend wouldn't let some ex-prick stand there like that."

"You might need to kiss my forehead to sell it."

I wasn't going to think about why in the world I gave in to it. Maybe it was because I wanted to know what her skin felt like. The town already thought we were dating. My family knew the truth, which was what mattered.

I leaned in and pressed my lips against her forehead. The zap I felt made me pull back immediately. I decided to ignore it. "Be right back."

CHAPTER
Twelve

Teale

My heart galloped in my chest. When Kane kissed my forehead, for a split second, something almost electric shot through me. *Stay calm. Keep it together.* It felt like I had run a marathon, and I worked on steadying my breathing.

Kane stalked up to Mason, got in his face, and said something. Mason took a step back, and Kane followed him.

Thank goodness all my STD tests had come back negative. After I found Mason cheating, testing had been the first thing I'd done. There was no telling how long he'd been cheating on me.

While Mason was still talking, Kane turned and walked away, completely dismissing him.

From the look on Mason's face, it seemed like maybe he'd leave me alone now. Beneath the surface, he was a chicken. I was sure he missed my pocketbook, which was the only reason he wanted to come find me. It had taken him a month to even make initial contact.

With Vanessa currently out of a job and Mason leeching off me for the last two years, I imagined funds would be running low over the next few months, depending on what Vanessa had managed to save. Rumor was no one worth a damn would hire her now. At some point, I was sure she'd find something, but I doubted she'd be headed to the Olympics any time soon.

Kane turned and our eyes met. Good grief, that was sexy. And now my mind was going to all sorts of places. Places I only allowed myself to think about at night. After feeling Kane's lips on my skin, I wondered what it would feel like to have his lips on mine.

As Kane got in the car, my phone beeped. I checked my email, and there was a Twiner Tellings update.

Kane Foster Fights for His Woman!

Oh. My. Gosh.

I peered out the window, trying to figure out where the Twiner sisters were lurking. They were nowhere to be seen. But there were several people peering out the window of the Red Onion, including the family members I'd just met. *Have they been there the entire time?*

Those Twiner sisters were my inspiration for when I got older. I wanted to be that sassy and full of life.

"What is it?"

Kane's voice startled me, and I jolted like I'd been caught doing something wrong. "I really don't think you want to know."

"Teale."

I scrunched my nose. "There might have been another

newsletter."

"Fuck. What does it say?"

The intensity pouring off Kane was insanely hot. "Umm… remember, you're driving."

"Teale." That one word was filled with so much emotion. Kane Foster had been pushed to his limit today.

"It says 'Kane Foster Fights for His Woman.'"

His knuckles went white on the steering wheel, and he grew quiet. Too quiet.

I opened my mouth to say something but closed it, changing my mind. Maybe he needed a few minutes to process everything.

We left the town limits and began our trek back to his cabin. I pulled out my phone and busied myself so I wouldn't speak. And honestly, I'd been so focused on what happened with Kane that I hadn't given Mason's surprise arrival much thought.

But it *was* a big deal. And creepy. And irritating.

I texted my mom. Once I'd gotten settled at Kane's, I'd told her everything that had happened with the cheating and the money. I wanted my family to hear it from me and not from second-hand gossip. The skating world was small and at some point they would have found out.

Me: *Mason showed up! Gah!*

Mom: *What? How did he know where you were?*

Me: *He logged into my online account and saw where I was shipping stuff to. I've already changed my passwords.*

Mom: *Bastard. What are you doing?*

Me: *Well, Kane's agreed to be my fake boyfriend so Mason will move on. I think Mason is scared of Kane. Mason basically wanted money.*

Mom: *Oh, my word, Teale. Do you need us to come up there? What have you gotten yourself into?*

Me: *Oh, Mom, it's fine. Kane's fine. He's a gentleman. I'll call later and tell you everything. But I am loving Skagway. It's just what I needed. And now hopefully Mason will leave me alone.*

Mom: *Where is your mind at on skating?*

Me: *I just don't know. I don't want to commit to an answer yet.*

Mom: *Fair enough. We'll support you either way. We have a month to tell your sponsors.*

Me: *I'll let you know.*

I put my phone away as we pulled up to the cabin. Kane still hadn't said a word, and he looked like he was going to bust a vein in his neck. I chucked him playfully on the shoulder, trying to relieve some tension.

"So, we've had a pretty productive morning, and it's barely lunchtime. I met the Twiner sisters, your two brothers and one of their wives, got to step into the Red Onion without actually eating, I introduced myself to most of the town, saw my ex-boyfriend, got a fake boyfriend, and was featured twice in the Twiner Tellings newsletter. Oh, and I got lots of packages. Not too bad, eh?"

Kane looked my way with a smile playing on his lips.

"Not too bad?"

"I mean, we could have been stuck indoors because of all the snow."

"Not too bad?" he repeated.

This wasn't working. I needed to keep going. "Oh, and you got issued a frequent luggage carrier number. That's super-duper special."

"I have managed to go my entire life without being featured in a Twiner Tellings newsletter. My entire life. And after only two hours in town *with you,* I'm in the damn thing twice."

"You're welcome?"

He laughed. "Thanks."

Are we past it already? I figured we were, or he would have filled the truck with all sorts of cussing and kicked me out as a roomie. But I wasn't going to press my luck.

He grew more serious and turned my way. "You okay?"

I was sure he was referencing my cheating ex being in town. "Yeah, I am. I'd have hit him with a frying pan if he'd just showed up at Butch's cabin. But, yeah, I'm okay. He's a wuss, so I'm hoping he leaves me alone now that he thinks I'm your girlfriend."

"I can't tell if you're putting on a front or not. With most people, I can. But not this time, not with you."

That seemed to bother him. So I decided to be completely honest with him. "I'm not putting on a front. I'm actually really okay. When I saw him, I felt nothing except sadness at too many years wasted. We were over long before he cheated. I just didn't want to rock the boat. The routine of our relationship worked, so why mess it up, ya know?"

"Yeah, I get it. Well, I guess I do. I've never really done the relationship thing."

I wondered what had happened to Kane to make him so against getting involved with anyone. Maybe at some point I would find out. I didn't imagine it was something he divulged easily, if ever, considering how private he was.

I petted Mariah's head where it rested on my shoulder. I was so used to her being Kane's shadow sometimes I forgot she was there. It grew colder in the truck as we sat outside with the engine off. Kane was deep in thought.

"So, what do we want to do?" I asked. "We have like two and a half hours before it gets dark."

He seemed to consider that for a second before turning my way and giving me a wicked grin. "Let's blow some shit up."

"Like dynamite? That's allowed?" I mean, we were in Alaska, the rugged frontier. But dynamite seemed a little drastic.

"Let's go shooting. You ever shoot before?"

I thought about it and shook my head. "It wasn't really something I could fit in my schedule. This will be a lot of fun. But I'm not getting any vict—I mean, trophies to add to your wall."

"Duly noted. That wouldn't be expected. Let's get some lunch, and we'll go shoot some shit."

I grabbed his arm before he got out of the car. "What type of outfit do I need? Should I be like a total combat chick or cool winter hiker? I might have something to pull together a chic hunter person, but I don't want the animals to think I'm in the same league as you."

The Kane I'd gotten used to over the last couple of days was back; he became visibly less tense and more like what I imagined his true personality to be. "Just wear warm shit."

"Warm shit. I think I've got some of that." I laughed. "You cuss a lot."

"So my mother says."

Tilting my head, I tried to imagine the woman who'd raised three sons. She had to be tough. "Aww. I really want to meet Mrs. Foster."

"She'd like you. And she's already requested a family dinner. My phone won't stop vibrating, which probably means it's planned. That also means she's read the Twiner Tellings, heard from my brothers, and needs to make a decision herself."

"So, is that my invitation?"

"Why not? She'll see the truth and set my brothers straight, which will make this a hell of a lot easier."

"Kane, I really do appreciate what you did. It means a lot. I promise I'll be a good roomie."

He winked. "It's not so bad. But to make us square, I'll let you make lunch."

"Deal."

CHAPTER
Thirteen

Teale

I missed again and groaned in frustration. "Seriously, that can is moving."

As I spoke, puffs of white from my breath filled the air.

"It's not moving." Kane aimed his gun and, one by one, picked off the line of cans. "See, they aren't moving."

"You suck."

He hit the next row of cans. "I don't think I suck."

That row of cans was gone, and I hadn't hit a single one. "You really can shoot."

"It's what I do for a living. One day, I'll have to see if you really can skate."

"Touché." I aimed the gun, fired, and missed again. Stupid, stupid can.

"You're tensing too much. Relax and barely pull the trigger."

I took a few deep breaths, tried to do what he said and pulled the trigger. Another miss. "Son of a biscuit eater!"

Kane chuckled. "Why not just say 'son of a bitch'?"

"Because you curse enough for the both of us. I'm lending you my curse-word allotment. I've decided I'll be creative with my cussing."

He blinked. "Well, that's considerate of you."

"I try. After all, I kind of made a mess of your life. But, good grief, I had no idea news would spread that fast."

"Welcome to Skagway."

I pointed the gun, fired, and missed again. "Shitake!"

"Here, let me help you."

Kane stood behind me, his arms coming up on either side of my body. He gently grabbed my hands and helped me aim the gun. "Keep this arm firm but don't stress too much. Now, look through the sight."

I did as he said.

"Now gently squeeze."

I pulled the trigger, and the gunshot rang through the air. The can fell off the log.

"Oh my gosh! Oh my gosh! I did it! I did it!" Kane grabbed the gun before I started to run around with my hands in the air like a crazy person. "Kane, I hit the can! I hit the can!"

"Yes, you did." He was enjoying watching me make a fool out of myself.

I was so excited. And in the exhilaration of the moment, I jumped into his arms, cheering like a madwoman. Of course, he caught me. But then I stopped cheering, and we were eye to eye. His gaze darkened as he took in my face, and then it shifted down to my lips.

We leaned closer to each other, and my breath caught as I waited to feel his lips touch my skin again.

Snap.

A loud sound broke the connection. I shifted my eyes to the ground as Kane commanded, "Mariah, check it out."

The husky took off, and Kane set me down gently. "Want to stay here or come with me?"

His voice was softer this time. I glanced up to find him focused on me. "Was that an animal?"

"Could be. But from the snap, I imagine it was something breaking from the weight of the snow."

If there was more than one animal, I'd be bait. No thanks. "Yeah, I think I'll stick with the hunter guy. My aim isn't the greatest. And if I tried to shoot, I might hit you instead, which would be terrible."

"It would only complete the afternoon if you shot me. I mean, then we could meet the doc, too."

"Kane Foster! Take that back!"

He started walking away, and I ran to catch up. "Take it back."

"Never."

I smiled to myself. I loved this side of Kane: fun yet protective. I followed him for about twenty feet to where Mariah stood. A branch had broken off a nearby tree and lay in the snow. "Thank goodness."

Kane took a few steps. "There're some tracks not too far from here. Let's head back to the cabin. The sun's going to be setting soon."

It was hard to get used to the sun setting at around three in the afternoon. "Tracks? Are we safe?"

"Yeah, we're safe."

I stayed next to Kane as we walked back to the cabin, my eyes darting back to the forest as if something was watching me.

CHAPTER
Fourteen

Lumberjack

I grit my teeth and throw another log on the fire. The need to kill... it's starting to take over.

I drag my knife over my cheek as I remember her face.

It's not her time yet. I need to find someone who will curb my appetite until I can fully satiate my hunger.

She's an angel. A perfect addition to my collection. I stroke the differently colored strands of hair. They were all so beautiful. Even as I choked the life from them.

I'll keep her alive a little longer. I'll play with her. She deserves the best.

They all thought they'd found the one, but they hadn't. They'd been waiting for me.

At the perfect moment, I'll take her.

CHAPTER
Fifteen

Kane

Winding down later that evening, I was still out of sorts from what had happened earlier. I had wanted to feel her lips on mine. I wanted to make her come so loud she screamed my name.

Not in my house. Not in my town.

If the branch hadn't broken, I probably would have done something stupid.

For the first time in a long time, I was enjoying myself, and I wasn't sure what to think about that. With that prick Mason in town, Teale wasn't going anywhere. That guy really rubbed me the wrong way. He was a pussy. I doubted he was going to make trouble, but I wasn't sure.

I threw another log on the crackling fire; Mariah slept on her bed a few feet away. Teale walked in, freshly showered and wearing those shorts that drove me wild. And tonight, she had on a thin sweatshirt that said *Montana* across her chest.

"You know it's winter, right?"

She looked down at her clothes. "Is it? I thought it might be summer."

I shook my head and poked the fire, fighting a grin. I loved that smart-ass mouth of hers.

"What's got you all worked up? Maybe you should use the sauna. It feels amazing, by the way. Thanks for letting me use it this afternoon. I want to use it every day."

The images of her in there naked and sweaty weren't good for my state of mind. This woman was testing every ounce of my self-restraint.

And my brothers would not stop texting me. I refused to acknowledge or respond back to anything either said. I had caught that there was a family dinner at Kory and Hayden's in two days. This was Mom's subtle way of getting to meet Teale. If Mason left before then, I would show up by myself just to irritate them.

"So, first day of roomies went pretty well, eh?" I raised my eyebrow in response, and she giggled. "I wonder what sort of mischief we'll get into on day two. Oh, can we get my rental car? Kory and Alexa invited me over for a girls' night. We're having a slumber party."

That had *terrible idea* written all over it. "Hell no."

She looked at me like I had grown a second head. "Why ever not? You aren't my dad."

"Because when those two and Devney get together, it's trouble. Last time they did, they got into some group text thing, and from what I heard, it was a disaster. Our personal shit is not going to be broadcasted in a group text."

"Well then, that settles it. I'm going."

Did she not hear a word I just said? "I think you argue

with me just to piss me off."

"Or maybe you start arguments with me just to get pissed off."

That made no sense but still made me smile. It was time to change the subject. "If you don't go back to skating, what will you do?"

She shrugged. "Maybe give lessons. I don't know. I've invested wisely, so I have time to figure out what I want to do. Or not do, really. But I don't want to be idle. I figure I'll know when it happens. For now, I'm just living in the moment instead of worrying about the future. For years, my life was all about the next regional, the next national, qualifying for the Olympics. Every moment was planned and scheduled. Now, I don't have anything planned, and I'm enjoying it. So we'll see."

She stood and stretched, her shirt creeping up above her belly button. Her stomach was flat and paler than her legs, which were toned and tan. Today, when she wrapped those legs around me, I could feel how strong they were.

"Eyes up here."

My eyes shot to hers. She was smiling.

"What?"

"Well, I've been standing here asking if you want to play cards again, and you've been staring at my legs. Admit it, Kane Foster, you've been caught red-handed."

"I—you—Maybe you shouldn't wear things like that."

She raised her eyebrow. "Really? That's the best you've got? I mean, each morning I've had to deal with you in sweatpants, shirtless, in all your muscled glory with biceps bigger than my legs. And yet somehow, I've been able to carry on a conversation."

Deep breath in... let it out. She was right, I had been caught red-handed. "I apologize. I wasn't trying to be a dick."

She sat on the arm of the chair next to me. "You run hot and cold, Kane Foster. One minute you're cold as ice, the next minute you're staring at me as if you'd like to devour me. Why is that?"

"Do you not filter *anything?*"

She shrugged. "Not really. I figure honesty is the best policy... kind of like you, but not so crass and grumpy-like. And, of course, with the exception of Mason and everyone in town thinking you're my boyfriend."

I scrubbed a hand down my face, feeling like a total ass. "I'm not a complete dickhead. I'm sorry. I would never do anything. I swear."

She stood and smiled. "Pity. I thought we might have some casual fun."

What. The. Actual. Fuck?

I needed to put some space between us. "I'm going to use the sauna."

"Sounds good. Have fun sweating out your frustrations."

I stood, running my hands through my hair. *What is this woman doing to me?* I went back to my bedroom, stripped down, and entered the sauna. When I was stressed, I sweated it out. *How did she know?* I turned up the heat and tried to relax.

Did I hear her right? She was so sweet and, in some ways, innocent, yet she was also confident in herself and cared little what others thought. Somehow, she'd managed to become my roommate, and the entire town thought she was my girlfriend.

A shadow passed in front of the door. *Is anything in my house not sacred anymore?* "Teale?"

"Who else would it be?"

Smart-ass. "What do you want?"

"To talk. You decent?"

"No."

The door opened, and she threw the smallest towel I owned at me. "Get decent. I'm coming in."

She gave me all of five seconds to cover up before the door opened and she walked in wearing a very skimpy bikini. The thing was better described as dental floss.

"Oh man, this feels amazing. I love it in here."

She sat on the bench across from me, and I got a better look at her body. Her breasts were the perfect size. I liked what I saw. A lot.

"You wanted to talk?" I asked.

"I did."

The sweat began to bead on her chest. The first droplet moved toward her nipple. Lucky fucking droplet.

She hadn't said another word. "What did you want to talk about?"

"You left in the middle of the conversation."

"It seemed like we were done."

That intensity we'd experienced earlier returned in full force. I had two choices: get up and leave or see this out. I stayed put.

"Oh, I thought you just stormed off after I gave you a compliment."

"I did not storm off."

Teale closed her eyes and got comfortable.

"What are you doing?"

"I'm steaming with my roomie. I seriously love this thing, and I'm going to get one when I go home."

"Your roomie, who only has a hand towel over his dick."

She cracked one eye open. "Well, with the tent you're making, my assumption about it being tiny may have been a miscalculation."

Things were definitely shifting. And fuck it. I was done. If she wanted to play, I'd step up to the plate.

"But you have me at a disadvantage."

"So you're saying you'd want to steam together if I take off my top."

"That's up to you, Teale."

Her chocolate eyes flickered with lust, and her nostrils flared. She reached up behind her neck and untied the scrap of fabric she was wearing, not once breaking eye contact. Man, I wanted this woman and her smart mouth.

Before she let her top go, I needed to be straight with her. "I need to be absolutely clear about something before this goes anywhere."

"You don't do girlfriends."

Okay, well, that was one thing. "Correct."

"This isn't a relationship."

And she made another valid point. "Correct."

"Your family won't know we have a benefits clause in our fake relationship."

Damn, she was good. "Correct."

"Did I miss anything?"

She let the top drop. Her breasts were perky and firm, and I swallowed hard.

This might actually work. We'd both have a fun winter and then go our separate ways come spring. "There are some ground rules."

"Of course there are." She stood against the door, her

hand traveling up her stomach toward the bottom of her breast.

"No sleeping in each other's beds at night."

I didn't want her to get the wrong impression. Watching her closely, I didn't see any disappointment.

"Sounds good."

"And until this is over, it's exclusive," I stated.

"Perfect."

"I mean what I say, Teale. I don't want there to be any misconceptions."

She rolled her eyes. "Trust me, Mr. Grumpy Pants. You and me in a relationship would be like oil and water. But wouldn't it be nice when you come home to have a way to let off steam from the stress of the day. I can't imagine clients from the city have you skipping around and singing."

I chuckled. "No, they don't. That's why I have this place."

This might be nice. I'd been crystal clear about the rules. There was no way they might be misinterpreted. I stood, discarding my tiny towel. Her eyes immediately darted to my stiff dick as I stroked it once. I swore she gave a little moan.

"I was dead wrong about the tiny dick."

The hunger in her eyes fueled my own desire. "Time for talking is over unless you want to change your mind, angel."

She shook her head, and I captured her mouth.

CHAPTER
Sixteen

Teale

My heart hammered in my chest. This was unlike anything I had done before in my life. But I wanted... I wanted it so bad.

Kane's tongue took my mouth with such fervor, I thought I would orgasm on the spot. Mason had never been passionate about anything, including sex.

His rough fingers trailed up my body. My core throbbed for a touch, a flick, anything. "I'm going to fuck you so hard, you won't be able to see straight." His voice was husky and set my nerves on fire.

"Oh, I hope so."

His mouth moved down my cheek to my collarbone. Sweat dripped off my skin, yet goose bumps were forming all over. I loved the mixture of feelings. His tongue licked my nipple, and I arched into him, sure I had never felt this good in my life.

He took a step back, and I felt the loss of him immediately. Kane picked up my bikini top and returned to me. "If I do anything you don't like, tell me."

"I promise. But right now, I just want to come. I need to come."

"Hands above your head, angel."

I put them above my head. Kane leaned a little closer. I pushed my breasts against his chest and kissed his neck as he used my top to tie my hands to one of the beams above my head. I loved it.

The ache between my legs grew. Kane's hands found the sides of my bikini bottoms and untied one side and then the other. The condom packet I'd tucked into the back of my bottoms fell to the side and Kane quirked his eyebrow. "I like a prepared woman."

I leaned against the cool glass. "I like a man who gets a woman off and doesn't leave her hanging."

He chuckled, and the deep promise behind it did things to my insides. I'd never done anything like this before, but being here with Kane had me feeling wanton. His finger brushed against the most intimate part of me. I groaned as he slipped his finger inside of me. His lips trailed kisses down my shoulder. The feel of his beard was scratchy but soon soothed by his lips. He worked his way back up to my ear. "I'm going to make you come so many times you'll beg me to stop."

"We'll see."

His teeth nipped my neck as his second finger entered me. The tension inside me was building faster than I thought possible. When he bit my nipple, I flew right off the edge, my orgasm rolling through me. My eyes flew open. "My word, you're good at this."

"I'm happy to oblige."

I leaned up and kissed his neck. "Something you should know about me, I have a lot of stamina. You're going to have your work cut out for you to keep me satisfied. Are you sure you're up to the task?"

He hoisted me up, and my back found the cool glass again. His dick was poised at my entrance. "I think I can handle it."

There was so much lust in his eyes as he stared into mine. His dick teased my entrance. I moved my hips, tightening my legs around him to give myself the perfect amount of friction to heighten my torment.

"You okay?" he asked.

"If you don't start moving, I'm not going to be," I bit out.

Kane plunged in and pulled out just as quickly. With just a few more thrusts, I was going off again. Damn he was good.

Kane untied my hands and rubbed my arms as he lowered them from over my head. "I'm taking you to bed, angel. That should hold you over while I taste every inch of you."

We were a sweaty mess when we came again, breaths labored and chests heaving. Kane pulled out, sat up, and disposed of the condom. There was no spooning or holding after sex, which was fine because I knew this wasn't long term. It would run its course, and we'd go our separate ways.

"We're going to run out of condoms."

I giggled. "We've been going at it like bunnies."

Checking the time, I saw it was past eight in the evening. I stood and put on the shorts and sweatshirt I'd been wearing.

"I need sustenance."

Earlier in the day, I'd put a roast in the Crock-Pot with some vegetables.

Kane pulled on some jeans. "I'm going to go check things out with Mariah unless you need my help."

"No, I've got it. What do you check out?" I wondered what Kane did when he was outside for long periods of time. He knew every inch of his land.

"I check for tracks or anything that's out of place. After seeing those tracks earlier—and closer to the cabin than I'd like—I just want to make sure the wildlife isn't encroaching too much."

"Have fun."

Kane threw up a hand in response as he took Mariah out. I wondered why he was so meticulous. *Would animals really come that close to the cabin?*

I checked my phone and saw I'd gotten a text from my mom about thirty minutes earlier.

Mom: *How are things?*

Me: *Good. Kane took me shooting. He's not so grumpy when he's away from people. Haha!*

Mom: *I can't wait to meet him. He sounds like a good man.*

Me: *You know we aren't really dating, right? Like we are really friends and he's helping out with Mason like I explained. And I'm only living here because there really are no vacancies.*

Mom: *Oh, I know. I would still like to meet him. You sound happy and I like that.*

Me: *I am happy. Just being away from everything is helping. Love you guys.*

Mom: *We love you, too.*

The door opened and Kane came back in with his eyebrows drawn.

"What's wrong?"

"More bear tracks. Looks like the same one that's got a limp. Tracks are a little closer this time."

That creepy feeling came over me again, and I looked out the window. It was pitch black, and I couldn't see anything. "It can't get in the house, can it?"

"No, it won't. Bears don't open doors."

I threw the dish towel at him. "But they can bust through them."

"I think you've seen too many movies."

I hit at his chest, and he caught me. That familiar look in his eyes made me smile. "Not until we've eaten. I'm hungry. I'm not one of those girls who says they're hungry and then only eats a bite or two. Like, I'm legit hungry."

He smiled and took a step back. "You cooked. I'll serve."

As I walked to the table, Kane said, "Teale?"

"Yeah?"

"I won't let anything happen to you. Promise. Don't let the bear worry you. I'll always make sure you're safe."

"Thanks, Kane."

My heart fluttered with feelings that weren't supposed to be there.

CHAPTER
Seventeen

Kane

It had been a long night. I cracked my neck and took a sip of my coffee. A little after midnight, I'd received an email from the FBI asking for my thoughts on the case so far. It pissed me off that I couldn't see what I was missing. And of course, the FBI reminded me *again* of the deal I'd made regarding my brother, Hayden, and his wife, Kory. *Bastards.* I looked again at the photos of the crime scenes in my office. I'd looked at the pictures and evidence several times while Teale was exercising or ordering more shit online. Yesterday, she told me there were more boxes at the post office.

Somehow, I'd managed to keep us at my cabin for the last few days. The trick was keeping Teale busy. We hiked, shot targets, snowmobiled, and fucked. Yeah, we fucked a lot.

But today, there was no escaping seeing my family. Kory was having a dinner at her house. Well, it was technically Alexa's house. When Kory first arrived in town, Alexa had offered it to her and Hayden. Since Alexa lived with Drake in the cabin he'd built, not to mention the apartment over the Red Onion, Kory and Hayden helped keep the place up.

I'd known Alexa since high school. She had a heart of gold and wanted to help anyone she could. Kory was the same. They were good for my brothers. I had a feeling once Teale got into the mix, the shit I would receive from my brothers was going to be a new level of hell. They'd never seen anyone affect me the way Teale was able to disarm me completely. Hopefully, I'd be able to keep my shit together and wouldn't turn into some giggling, grinning fool.

I turned my thoughts back to the case. Over the last day or two, I had better focus than I'd had in months, so I stared at the pictures and notes again. The animal tracks and weather had obscured any human footprints. In some cases, by the time the FBI had found the women, there wasn't much left. The crime scenes themselves weren't going to give me much.

I dug through the files. The profile for this guy was pathetic. We assumed he was male due to the strength it would take to subdue his victims. He was able to use an axe, and all his victims were slim women with blond hair.

I picked up my phone and called Agent Douchebag. His cocky attitude continually drove me to the verge of telling him to fuck off. He acted as if he owned my ass.

He answered on the first ring. "Well, well, you finally decided to return my call. You're working late."

"They were all in new relationships." There was a pause. So, they hadn't added this detail to the short list of information we had on the killer.

"And?"

And if I could give this guy a swift kick in the ass, I

would. But his arrogance was wearing on me. "I don't put together the clues. That's your job. Or did you want to pass that off on me, too."

"I thought we had a deal. No need to be an asshole, Kane."

I gritted my teeth. I'd had enough. "There's nothing I can do for crime scenes you've let go to shit. If you're going to threaten me every damn time, the deal is off. Go figure it the fuck out on your own. I'll let Hayden and Kory know you want to see them."

I hung up the phone, seething. Yeah, I was calling his bluff. Too much time had passed for them to really do anything to Kory or Hayden. And I had taped conversations of Agent Pussy threatening me and was willing to use them, if needed. Their asses would be fucked. Butch was ex-military, and he'd be able to put me in contact with someone within the government. The only reason I hadn't told them to piss off was that there was a prick out there killing innocent women.

The phone rang again. *Bingo*. I picked up and said, "If you're ready to actually work together and not be a motherfucker, I'm willing to stay on this case. If this bullshit is going to continue, consider the deal off. And we'll see where the chips fall."

"Let's be reasonable." Agent Gathcart was uncomfortable now.

It was time to shit or get off the pot. "I'm done with the threats. You have yourself a serious problem, and if the timeline is right, he's due to kill again soon."

"I know." He let out a long sign. "No more threats. Regardless of what happens, Kory and Hayden are out of this."

That was a relief. The last thing my brother needed was

more drama. I remained quiet for a second. I had said more to this man in the last five minutes than the entire time I'd known him. If Teale's habits started to rub off on me, causing me to word vomit, I might have to punch myself.

"Kane, you still there?"

"I am. You need to inform the people of Alaska that there's a problem. Specifically, this area."

He hesitated before speaking. "We don't want to alarm the public."

It had been the same debate the entire time. People's lives were at stake, and I was done messing around. "The people deserve to know. I'm not letting anyone in my town be killed because you didn't want to alarm the public. We both know he's moving south. That puts Skagway and the surrounding towns at risk. You need to warn the public, or I will."

"You have confidentiality clauses."

I said nothing. Those were my terms. He tried to wait me out, but I wasn't budging. "Kane, we don't want this guy to know what we have."

"Which is absolutely nothing. Maybe if people know, they might have additional information to help us or they might see something. You guys have had zero leads. The people deserve to know."

"Fair enough. I'll run it by my boss."

This time, I wasn't going to accept the runaround the way I had the last few times I'd suggested telling the people. "I'll expect to see it on the evening news. Don't mention my name." The last thing I needed was everyone asking me, "Who dunnit?" I had no idea, and it would take my focus off the case.

"I'll let you know when it's done."

"Thanks."

It seemed like the conversation had ended, but Agent Gathcart said nothing. I expected he had something else to say, so I waited.

"Our team received something today. It's been cleared to share with you."

"What's that?" These fools were completely incompetent. They spent more time focusing on the red tape than the actual problem.

"We got a letter that said, 'I know you're working with Foster.'"

My name was being brought into this? "What the fuck?"

"Yes. You got anyone who might have a beef with you?"

"No. Have you told anyone I'm involved?"

"Just those on the case you already knew about."

I let out a breath. There were two options; the FBI had a rat or whoever this asshole was had eyes on me. Either way, it pissed me off.

"Kane, you still there?"

"Yeah."

"Let me know if you think of anything."

"Will do."

After I hung up, I looked at the evidence again, needing to get my thoughts straight now that the killer knew about me.

So far, the killer gave little to no clues. The guy had left an ax embedded in a tree trunk at every crime scene.

I leaned back in my chair and stared at the map of all the confirmed kills on the wall. The pins looked like a giant F. The asshole was probably telling us all to fuck ourselves.

Based off the timeline and the locations, the next kill would be around Skagway or the surrounding towns. And if the killer knew about me... he most likely knew about my family. My brothers and dad needed to know. I pulled out my phone and three-way called my older brothers. It was three-thirty in the morning, and they'd probably be pissed, but what the hell. It needed to be done.

"This better be good, asshole," Hayden's sleepy voice answered first.

"Kane, some of the world sleeps," Drake muttered.

"Can you guys get away from Alexa and Kory?"

Last month, both of my brothers got married within days of each other. That life was not for me. I loved Alexa and Kory like sisters—I would die for them—but relationships were stressful. The ups and downs had taken a toll on my brothers.

It took a few seconds before Drake came back on the line after Hayden let me know he was ready. "What's going on, Kane?"

"I've been working with the FBI. There's a serial killer in Alaska."

They both swore on the other end of the line. Drake responded, "What can you tell us?"

It took a while to bring them up to speed on what I knew. I was confident anything I told them would stay between us. After I finished, they were quiet, and I let them process. It was a hell of a lot to take in.

"Be on the lookout for anyone strange. Anything strange. It should be in the evening news, so make sure your wives don't go out alone. The asshole knows I'm involved, so there's either a snitch or he's had eyes on me."

"Jesus," Hayden said.

"We'll keep the girls close," Drake added. "What do you need from us?"

This was going to cause me hell, but I needed to have a plan. "If I have to go out of town, Teale is going to need a place to stay."

"We'll make sure she's okay. You ready to answer any of our questions yet?" Drake asked.

Of course they wanted answers. But they weren't ever going to get them. They could say whatever the hell they wanted. "Nope. It's been explained. I'll call Dad in the morning. Thanks for helping with Teale. Night, dickheads."

They chuckled, and we hung up. *Assholes*.

I wanted to find this guy. *Where is he? What is he thinking?* I kept staring at the pictures, willing something to come to me. Before the news broke, I would need to tell Teale.

CHAPTER
Eighteen

Lumberjack

I *stare at her, my latest love.*

Her hands and feet are wrapped.

She's squirming near the fire in anticipation of what's to come. I see the desire. They all have it.

She's a random I found. Not the type I normally like. That will throw them off. It'll buy me just enough time.

I take a step forward and watch her eyes widen. I'm coming, sweetheart. It's time. I've kept you waiting long enough.

I need this one to last. It might be awhile before I'm able to indulge in the sweet nectar of a woman.

I have plans. Big plans for his dark-haired beauty.

I need to be careful. Very careful. If I give Foster too much, he'll find me before I'm ready for it to all be over.

CHAPTER
Nineteen

Kane

"I swear I won't cause a problem this time." Teale giggled from the passenger seat.

I snorted. "I don't know if you can help yourself."

From beside me, I heard an exasperated sigh, and Teale muttered something under her breath. As we came down the driveway, I saw the entire family was already at Kory and Hayden's. I put the truck in Park and silently cursed. This was going to be hell. Hollis's SUV was there, too. Since coming from New York with Alexa to be the town's doctor, we'd adopted him into the family. He was a good guy. I respected him for what he was doing for our small town.

I took a deep breath and grabbed the hat from the glove compartment. A bet was a bet. I was ready for winter be over with, and then I was burning this hat.

"What's that?" Teale asked.

I smirked. "A hat."

I put it on, and Teale looked at me like I had two heads. It was one of those hats where the flaps could be tied up to make you look like a pussy or they could be left down and make you look like a dick. It was a pick-your-poison kind of deal. After I pretended nothing was wrong with this stupid-ass hat, Teale said, "O-okay, it just doesn't seem like your style. It's... I don't know..."

"Ridiculous."

She giggled. "I was going to go with *furry*. I mean, you could use it to trick the animals into thinking you're one of them as you find your next... trophy."

"We're going to go hunting."

She shook her head. "No way. You'll end up mistaking me for a poor little rabbit or squirrel. I won't look good mounted."

"You look good mounted on me."

In the dim light, I saw a blush creep on her cheeks. Fucking beautiful. Just thinking about it made me want her all over again.

"Well..."

"Did I fluster you? I remember this afternoon when you were riding me, you were calling out my name and begging me to thrust harder."

She pressed her legs together, and I could tell she was getting wet. Hell, I wanted her again. I was about to say something else when she reached for the door. Before she got out, she taunted, "I mean, you were good today. But I still had to get myself off before we came here. So, you must not have thrusted hard enough."

Teale scurried out of the truck. *Tease.* I would get her

back soon enough. I opened the back door to let Mariah out and walked around the truck to where she was waiting. "Did you really get yourself off?"

"Yes, in the shower. I used a vibrator. It's water safe."

I wanted to pull her back into the truck, but the front door opened, and Alexa stepped outside.

"Oh, good, you guys are here. Dinner is just about ready."

Yeah, right. They'd known from the truck lights the moment I pulled down the driveway. They'd been waiting to pounce.

Teale bounced up the steps. That woman had more energy than anyone I knew. "It's so good to see you."

"You, too. Come in and meet the rest of the family."

Things were definitely shifting between us. I wasn't ready to kill her and actually enjoyed her company. It was a nice, temporary change—at least until she left.

As soon as we cleared the door, I took off the stupid hat. Kory already had a bowl with water and food for Mariah.

It looked like a damned reception with everyone lined up to meet Teale. My brothers had shit-eating grins on their faces. It irritated me, but I didn't let them see that. If they thought they were getting to me, it would get worse… so much worse.

They looked at me, and I pointed to the dark-haired beauty beside me. "This is Teale. Now everyone can get off my ass."

Teale shed her furry coat. "Hey! It's nice to meet you guys. I'm the fake girlfriend who's wreaking havoc in Kane's life."

Well that was one way to put it out there. I had to work on not smiling like an idiot.

Mom took a step forward with a huge grin on her face.

Soon enough, they'd see that I wasn't some lovesick puppy like my brothers were. "I'm Kane's mom, Amie, and this is his dad, Ike."

Teale reached for my mom. "I need to hug the vegetable lover. You saved me while we were stuck at Kane's cabin. If it hadn't been for you sticking those vegetables in his freezer, I would've had only meat and potatoes. And I promise, as Kane's roomie, I'll do my best to get him to eat his veggies."

Mom laughed and tucked some of her blond hair behind her ear. Hayden looked the most like Mom. Drake was a mix of both parents. And I favored my dad. Mom said, "That's appreciated. Normally, I throw the old, freezer-burned vegetables away after a year and restock them, hoping he'll come around."

"Well, I've explained the importance of veggies if he wants to be strong like his brothers."

That earned more laughs, and I rolled my eyes. Hayden flexed like an idiot. "Spinach does a body good."

The prick hated vegetables, too. I nodded. "Be sure to get an extra helping tonight. It'll inspire me to try some after you finish them."

Hayden's mouth turned down for a second. He'd been caught. Beside him, Kory put her hand on his arm. "Aww, that's such a sweet older brother setting a good example. I think we've got some salad, squash, and green beans in there."

It was hard to keep a straight face. I said, "Eat a whole plate of veggies, and I'll eat some squash."

Teale was excited. "This is going to be monumental. I have tried everything while we were snowbound. Everything. Thank you, Hayden. Now maybe Kane won't be so obstinate about the protein shakes."

Oh, hell no. "You're adding shi—stuff like spinach and kale. That's not protein."

"I hope my son has not cursed too much around you. I try, Teale. Lord knows I try." Mom said.

Here we go. Teale winced. "Well… I've loaned him my curse-word allotment, so he's not that far in the hole."

Dad looked at me and smiled. *Yeah, I have my hands full.* She was a full-time job. I clapped my hands together before we got off track. "I'm ready to be inspired to eat my veggies. Kory, can you make sure and give my brother an extra helping of green beans?"

"For sure," she giggled.

Mom knew Hayden rarely ate vegetables and pressed her lips together. Drake sometimes did. *Pansy.* Mom turned toward the kitchen, ushering Teale. "Okay, let's get our plates fixed, and Ike will say grace."

As the rest of family went to the kitchen, Hayden and I flipped each other off at the same time. "Let me know how the green beans are while I'm eating roast." He pushed me, and I laughed. I added, "That'll teach you to be a show-off."

Drake came up behind us. "Because we all know I have the bigger muscles."

I turned to my two brothers, using one of Teale's lines. "For you guys to be so obsessed with your muscles, you must be trying to compensate."

"Whatever, dickhead," Drake responded.

"Ass," Hayden said.

It worked on them as well as it had me. We walked into the kitchen. I shrugged, saying, "Mom always says name-calling isn't nice."

Mom held a spatula. "Drake, Hayden, stop calling your

brother inappropriate names."

"Sorry, Mom," they said.

I grinned. "Get 'em, Mom."

Mom pointed the spatula at me. "Don't egg your brothers on."

"Never." I smiled and gave her a hug.

As we made our way to the dining room, Dad said to Teale, "We didn't get to meet officially. I'm Ike."

She hugged him. "It's so good to meet you. And I love your furniture. Like seriously love it. It's stunning."

"Well, thank you."

At that point, Hollis came downstairs in his city-slicker loafers and khaki pants. "Sorry about that. I was on the phone with Devney. I'm Hollis, the town doctor. It's nice to see someone else making the Twiner Tellings for a change."

"Well, I'm glad it helps someone. My word, where do those ladies hang out? They definitely have ninja skills."

Hollis laughed. "Fifth-degree black belt ninja skills."

"Fo' shizzle."

He leaned in conspiringly toward Teale. "Just be glad Ol' Man Rooster doesn't have any grandsons. Until I started dating Devney, he had me almost down the aisle with his granddaughter. It was a mess."

"Oh my. This town is amazing! Ol' Man Rooster? I think I might have to adopt him as my unofficial grandpa."

The family laughed. Hollis looked at me. "How's the hat? Keeping you warm this winter?"

"For sure."

Drake added, "I love mine."

I rolled my eyes. Of course he would say that. Hollis looked at Teale. "Has Kane been wearing his Paul Bunyan hat?"

"What's a Paul Bunyan hat? Like a knitted beanie?" she asked.

Exactly. Finally, there was something we could agree on. I added, "Yes, in folklore, Paul Bunyan's hat looks like a beanie."

Hollis walked over to his coat and pulled out the stupid hat that was just like mine, but in red. "Well, if this hat had been around when Paul Bunyan was cutting trees with Babe, his blue ox, he would have opted for its versatility."

Hollis put the hat on and demonstrated the flaps down and up.

Teale nodded. "I can see that. It's definitely an upgrade to the beanie. Why does Kane have to wear this hat?"

"He lost a bet, I'm afraid. I was proven to be more Alaskan than him in a fishing contest." Hollis puffed out his chest.

I gritted my teeth. The man was obsessed with being an Alaskan. Unfortunately, he was about as city slicker as they came. But then the mayor had gone and given him a certificate as an official Alaskan. The world was coming to an end.

Teale looked at me, shock clear on her face. "Someone bested you hunting? Were you sick?"

The side of my mouth tried to lift, but I forced it not to move. "Fishing. And no, I wasn't sick."

I swear that fucker cheated. No way he could catch that many fish that fast. It was like the damn things had been jonesing for his hook.

Teale patted my shoulder. "The hat is very, um... manly. You should embrace it."

I raised my eyebrow in warning. "Don't."

She put her hands up. "Okay. I won't mention to Hollis

that tonight is the first time I've ever seen that hat."

Oh fuck, I'm in trouble. Teale grinned, secure in the knowledge that she'd just thrown me to the damn wolves, and man, I liked it… more than I should.

CHAPTER
Twenty

Kane

"You need another beer?" Drake called.

"Yeah," Hayden and I answered.

We survived the dinner with my family. My mind kept drifting to having Teale again after the stunt she pulled in the truck and that sass about my hat. If we could leave without raising suspicions, we would have been gone long before now.

At dinner, Teale sat with Mom and Alexa. My brothers looked disappointed, which pleased me. I would never let there be more between Teale and me. Never. Hayden looked a little sick as he nursed his beer. The vegetables had done him in. He hadn't finished, so I'd gotten off scot-free.

We were sitting around the table, eating some chocolate pie Kory had made. It was damn good. Of course, Teale hadn't eaten much since she'd been talking about everything and nothing at all. I sat back and watched. She had the ability to draw people in and make them feel like they'd known her for a million years.

"No way! Are you serious? Kane Foster, I have a serious bone to pick with you," Teale called from across the table.

"What the hell did I do?"

Mom chided, "Kane, language."

"Sorry, Mom. But she yelled at me, which startled me and caused a curse word to slip out."

Mom closed her eyes. "Ike, this is your fault."

"My fault?" Dad responded.

"This is my payback for something you did in your past life. I was an angel."

Dad leaned over, put his arm around Mom, and smiled at her lovingly. I admired my parents' relationship. I had been lucky to have them as I grew up. Dad kissed the side of Mom's head. "I'm sorry, dear."

Teale cocked her head. "Aww, it's so sweet to hear you apologize to your mom like that. Can you say 'Sorry, Teale' in that same nice tone?"

Mom looked my way. "Kane, I hope you're using the manners I taught you."

"Oh, he is. He just gets a tad grumpy sometimes."

Drake leaned forward. "A real Mr. Grumpy Pants, I've heard."

Teale high-fived my brother from across the table. "Yes! The name is so fitting. He stomps and grunts and uses one-word answers."

Hayden laughed. "Teale, I've decided we're going to adopt you into this family."

She giggled. "I can be the sister you guys never had."

"Yes!" Hayden gave a fist pump.

That would be my worst nightmare coming to life.

Mom switched topics before she took another bite of pie. "Are your parents coming up to visit any time soon, Teale?"

"As soon as this town gets some vacancies. There is not one opening anywhere. I've tried everywhere. Nothing. And supposedly, per the Twiner Tellings, Mason is still here."

We hadn't heard a word from him since that first day. Samoane and Jane had been seen entering Mason's hotel room. They were the girls who *liked* the visitors in town. It was hard to picture Teale with that prick. And the thought of her sitting at the dinner table like this, but with his family, rubbed me the wrong way. Probably because he was such an asshole. *Yep*. That was definitely the reason.

Mom put down her fork. "They could stay with us."

"Oh, I wouldn't want to impose my family on you guys," Teale said.

"It wouldn't be an imposition. Not at all. We'd love to have them. I don't think they're going to find an open room anytime soon."

I wanted to cut Mom off as she made the offer, but the manners she'd taught us were ingrained. This had *bad idea* written all over it. Teale would want to stay with my parents so she could see her parents, which meant she wouldn't be at my cabin and in my bed. I wasn't fond of that idea. But there was nothing I could do.

"That's really nice. I'll let them know."

Kory leaned forward. "When are we doing girls' night?"

My brothers and I exchanged a look. The girls alone in any of our houses wasn't an option with a serial killer on the loose. The FBI had announced that there was a serial killer in Alaska. I knew the girls knew, but people never figured they were in harm's way in their own homes. And with him identifying me, it had me more on edge.

"How about this Friday?" Alexa offered.

I intercepted before this spun out of control. Teale being exposed like that—hell, any of them being exposed like that—wasn't going to happen. If I had to tie her up, I would. "Why don't all of us get together? Guys can hang while you girls do... whatever you girls do."

The entire room fell silent, and all eyes turned to me.

"What?" I asked.

"Nothing," everyone seemed to mutter at the same time. Teale looked perplexed, too. It was odd.

Alexa smoothed over the situation. Thank goodness. She was always Switzerland. "Sounds great. Devney will be back by then. She's visiting her mom in Washington and hasn't been able to get back because of the weather. Hayden's going to get her tomorrow as long as the weather holds. You'll love Devney. She works part-time at the clinic but also teaches music at the high school."

"Perfect! I can't wait to meet her." Teale put her hands up. "Now that we have this settled, let's back this horse up for a second. I still have a bone to pick with you, Kane Foster!"

"What did I do this time?"

She flattened her lips. *Oh shit, I'm about to get it.* "You have been withholding information. There is a Starbucks here? An actual Starbucks? Like a legit, certified Starbucks. The heavens are opening up and singing Hallelujah from the sky."

"Yeah. It's in the fu—freaking jewelry store."

Mom raised an eyebrow at my near slip.

"I don't care if it's in Timbuktu. I've been living off that yucky coffee at your house until my espresso machine comes.

And I could have been coming to Starbucks every day. I'm a rewards member."

Hollis grinned. "Welcome to the club, young Starbuckian. Pretty soon we're going to outnumber the natives. And then they might give us an actual building as opposed to hanging in the diamond-ring section while ordering a double espresso."

Kory added, "I feel the same way. But I've learned only the tourists go there. Hollis and I alternate who goes so we don't appear as addicted. Sometimes, we get Alexa or Devney to pinch-hit and do a coffee run. I think we're slowly bringing them to the dark side."

Teale clapped her hands. "Oh, this will be fun. We'll convert the entire town."

I groaned, and my dad covered his mouth to hide his laughter. Everyone was enjoying my discomfort. I shook my head. "That won't happen."

As if I hadn't spoken, Teale continued, "My first conversion will be Mariah."

Everyone looked at me. Yeah, she had gone to the one thing that would never happen. "Leave my dog out of this. She's not drinking coffee."

Teale came around the table and knelt in front of Mariah. "Tomorrow, I'm going to get you a puppuccino. You're going to love it." Teale raised her head and looked at everyone at the table. "Who's coming with us? My treat."

I'll be damned if every one of the traitors raised their hand.

"I've got to see this," Hayden said. "Kane at a Starbucks."

I folded my hands over my chest. "I'm not going. Mariah's not going."

"Oh, this is going to be fun!" Kory exclaimed.

Teale jumped up. "Does eight work for everyone?"

"Teale," I said firmly.

No one was listening to me.

My family all agreed on the time. Teale confirmed, "So, eight it is."

I tried again. "Teale."

She turned and gave me that oh-so-sweet smile. "Yes, Kane?"

This was never going to end. And if I refused, she'd kidnap my dog. "Never mind."

Later, in the bedroom, I would spank her ass for this little stunt. And I wasn't sure who would be more turned on, me or her. Teale had a ferocious appetite and neither of us had slowed down.

Again, my family stared at me in amusement. I let out a breath. "Trust me, after living with her for a week, I've learned that some things are just easier to let go. There's a reason why I live alone."

Teale laughed. "You don't live alone. You have all your vic—I mean trophies." She mock-whispered to my mom, "I'm not allowed to say *victims* as part of the house rules. But all the dead things staring at me all the time is a little over the top. I had to put a towel over the ones in my bedroom."

Dad let out a hearty laugh along with Mom.

Fuck my life. They loved her.

CHAPTER
Twenty-One

Kane

After dinner was over, the men cleaned up the dishes, which was something my father had taught us as children. If Mom spent her time cooking, we could pick up. I liked the concept.

The space heaters on the porch were on high as I sat on a chair in my stupid penis hat and drank a beer. The rest of the family was inside, chatting away. I needed some space for a few minutes. Mariah sat beside me, eyes closed as I stroked her head.

The door cracked open, and Mom came out. "Mind if I join you?"

I got up and dusted the snow off a second chair for her. "Of course not. What's everyone doing?"

"Just chatting. Alexa was telling Teale the story of how the clinic came to be. And Kory was talking about her party-planning business. Our family has been busy these last few months."

Alexa's father had been killed in a logging accident about two and half years before. If Skagway had had a doctor, her dad might have lived, but it was expensive to airlift someone to the hospital and sometimes the weather wouldn't allow it. Alexa had opened the clinic and brought Hollis back with her from New York. That was how he came to be the town doctor.

The rocking chairs crunched the little bit of snow on the porch as we rocked. I knew Mom wanted answers, but she wasn't the type to push. I'd been lucky to have the best damn mother anyone could ask for. But I also knew Mom had dreams for her boys. She wanted us to be married and happy. And Mom had always wanted lots of grandkids.

I wanted to make sure she wasn't getting the wrong idea about Teale and me. "Mom, Teale and I really aren't dating."

"I know."

I blew out a deep breath. "It's just everyone keeps staring at me like I'm two seconds from proposing and being tied down for the rest of my life. I just don't want people trying to see something that isn't there."

"Do you want to know what I see?"

"Sure."

I really wasn't sure.

"I see a man who's letting this huge wall he's built come down just a little. I see a man who's enjoying himself in the company of others. It's not bad, it's just different from what we're used to."

I thought about this for a minute and was able to see her point. "I get it. But Mom, it'll never go further than this. I don't want to get your hopes up."

"And that's fine. But I think you've got a friend for life.

We can never have too many of those."

"True."

A friend for life. I thought about this for a second. It would be nice to reach out from time to time. But when Teale found a man to settle down with and got married, I'd have to cut it off. The thought of her with another man wasn't something I wanted to deal with.

Mom broke the silence. "I like her. Her energy is a breath of fresh air."

"And ability to drive me crazy. Mom, she would argue with a lamppost if no one was around."

She patted my leg. "You'll survive. You're tough. I'm sure a tiny girl like that isn't that scary."

Oh, she has no idea.

Suddenly, we could hear music coming from the other side of the house. I wondered what was going on. Mariah's ears perked up.

"Let's go see what they're up to. I heard them mention ice skating."

I got up and followed Mom around the porch where the family was gathered. "What's going on?"

"Teale asked if she could skate when we showed her the pond. I asked if she wanted some music, and she said to surprise her."

Teale was at the bench on the side of the pond lacing up. Back at the cabin, I'd mentioned there was a pond, and she'd thrown her skates into a bag, just in case.

Mom asked, "Are you guys going to join her?"

Alexa shook her head. "Not tonight. I didn't bring my skates."

Kory said, "I'm not a fan of skating when it's this cold."

I knew my brothers and dad weren't going to skate. We'd played hockey when we were younger, but that was it.

One song morphed into the next, and Teale took to the ice. She moved with a grace I'd never seen before. She glided across the ice and then began to spin, her arms out to the side at first and moving closer to her body as her spinning grew faster. Then in an instant she broke out of that and kept skating. It was like she was part of the music.

"What song is this?" I asked.

"It's called 'This is Me.' We had a *Greatest Showman* themed party here a couple of days ago, and this was the last thing I played. It's a musical."

I'd never heard of it. But I wasn't one to regularly listen to music, much less a musical.

Teale's face was beautiful as she skated. I was riveted in place as I watched her. The air blew her dark, messy hair loose from its bun as she changed direction. It was unlike anything I'd seen before. She jumped with some twirl and landed perfectly. My family gasped as Teale skated faster and harder. She was a true champion.

The song ended, and my mother said, "That was amazing."

"She's an Olympic champion."

I heard people gasp. Without thinking, I took the stairs two at a time down to the edge of the pond where Teale was skating. Her abrupt stop shot some of the ice onto my pants leg, and I smiled.

"You really can skate." I echoed her words from when we'd gone shooting the first time.

Teale gave a little push back and then forward. "I really can. Want to join me?"

"I don't have skates."

She thought for a second. "I'll order you some. It's only fair—if I shoot with you, you skate with me."

"Fair enough."

Am I actually agreeing to this? What the hell. I looked back up to the rail, and the family had gone back inside. Good, so they were letting us just be friends.

Teale twirled a few times. "I didn't realize how much I missed this."

I sat on the bench to watch as she skated some more. I imagined these simple movements were amateur, but damn, they looked complicated. I would be lucky to not bust my ass out there. "You think you want to return to skating?"

"No, I want to retire. But I don't want to give up skating completely, either. I think I want to teach or something. Maybe hold some different types of camps."

"That sounds like a good idea. Will you teach at your rink in Montana?" Teale fed off the energy of other people. She would make a good teacher.

She did another small twirl. "Probably. I like being close to my family. They remind me of yours. Well, there's only me, but the atmosphere here reminds me of home, if that makes sense."

"Yeah, it does."

Family was everything. Seeing Teale in her element broke down another wall between us. *Friends for life.* Mom had a good point. Teale moved around on the ice some more.

"Your ass looks great, by the way."

"Oh, you think so?"

She did another spinning thing. Yeah, I wanted her again. "I do think so. I also think it's time we left."

"I like that idea. But you better play it cool and not drag me out of here. I don't want your family to know we're sleeping together. It'll just muddle things."

She had a good point. And neither of us wanted complicated. "Agreed. Get inside, say good-bye, and let's leave. Don't fuck around."

"Yes, sir."

Teale gave me a smart-ass salute. Part of me liked egging her on to defy me. And I wasn't sure why.

CHAPTER
Twenty-Two

Kane

I swore Teale was taking her time just to piss me off. She was now exchanging numbers with my mom and sisters-in-law, had asked if she could come to the quilting circle cook-off this spring, and solidified plans for the girls' night out.

Enough was enough. "I'm going to head out. Teale, you ready?"

That mischievous smile confirmed that she was doing this intentionally. And man, it was hot when she defied me. More than I would admit.

Before Teale could respond, my mom offered, "Teale, if you're not ready to go yet, we could bring you home." If she took them up on it... I wasn't sure what I was going to do. If I protested, it would draw attention.

Teale stood. "That's really sweet of you, but I don't want you to drive out of your way. I'll just remember to bring my rental car next time."

Or not.

Being on the roads this late with a killer out there wasn't going to happen. She stretched with a yawn.

If she's too tired, so help me.

Teale hugged every damn person in the room. I'd never ever taken this long to leave *anywhere*. And, of course, there were more conversations. At the door, my family told her good night... again.

"Night guys. It was great meeting you. Can't wait for tomorrow." She gave a little wave, and I herded us out the door. If we waited around, they'd find something else to talk about.

Hollis said, "Don't forget your Paul Bunyan hat!"

Son of a bitch.

"More like dick hat," I grumbled and begrudgingly turned around to grab it. I put the stupid thing on. Teale smirked at me, and I had to take a deep breath. "Let's go," I commanded quietly.

From behind me, Hayden said, "You look so... tough in that."

Teale giggled and said, "Night, see you guys tomorrow for coffee."

As we went down the stairs, I muttered, "I think that's a record for good nights."

"A little anxious to get home, are we?"

I opened the truck door, and Teale put her finger to her chin. "Maybe I should go back in there and say I forgot something. We could start this process all over again."

"Get in the damn truck, Teale."

She thought for a second more, but my patience was gone. "Now."

"Man, you're feisty."

"No, I'm not feisty. I'm ready to sink my dick into your sweet pussy. I'm hard as fuck. Don't test me. Mariah, load up."

Her eyes widened, and I saw the desire flare. Without another word, she hopped into the truck. Finally, the woman listened to me. I had been about two seconds from throwing her in the truck and peeling out of there like a madman.

I got to my side of the truck, ripped my hat off, and threw it on the dash. Teale's laughter only fueled me more. Wisely, she buckled her seat belt and said nothing as I drove down the street.

About a mile down the road, she reached across the console and grabbed my stiff dick. "Someone was ready to leave, I see."

"You know I was."

Her hands messed with the buttons on my jeans. With little resistance, I was freed. "Well, I could make it up to you if you want."

"How's that?"

Teale leaned over and brought my dick into her mouth. I jerked the wheel to one side before correcting and turning down a road no one would be on. Down another road, I pulled over to the side. Her mouth was warm as she worked me up and took me deep. "Fuck, that feels so good."

My balls drew up. She sucked harder. I pulled her up and saw the hungry look in her eyes. "Take off your pants, angel."

While she got her tight-ass leggings off, I put on a condom. I wanted to sink into her heat. Teale crawled on top of me, and I grabbed her hips just before she sank onto me.

"Kane." Her voice was breathy, needy.

I cupped her, feeling how wet she was. "Someone's almost ready."

"I'm ready."

I teased her entrance with my tip, and her moans grew louder. "Don't sink down. Not yet."

"Kane."

I released her hips to see if she'd move. I'd found in our short time together that Teale gave me control in the bedroom.

Good girl.

I took the bottom of her flannel shirt and ripped it open, buttons flying everywhere.

"Kane, I liked that shirt."

I pulled down her bra, exposing her. "And I like your breasts."

"I thought it was my nipples you enjoyed."

I leaned forward and licked the tip of her pointed nipple while my hand found its way to her core.

"Kane, I swear if you don't get inside me right now, I'm going to get myself off and leave you hanging. I'm ready, dammit."

Oh, she's feisty. I sucked her nipple hard, and she let out a moan. If we were home, I would make her wait a little longer, but I couldn't wait. I pushed up, and Teale sank down hard and fast.

"Yes!" she screamed.

It was a race to orgasm as she rode me like her life depended on it. Her nails dug into my shoulders, and I moved my hips faster. As I released, I gave a low, guttural grunt.

Teale collapsed against me as our heavy breaths filled the silence.

I had a feeling winter would be over before I was ready.

CHAPTER
Twenty-Three

Kane

How in the world did she talk me into this?

I rubbed my eyes, wishing it was all a bad dream.

"Oh, it's not that bad. Good grief. Stop being a baby."

I looked at Teale, who was wearing those leggings that drove me crazy under a long flannel shirt. "I'm not being a baby. This is ridiculous. We're going to the local jewelry store for coffee as an entire family."

I gave a sigh as my brothers and my parents pulled in behind me. They were all in separate vehicles. A Foster family caravan. *Just great.* Everyone in town would surely notice all our trucks parked in front of the Starbucks. Deep down, I'd hoped they wouldn't show. Moments later, Hollis pulled up. *Motherfucker.* Everyone had come to this circus.

Teale clapped in excitement. "Everyone's here!"

Unfortunately.

We were going to be the talk of the town. *Entire Foster family visits Starbucks to get a puppuccino.* I pinched the bridge of my nose. We were going to make another newsletter, for sure. *Kane Foster loses his dignity.* I looked at Mariah where she rested her front paws on the console. Teale was loving on her. "You're about to get the bestest treat you ever received in your life. Are you ready?"

I refused to acknowledge any of it. If I said nothing, then I wasn't part of this idiocy. Teale put her hand on the door. "Oh good, the Twiner sisters are here—right on time, too. I figured we could do a family photo."

"What?" I jerked my head around, looking for them.

She laughed. "Gotcha."

I tried to hide my smirk, but it was useless. Teale's sense of fun was contagious. "Do you want to come in?"

But she never gave up. "Teale, it's a damn miracle you got me this close. Don't push your luck. Or so help me, I will take my dog and leave."

"Someone needs some caffeine, Mr. Grumpy Pants. What do you want to drink?"

Ignore the dig. Just ignore it. "I'm not drinking anything that comes in a white cup with that stupid green emblem on it. No. Way. Go do your thing, and I'll be right here."

She gave me that sassy salute. "Sure thing. Wait here, Mariah, *pretty please.* I'll be back with your goodness."

Mariah wagged her tail. *Good grief.* Everyone except Drake went inside. He approached my truck. This was going to be good. He leaned on my door. "You not going in for coffee?"

"I would like to maintain some of my dignity."

He chuckled. "Yeah, I just came here to watch your face

when Mariah gets her first *puppuccino*. I didn't know that was a thing."

"Don't say another word. After this, we're going shooting or fishing or something. Hayden is on his own after actually stepping foot in there." I could feel a headache coming. *How did she talk me into subjecting my dog to this?*

"I'm curious… should I call you Sir Grumpy Pants or Mr. Grumpy Pants?"

"Shut up."

"Real mature of you. Next thing you know, you'll be calling me a *meaniehead.*"

I gave him the bird, which only made him laugh harder. *Asshole.* This was taking forever. Maybe they had to harvest the beans.

Drake shifted his weight, becoming serious. "Any news on the serial killer?"

I shook my head. "No. Whoever it is knows what he's doing. I still have nothing. And he hasn't sent anything that I know of. It still makes no sense why he wanted them to know he knew about me. I need a fresh crime scene if I'm going to be able to track him, but I don't want one—if you get my drift."

"Yeah, I do."

It was frustrating. I felt like I was missing something big. "If there's anyone who can catch him, it's you."

I wasn't so sure about that. I was able to track almost anything, but this had me stumped. "How are the girls dealing with it?"

"Fine. They understand. Since we found out Lex is pregnant, she's being extra cautious."

"What? She's pregnant?"

Drake's face dropped when he realized what he'd said. "Fuck, I wasn't supposed to say anything."

Holy shit. My brother's going to be a dad. I'm going to be an uncle. I smiled. "Congratulations, man! That is the best news."

Drake rubbed his neck, visibly worried. "Don't say anything, okay? Lex isn't ready to tell anyone yet."

If I knew my brother, he was bursting at the seams for everyone to know. He'd always been the one who talked openly about having kids one day. Drake had never been afraid of his feelings. Hayden, on the other hand, had been a wild card for a while. When Kory came into his life, everything changed. I would always be a bachelor. I'd given love a try once. The heartache wasn't worth it.

Drake's smile brought me back into the conversation.

"So, you're good?"

Regardless, this had to have been a little daunting. Soon Drake would be responsible for another human being's life. Big fucking responsibility.

He nodded. "I'm great. More than great. I want everyone to know. We weren't trying, but we weren't doing anything to stop it, either. Happened faster than either of us thought it would."

"You better make sure it's a boy. The Foster line is counting on you."

"That's what I told Lex." Drake chuckled. It was something we joked about a lot. The men outnumbered the women, so we got our way most of the time, like watching action movies on movie night. I would never marry, so as long as my brothers kept up their ends of the bargain by having boys, we'd be good to go.

The family came with their coffee. Teale laughed, holding two cups and talking with Alexa. It was hard to take my eyes off her.

Drake slapped my shoulder. "Remember—not a word about Lex being pregnant."

"Got it."

"Kane, did you hear me?"

I looked at Drake. "Not a word. Promise."

He nodded.

My brother was going to be a dad. I watched Hayden come out with his arm wrapped around Kory and wondered how long until he had a kid, too. He probably wouldn't be that far behind. Things were changing and moving forward. It would never be the same.

I wondered where I would fit into all of this, and if I was okay with it just being me. I wasn't sure what the honest answer was. I shook my head, cursing myself for the thought.

Teale bounded up to the truck with a white cup. In the middle of the cup, where the Starbucks emblem normally was, had a black circle drawn in marker. "Venti Café Americano in a white cup with a black circle."

What language is that? I stared at the cup like it was poison. "Café what?"

She rolled her eyes. "Large black coffee."

"Then why not say that?"

Hollis said, "It's Starbucks. You can't just go up to the counter and say large black coffee. You have to speak the language."

I shook my head. "There must be drugs in the coffee. Do you guys hear yourselves?"

Teale giggled as she opened the back door. "Just drink

your coffee and stop being grumpy."

Kory and Alexa had their phones out and were already taking pictures. I would never live this down. I got out of the truck like a stupid ass, holding a white cup with a black circle, and took a sip.

It wasn't bad, but I would never tell.

Mariah looked at me, and I nodded.

Hollis coughed under his breath. "Hat. Get your hat."

Fuck my life.

I grabbed the hat from the console where Teale had put it that morning. As I took another sip, Teale yelled, "This picture will be perfect for the Twiner Tellings."

"Teale."

Completely ignoring me, she knelt in front of Mariah. "Here you go, sweet girl. Try this. It's a puppuccino."

Mariah gave it a tentative lick before devouring the cup of whipped cream.

Traitor.

Everyone had their phones out, taking pictures.

Hollis cheered in victory. "We have another Starbuckian joining our forces," he said as he petted Mariah's head. Mom handed Teale a cup of coffee.

In unison Teale, Hollis, and Kory held up their coffee cups to each other. They cheered. "Hear, hear."

Dad and Mom took a sip of their coffee while Ol' Man Rooster sat across the way, staring at us. He rubbed his eyes like he couldn't believe he was seeing what he thought he was seeing.

He yelled, "Has hell frozen over?"

I deadpanned back, "I think it has, Rooster."

Of course, everyone around me found that hilarious.

Teale's eyes widened when she recognized the name. Without saying a word, she walked over to greet him. Probably introduced herself as my girlfriend and told him the way we'd met, as well. They were probably exchanging life stories. The next thing I knew, he took the cup she offered and drank from it.

The world was ending.

It had to be.

That was the only explanation.

It couldn't have been the dark-haired ice skater who had rocked my world.

CHAPTER

Twenty-Four

Lumberjack

Relief washes through me with the rush of the kill.

Her body lays lifeless beside me. She was sweet and innocent, and I devoured her screams as she begged me to stop.

This one lasted a little longer than the others. She thought she had a chance to escape. It's all part of the game, the thrill of the chase.

Now, I'm changing the game.

CHAPTER
Twenty-Five

Teale

A month's worth of packages arrived over that week. With the weather, some of my purchases had been delayed. Unfortunately, we'd also had to cancel our girls' night. The snow had everyone stuck inside, unable to travel.

I was relatively sure Mason had left. I'd gotten notice from the landlord that he'd moved out of the apartment. Word was he and Vanessa had split up, too. *Oh well*... I hoped it had been worth it. When I'd mentioned that Mason had left, I'd expected Kane to ask me to move out, but he hadn't said a word.

I opened packages while Kane was out doing rounds with Mariah. Things were becoming easier between us. It was nice. But he was still an enigma, and I couldn't figure out why he wanted nothing to do with relationships. It made no sense, and he offered no insight. Maybe someday... but I doubted it.

It was going to be interesting to see what happened when my mom and dad arrived at the end of the week. They were going to be staying with the Fosters. At one point, I'd mentioned staying with them, too, but Kane had distracted me with that amazing mouth of his. We still hadn't discussed it, but I was going to stay with my parents to spend time with them.

As I changed the laundry, I pulled one of Kane's thermal shirts out the washer and just stared at it. As the days passed, I knew it would be easy to let myself fall for Kane. I had to remind myself this was a winter fling. There were times I felt it could be more.

But it wasn't fair to change the agreement we'd made. And Kane had explicitly said relationships weren't his thing.

I started the dryer and aimlessly walked around the house, my thoughts consuming me. I paused at the door of his office, catching a glimpse of the board Kane was working on, which was covered with a sheet. There were crime scene photos on the board, and he covered it so I wouldn't accidentally see them. Some things were better left unseen.

Kane was working long hours, trying to find the serial killer. It creeped me out to think someone was out there snatching women to torture and then kill them. Kane was stressed he hadn't been able to find any more clues from the pictures and that the killer would strike soon. Thank goodness, no additional bodies had been found. But it felt like a clock was ticking as we waited for it to happen. It seemed odd for the man to stop all of a sudden.

The back door opened, and Kane came in the house, shedding his coat, and hung it on the hook by the door.

"Where's your hat?"

He looked at me and winked. "In the truck. I don't want

to scare the wildlife to death. Can't be adding any more victims to my wall."

"You can be a funny guy when you want, Mr. Foster."

Kane ignored what I said and walked over to the open boxes. He pulled back one of the lids and asked, "Did anything good arrive?"

"Some clothes, pair of shoes, and a yodeling pickle."

"A *what*?"

I pulled the green plastic pickle out of the box behind me. "A yodeling pickle. I found it in the 'interesting finds online' section. And the description hooked me right in."

Kane looked at me like I was crazy. "And what does it do?"

"It yodels." I pressed a button, and an obnoxious yodeling began.

"That needs to go into the trash right this second."

I snickered. "I have to admit, it sounded more fun online."

"How in the world can a yodeling pickle sound fun?"

"Umm... well... I was half asleep." He waited for me to elaborate. "The ad asked if I was tired of trying to convince my regular pickles to yodel using mind bullets. I was, so I ordered it. Well, I've never tried to get pickles to yodel, but I could see how tiring it could be and I thought, 'Why even try the mind bullet process?' So, I went straight to a yodeling pickle."

He stared at me with one brow lifted. "That's what I call wasting money."

I jumped up onto the counter with a shrug. "Or being able to check off 'heard a yodeling pickle' from your bucket list."

Kane positioned himself between my legs. His lips found mind for an intense kiss before he pulled back. "I can show you a yodeling pickle that will be much more satisfying."

"Oh no, you didn't just call your penis a yodeling pickle. That's just... *Ew*."

He nipped my lip, and I opened my mouth to his. It was moments like this when our casual arrangement felt like more. So much more. He gruffly whispered, "Yodelayheehoo!"

When I pushed him back, he was grinning. "I made you breakfast. Bacon, eggs, hash browns, and a protein shake. Then we'll see about the yodeling."

"Teale..."

"Just try it. It's a great way to get your veggies in without even noticing. And it helps with stamina. I mean, I have one every day and I haven't heard any complaints from you." I ran my hands up his chest, and he pressed himself against me. "I promise to reward you if you try it."

He trailed kisses up my neck. "What kind of reward?"

"Anything you like."

"Deal."

The ringing of his cell phone broke the moment. He looked at who was calling, and his eyebrows pinched together. "Let me get this."

"Of course."

Kane stepped away and accepted the call. "Yeah?" There was a long pause, and all playfulness dropped from his face. That wasn't good. My stomach knotted. "Fuck. Where? Give me two hours. I know, but I'm almost an hour from there. Don't let anyone on the site. I need it just as you found it. Yes."

I felt an enormous sense of dread as I listened to his side of the conversation and assumed the worst. "He struck again, didn't he?"

"Yes." He paused for a second. "I need to take you to my parents' place. You'll be safe there. Pack enough stuff for a few days, just in case."

I nodded solemnly and slid off the counter. As I passed him, I caught his scent and froze. Something could happen to him. I turned around and threw my hands around his waist, needing the connection. "But what about you? I don't want you to get hurt, Kane."

"Angel, I'm what the darkness is afraid of. I'll be fine."

I could feel the dangerous undertones in Kane's voice. Kane never said anything he didn't mean. I held him tighter. There had to be something Kane was afraid of, too.

CHAPTER
Twenty-Six

Teale

The entire way into town, Kane shot off rapid-fire instructions to his brothers over the phone. The whole situation had me more on edge, and I wasn't able to block it out. Drake, Alexa, Hayden, and Kory were coming to Ike and Amie's while Kane went to the crime scene. Everyone would be there within the hour. I understood that it was safer. And there was no way I was going to stay at Kane's cabin by myself.

The crime scene was about twenty-five minutes from his parents' place. The serial killer had been just on the outskirts of town, which I knew troubled Kane. The killer had been within reach, and Kane hadn't been aware of it. Now someone was dead. I could sense that Kane blamed himself, at least in part.

We pulled into Ike and Amie's driveway in silence. Normally, I loved coming here, but today was different. Kane would be leaving the safety of the family and heading into danger. We got out of the car without a word. There was so much I wanted to say, but I remained silent. As soon as we walked through the door, Kane headed to his dad's office. "Need to check security. It'll just be a minute."

I imagined he wanted to talk to his dad alone, as well. Amie gave me a hug. "I'm going to take your bag up to the guest room. Make yourself at home."

"Thanks, Amie."

I should have offered to do it myself, but I was afraid I would miss Kane leaving. I wasn't sure what I wanted to say, but I was scared. I could hear Kane's phone going off. It seemed like every few minutes, the FBI called to check on him, which only added to the stress.

Amie came down the stairs, grim lines on her face. She was worried, too. "Would you like some tea, Teale?"

I nodded. "That would be nice. Do you need any help?"

"No, I've got it. You just sit down and relax. I think Kane is leaving soon."

I let out a sigh of relief. If I was in the kitchen, I might not hear Kane. "Thanks, Amie."

It was a struggle to keep my emotions in check. Before we left, Kane had grabbed a gun and put several knives into different holsters all over his body. That meant the situation was dangerous. The thought of never seeing him again was almost more than I could bear.

Kane stepped out of the office and into the hallway. He was dangerous and rugged and rough around the edges, but I was drawn to him. "I need to go. Walk me out?"

"Okay."

Outside, the air was eerily calm. We said nothing for a

few seconds; things felt different than they had before. I couldn't describe it. Finally, I said. "Please be careful, Kane. Please."

That was all I could say. Anything else would reveal more than I wanted to. Kane put his hands on either side of my face, which surprised me. It was gentle and loving, and anyone might have seen us. At his house it was different, but in public, Kane kept his distance. If anyone saw us at that moment, they would know there was more to our relationship.

"You're going to be fine, Teale."

"He struck so close." My voice was barely a whisper. There was so much to process, and I wasn't able to say what I wanted.

"I know. Please listen to me just this once. Do not go anywhere without telling me. Promise me."

"I promise."

He chastely kissed my forehead before stepping back.

"Kane…"

"Yeah."

I stared into his dark eyes; there were so many upspoken emotions there. I needed to change the subject. There were other things I wanted to say, but it wasn't the right time, so it was probably best to keep things light. "I know you didn't get breakfast, so I put the protein shake in the cup holder of your truck. Will you please give it a try?"

He smiled. "Thanks, angel. I will." He turned his focus to the dog sitting beside me. "Mariah, it's time to go hunting."

Those words were like ice in my veins. Kane would be in danger from a killer the FBI hadn't been able to find.

Mariah followed Kane to the truck, on high alert.

I wrapped my arms around myself as he drove away. I

was grateful his brothers and their wives hadn't arrived yet as the tears began to fall. Soon, they were coming so fast, I couldn't stop them.

As the truck disappeared down the drive, I felt Amie's arms come around me. "Now, now. It's okay."

I turned around and held onto her. I wasn't sure what had come over me. But having a mother figure was exactly what I needed.

She squeezed me tight. "Let's go inside and talk. Drake and Hayden will be here any minute."

"O-okay."

Amie led me up the stairs to a room that seemed a bit stark compared to the rest of the house. "Whose room is this?"

"Kane's. I made a point not to change my boys' rooms when they moved out. I wanted it to always feel like home when they came here. He asked me to put you in here." On the wall were a few of his *trophies*. They were likely some of his first. "So tell me what's going on?"

Why did he want me in his room? It was so confusing. I looked at Amie, and I wasn't able to hold it in any longer. "I've fallen in love with him. It wasn't supposed to happen. I promised him I wouldn't. But I did and now... I just don't know."

I couldn't hold back the sobs any longer, and Amie held me for what felt like an eternity. I wished my mom was there. Oh, how I wished, but I was grateful I had Amie.

As the tears subsided, I jerked back and started to panic. "Please don't tell anyone. Especially Hayden and Drake. I just don't want things to change."

"I won't tell a soul."

Downstairs, the door opened, and we heard Drake's voice

first.

"Let me go see them so you can have a moment. I'll let them know you'll be down in a bit."

"Thank you."

At the door, Amie stopped and looked back at me. "If it's any consolation, I think he's fallen in love with you, too."

Oh, how I wish that were true. But I remembered his words in the sauna so clearly. "He hasn't. I promise you, he hasn't. And he's been nothing but honest with me, Amie. You have an amazing son. It's my fault I let my heart get involved."

Before she opened the door, she paused for a second. "I don't think he knows it yet, but he has. Just give him time."

It would take Kane an ice age to change his stance on something like love. And my heart was breaking at the knowledge that I would never have any more of him than I did now.

CHAPTER
Twenty-Seven

Kane

Damn it all to hell.

This son of a bitch had been in my town, within fifteen miles of my fucking home. The girl was a tourist. And from the information we'd gathered, she was single. That wasn't part of the limited MO we had. *Motherfucker.* Everything about this scene felt wrong. The location was too obvious. The others had been off the beaten path. One thing was for sure... he wanted this body to be found fast. *Why?*

The image of Teale's face as I pulled away still lingered in my mind. She'd been so scared for me. And I'd wanted to reassure her. It hadn't mattered where we were or if anyone could have seen us.

Later.

I refocused on the scene in front of me. Mariah and I had walked the perimeter, but I was not letting anyone near the body. There had been no footprints. Only animal tracks like the other scenes. *What the fuck?* The killer hadn't airdropped the victim there. Based on the photos of the previous crime scenes, I'd thought the human footprints had been obliterated due to wildlife and the elements. I meticulously checked the different tracks.

Mariah was smelling the area but hadn't been let near the body. The smells were muted by the snow. I came upon the next animal track and froze. The limping bear. The same one that had been at my cabin. That wasn't a coincidence. That was how the man got around. I turned to Agent Gathcart. "Get good photos of each of the tracks. I'll be back. No one get near the body. Mariah, come."

I followed the tracks with Agent Douchebag hot on my tail. "What did you find?'

"I need to follow this animal track. Make sure they don't fuck up the scene. It might be our only shot."

I picked up my pace, and the agent followed. "I'll need to know what you've found."

"And you will. But if I don't have that scene preserved, I won't be much help. Keep at least ten feet back from all sides."

Agent Gathcart stopped and turned the other way. I drew my gun from the holster under my shirt and turned off the safety. Carefully, we walked through the forest, Mariah a few paces in front of me as she followed the trail. The snow slowed down our pace, but it was densely packed, which made it easier. The woods were deadly silent. We headed due north toward a road, and the tracks ended at a fresh set of tire prints. *Fuck.* The killer was gone. I snapped a few pics with my phone in case the FBI screwed up the pictures.

The girl's car had been reported stolen, and I imagined

these tire marks had come from her car. The FBI would probably find it dumped somewhere. *Is he using their vehicles to get away after ditching them?* It was something to add to the list to look at. "Get the scent, Mariah."

I pointed to the bear tracks and Mariah sniffed. Nothing felt right. The man could have used the car as a decoy and then doubled back. But I kept the course. Later, I would need to check how far the other scenes had been from a main road. My adrenaline was pumping as we searched, hoping to find something. Anything. After doubling back and searching the other way, I decided to return to the scene.

No scent. No trail. Nothing.

Son of a bitch.

I tried to take it all in to see if there was anything obvious. Another clue, perhaps. *Nothing.* Agent Gathcart approached as I made it back to the crime scene. Before he had a chance to bombard me with questions, I said, "On the rural road due north, there are tracks from a car that took off. We need to see where it wound up. I covered five miles and found nothing. I imagine he took the victim's car. We need to find it and process it."

Agent Gathcart dispatched some agents, telling them, "Keep me posted on anything you find." He pushed back his shoulders and focused back on me. "So, he's impersonating a bear to not leave footprints as he escapes?"

"Yes. Those bear tracks lead to the woods and disappear on the road. That's him. I think the other tracks are his, too. Each of the scenes have been staged like this."

At that point, it wasn't necessary to say the prick had been at my place. I trusted no one. And since he'd been on my land, that made things personal.

Agent Gathcart cleared his throat. "There's another problem."

I looked around the body to see if there was anything else. "What's that?"

"The killer called you out."

Spinning around, I said, "Come again?"

Agent Gathcart brought me to a tree and pointed to a picture of me with a knife through the forehead.

"What the *fuck*?"

In sloppy handwriting underneath, it said *"Catch me. I dare you."*

He wants me to catch him? Why?

From my research, I'd found that some serial killers wanted to be caught to claim what they had done, like Sean Gillis, also known as "The Other Baton Rouge Killer." Others, like Edmund Kemper, otherwise known as "The Co-ed Killer," were done killing and ready to be caught. For some reason, I'd caught this guy's attention, and he wanted to play with me.

The murders had been going on for the last year, before the FBI contacted me to help. The man killed every five weeks—except this last time. The killer had been at my fucking house twice. And Teale had been there.

"Give me a second." I took out my phone, needing the contact with her, and walked away for privacy.

Me: *You okay?*

Teale: *Yes, just watching* Ghost *with the girls. I'm taking notes in case you send me back to Butch's.*

There was no chance in hell she'd be going anywhere by herself.

Me: *You don't have to worry about that. My brothers there?*

Teale: *Yep. Your mom made us popcorn. I'm not supposed to say anything, but they're watching the movie with us.*

Me: *That's good ammo to use against them. Thanks, angel. I'll be there soon.*

Teale: *Sounds good. You did not hear it from me! Did you drink the shake?*

Me: *I did. It wasn't half bad.*

Teale: *Veggies are amazing. I'll make you another tomorrow.*

Me: *Let's not go that far. Okay, I need to get back to work.*

Teale: *Be careful. I packed a snack for Mariah in the truck if she gets hungry.*

Me: *Okay, I'll give it to her.*

I took a deep breath and messaged my brothers.

Me: *Everything okay?*

Drake: *Just fine.*

Hayden: *You good?*

Me: *Just keep an eye out. Things have taken a turn. I'll explain later.*

Drake: *Of course. Need anything?*

Me: *Not yet. I'll be there as soon as I can.*

She was fine. That was a relief.

"Why would the killer call you out?" Agent Gathcart was inches from me. He was not a patient man.

I blew out a breath and turned around. "I don't know. But I intend to find out. I'm not tied to this in any way. What do your psychologists think?"

"I'm waiting for their assessment. I'll send it after I review it."

Fanfuckingtastic. It would take time we didn't have. I nodded. "Let's process the scene."

We spent the next few hours photographing every inch of the place and examining the body. It was nearing sunset, and the FBI was bringing in lights so we could continue working. The poor woman had been kept alive and brutalized for what appeared to have been several days, based on the bruising. The coroner had said five, at least.

Sick motherfucker.

My phone rang, and I checked the screen to see it was Drake. It had been a couple hours since I'd checked in. "Yeah?"

"You need to get home. Something's happened to Teale."

I ran to my truck. Nothing else mattered.

CHAPTER
Twenty-Eight

Teale

Shock.

I had to be in shock.

The memory of the package I received sent a chill through me. Amie held my hand, and Kory and Alexa sat on the love seat adjacent to the one I was sitting on. *Maybe I'm numb?* The guys were at various spots around the house, keeping watch. The only sound that could be heard was the ticking of the clock.

The images I had seen would be with me forever.

Outside, tires squealed.

"It's Kane," Drake called from the other room.

I jumped up as Kane burst through the door. "Where is she?"

"I'm in here."

Kane appeared in the doorway, relief all over his face.

He was fine. Nothing had happened. Everyone told me

they'd been in contact with him, but after what I'd seen, I needed to see him for myself.

I ran into his arms. He picked me up, and I buried my head in his neck, savoring his crisp, woodsy scent. As he held me, I began to sob, my body shaking. I knew I shouldn't be acting like that in front of everyone, but I needed to feel him.

"Shh, I'm here. Nothing is going to happen. I won't let anything happen to you."

I nodded into his neck. No one said a word, which was wise. I was strung tighter than I'd ever been.

"Can you walk me through what happened?"

"Yes," I whispered.

Kane said, "I'm taking Teale upstairs. We'll be back down in a bit."

That was Kane's way of saying, "Don't disturb us."

Kane carried me upstairs to his room and sat down on the bed, still holding me. He checked me over as I sat in his lap. I was trying hard not to cry.

"Tell me what happened."

"Right before lunch, I called Andy at the post office to see if he could bring my mail out to your parents' when he brought theirs. I knew he had some boxes for me. I also got a sealed, letter-sized envelope. It looked normal. I thought it might be some sponsor contracts my mom sent, so I opened it without thinking." My throat grew thick as I thought about it. "I opened it up and Kane... it was just terrible."

I buried my head in his shoulder and sobbed. All those dead women's bodies. They'd been brutalized. All but one. One looked like she was sleeping. The last picture was of me outside of Kane's cabin with writing that said I'd be next. I wrapped my hands around his neck and held him tight.

"Shh, I've got you, angel. I've got you. No one is going to get you."

I hiccupped, trying to catch my breath. "Why does he want me?"

"I don't know."

I shivered when I saw it was already dark outside. "Don't get mad at what I'm about to ask, okay?"

"Of course not." Kane was being sweet and tender, which was a part of him I saw sometimes, but not frequently.

"I don't want to be by myself tonight. I know we're safe here, but I can't do it. Can I sleep on the floor in here? I know it's against the rules, and I won't make anything of it. I just don't want to be alone."

He pulled me back. "You'll be in my bed until we catch this son of a bitch. Not on the floor. In bed. With me."

I clung to him, relieved, and my love for him only grew, which was bad. I wanted him to want this not just because I was scared out of my mind, but because he loved me, too.

CHAPTER
Twenty-Nine

Kane

Teale was upstairs with the girls, watching some chick flick in the spare bedroom. It had been hard to leave her, but I needed to see the photos that had been sent to her. I would have watched any movie if it helped her calm down. I hated seeing her upset. Inside I raged. The asshole knew who Teale was and probably thought we were together.

But why target me? I had no answers. I couldn't think of anyone who would go to these lengths for any reason.

Dad handed me the stack of pictures. "We put them in Ziplock bags with tongs. We weren't sure what you'd do with them. You going to hand them over to the FBI?"

It had been a thought. But this killer had made it personal. The last thing I needed was to be bogged down in an endless array of questions when I just needed to find this guy. One slipup from me, and the killer would try and take Teale.

One. Mistake.

I thought about what I should do. "I don't know yet."

I took the pictures from Dad and looked at them, one by one. I ground my teeth and tried to remain calm in front of my family. But this wasn't good. Not good at all. There were over thirty victims in those pictures. Fuck. The killer had been at this for a long time. Longer than anyone had given him credit for. Much longer than the year the FBI had profiled. All his victims were petite blond women. But today, the victim had dark hair. Teale had dark hair. *Is it because of Teale he switched hair color? What made him go for blondes to begin with?*

The last picture brought me up short. It was her. *Her.* The reason I'd sworn off ever having a relationship.

An entire gamut of emotions ran through me. More than I'd ever experienced, but I kept it together.

"What do you see, Kane?" my father asked.

I wasn't ready to divulge anything until I sorted out my head. If I gave away too much, there would be questions. And that would only muddle my thoughts. If I said nothing, they would know something was going on. I needed to give a little. I put the picture down and looked at my brothers and dad. "This victim was someone I knew a long time ago. She was a friend. I didn't realize she'd been murdered."

Well, that was a spin on the truth and enough for now.

"Why would he go after your friend?" Drake asked.

That was the question that bothered me. "I don't know."

Dad brought it back full circle. "You going to give this to the FBI?"

Teale was my priority. I shook my head. "Not yet. If they find out about this connection, they might try to use Teale as bait. And then I'll be hauled off for endless hours of questioning. Ain't no fucking way I'm letting that happen."

Hayden leaned forward. "So, what's the plan?"

"We find him before he makes a move. Dad, can I use your office to lay things out? I'm going to be receiving a lot of evidence from the latest victim. I need someplace to work so the women don't see."

Not that Teale, Alexa, Kory, and Mom weren't strong, but some things didn't need to be seen. They wouldn't want to see.

Dad nodded, scratching his chin. "Of course, son. We'll keep it locked if you need."

"That'll be good." I stood. "I need to go check on Teale and see how she's doing."

I waited for my brothers to give me shit, but they said nothing. *Good.* The last thing I wanted to do was explain myself to them.

I climbed the stairs and met Alexa on the way up.

"Hey, Kane. Teale went to bed. I think she's still in shock."

"I'll go check on her. Thanks for trying to keep her distracted while I looked at the pictures."

I saw the worry in Alexa's eyes. She was such a caring soul. And now she was going to be a mother. She'd make a brilliant one. "Is there anything I can do?"

"You've been amazing. I'll let you know. My brother is one lucky bastard."

Her cheeks went pink. "Thanks, Kane. I'm glad you introduced us to Teale. She's an amazing person. I'll be sad when she leaves once winter is over."

That wasn't something I wanted to think about. But I had to say something. "Yeah, the Twiner sisters will have to work a little harder for their news."

"Yeah, they will." She started down the stairs. "Kane?" I turned. "Make sure you take care of yourself, too."

I'd be okay, but it wasn't worth arguing about. "Thanks, Alexa. Night."

"Night, Kane."

I cracked my neck to the side, needing a second before opening the door. *Who is it? Why me?* It was a big fucking riddle, and I hated riddles.

I slowly opened the door and found Teale sitting cross-legged on the bed in the dark. I closed the door before asking, "You okay?"

I flipped on the light, and she shrugged. It was weird seeing her this out of sorts. Normally, the woman was never quiet. Now I wanted to hear her ramble on about anything. I gave her a minute to see if she would say anything.

Finally, she spoke. "I can't get their faces out of my mind. That was a lot of girls, Kane. More than the FBI knew."

"It was." I wanted her to guide the conversation. I still wasn't sure what I wanted to tell her.

Teale rubbed her eyes, then focused on her fingernails. "Why me? I still don't get it."

Fuck. I'd caused this somehow, and I didn't want her to feel like this anymore. She deserved to know what I knew. From there, we would decide who else to tell. Seeing her this vulnerable helped me make the decision.

I sat down in the black leather chair across from the bed. I needed to see her reaction when I told her. "One of the other pictures was someone connected to me. I think that's the key to all this."

"What? How?"

I'd never told anyone this story. "When I was a senior in

high school I went up to Ketchikan to work for the summer as a guide. While I was there, I met a girl named Janine."

Teale's eyes shot to mine. This made me hella uncomfortable, and I shifted. "Janine and I saw each other casually. Her parents were very strict, and she wanted to keep it a secret. She was a virgin when we slept together. The day after we did, I got a note from her that said she was breaking up with me. I tried to see her, but her parents said she'd left to go out of town. Because they had no idea who I was, of course, they refused to give me any sort of information. I played it off like we were just friends, but they gave me nothing. A week later, her body turned up. Investigators ruled it a suicide."

I swallowed hard. "I blamed myself for her suicide. I thought losing her virginity had sent her over the edge."

Teale clamored off the bed and onto my lap and placed her hands on my face. "That wasn't your fault."

I didn't want to argue about it, so I said nothing. What was done was done. I wrapped my arms around her waist and breathed in her sweet scent before continuing, "Well, if all those pictures are of his victims, it appears this sick fuck killed her. And this all started because of me."

"Is there anyone you could think of that would have wanted to hurt her?"

I hardly knew anything about Janine. After she died, I had done some research and found out that a lot of what she'd told me was lies. She'd said she had a brother, but when I checked, there wasn't a brother. Janine had said she was eighteen, but the newspaper said she was twenty-one. Her mother and father were actually her aunt and uncle. None of it made sense, so I punished myself the only way I knew how. "It was a long time ago—six years, in fact. In my mind, I blamed myself for her death. I never saw any sign that she was upset about us sleeping together. If I'd thought there was something going on, I would have dug deeper. I'm going to try to remember if anything odd had happened. But the investigation was open and closed. She overdosed on her anxiety medication, from what the coroner said."

It was hard to process the emotions I'd kept buried all this time. I punished myself for her suicide by closing off the possibility of ever having a relationship again. Teale squeezed me tighter, not saying anything but giving me exactly what I needed.

"I want you to know the sex was consensual. I would never force myself on a woman."

"That was never a doubt in my mind, Kane."

"I never told my family about the relationship. There just wasn't any need."

And now that Janine most likely hadn't committed suicide because of me, I wasn't sure where that left the promise I'd made to myself to never have another relationship.

"Why don't we go to bed? It's been a long day."

I should have gone back downstairs to work on the case, but I needed to make sure Teale was okay. "I may get up in the middle of the night to work on things, but if I do, I'll leave Mariah with you."

"Thank you."

Teale stood, and we got ready for bed in silence; neither of us seemed to know what else to say. I kept going through my memories of everyone I could remember from that time and wondering if they had been involved. Nothing was coming to me.

We got into bed, and Teale laid her head on my chest. I

pulled her closer. "Thank you, Kane."

"I will make sure you're okay. I won't let anything happen to you."

"I know."

Now, I had to make sure I didn't let her down.

CHAPTER
Thirty

Teale

"Hey, Mom, are you guys excited about your trip?" I knew it wasn't ideal to have them up here right now, but I wanted my parents around. Between the threat from the killer and the confusing feelings for Kane, I was pretty much a wreck. There weren't any smart-ass comments from his brothers, which told me they knew things had taken an unexpected turn in our relationship. None of the girls brought it up, which was another sign. I hated that everyone knew I'd fallen for him. I felt like a fool, and at times, I swore I saw pity in their eyes.

But I wanted my mom around. It would just help having someone else. She'd be able to give me advice after assessing the situation. I still hadn't told her about the complications with the serial killer on the loose. It would worry her with me so far away.

I realized the pause was longer than normal. "Mom, you

still there? I'm excited to see you guys."

"Oh, Teale, we're going to have to postpone two weeks. Your dad pulled his back working on the Zamboni. I told him the mechanic would be here in a day or two, but you know how he is."

I sat up straight on the bed. My parents were getting older, and sometimes they forgot they had limits. "Is he okay?"

"Yes, it's mild, but the doctor wants him to take it easy for a couple of weeks. Your dad wanted to know if it was okay to postpone."

Postpone. I took a deep breath, pushing my disappointment aside. "I don't want Dad to hurt himself. The Alaskan wilderness will wait for you. But I can't wait to see you guys. I miss seeing you."

"I know, sweetie. We miss you, too. How's it going with Kane? He still being grumpy?"

I wanted to sigh, but I stayed upbeat, ignoring the tear that slid down my cheek. "Good. He's been working a lot. So I've been hanging with Kory and Alexa. It's been nice having the girl time. Tonight, I get to meet Devney. She had some unexpected delays coming back from Washington because of her mom's illness."

It was sad. Her mom was fighting cancer. In so many ways, I was lucky—my parents were happy and healthy. It made things seem less dreary when I thought about it that way. At least I would see them in a couple of weeks.

"That's nice. I can't wait to put faces to all these names. Are you sure Ike and Amie are okay with us staying with them?"

"Yes, I promise. It's beautiful here. You'll love it. I think you and Amie will get along great. The Fosters are amazing."

There was a pause before Mom spoke again. "Are you sure there's nothing going on with Kane?"

Mom always could tell when something was going on. I wanted to tell my mom, but I wasn't ready yet. There would be a million questions. With everything going on, I was too tired to answer more questions. My emotions were already strung too tight.

Amie had caught me at just the right moment the other day on the porch. Other than that, I'd acted normal while each day, a little more of me fell apart inside. When I returned home, I would tell her everything. If I let myself start crying, I might not stop. "I'm sure, Mom. Just friends."

At least that was what Kane thought.

"Sounds good. Two weeks will go by in a blur. We'll be there before you know it."

I hoped so. I needed to hang up before Mom saw through my brave front. If she knew how upset I was, they'd try to make the trip. And Dad needed to heal. "Give Dad my love."

"I will. He's resting right now, but I'll have him call you."

"Sounds good. Love you, Mom."

"Love you, too."

I ended the call and sat on the bed. From downstairs, I heard someone calling my name. Lately, it was torture being in this house. Being part of something I would never permanently be a part of. My head was a mess. Lately, Kane was more openly affectionate toward me, which further confused me. *Is he coming around? Will there be a chance for us?* I was too scared to ask and upset the delicate balance we had.

"Teale, we need your vote!" Kory called from down below.

I went downstairs, making sure I had a happy look on my face. The brothers were on one side of the room while the wives were on the other. They wanted me to join the wives' vote, which made me sick to my stomach. I would never truly be on the wives' side. I was a friend—a friend with benefits for the time being.

Kane cocked his head at me, and I averted my eyes. "What's up? What am I voting for?"

Alexa held her hands in the air as Hayden started to speak. "We need to settle which movie we're watching, and you could even it up for the first time ever."

Because Kane has someone here. But I'm not really Kane's someone.

"What's it between?"

Hayden said, "*While You Were Sleeping*, also known as snooze fest, or *Indiana Jones and the Last Crusade*, also known as one of the greatest movies of all time."

"Well my vote would be—"

Kane rushed over and covered my mouth. "*Indiana Jones.* I heard it. She said it. It's done."

I tried to protest, but he kept his hand over my mouth. Kory put her hand on her hip. "Kane, let her go!"

"She's voted. Hayden, put the movie on."

Amie came down, looked at me wrapped in Kane's arms, and said, "Why don't the girls hang out upstairs and have a mini girls' night? It could be a makeup girls' night since the first one was missed. Then the boys can watch whatever they want to watch down here."

Thank goodness. Kane released me but kept his hands on my shoulders. It was the same thing I'd seen Drake do to Alexa a million times. The intimacy of it was brutal.

159

Kory and Alexa agreed. "Perfect. Devney will be here shortly."

Because of the situation, Hayden hadn't been able to get her. Hollis had hired a pilot from Washington to bring her home.

I stepped away when Kory grabbed my hand to go upstairs. I refused to make eye contact with Kane. When I reached the bottom stairs, Hayden said, "Hey, Teale. I've been checking the weather. Everything looks good for your parents to come in."

I turned to face him, fighting the tears. My lip threatened to wobble, but I kept it strong. "Umm... they can't make it now. Dad threw out his back. He has to rest for a couple of weeks. They'll let me know a new date."

"Oh, I'm so sorry, dear," Amie said.

I kept climbing the stairs, putting my hand up to wave it off. "It's not a big deal. I'll see them soon."

When we got to the door, I knew Kane was close behind. "Teale, can I talk to you for a second?"

The girls walked into the room and left me in the hallway. He looked worried. *Shit*. I hadn't been able to hide my emotions as well as I thought.

"You okay?"

I kept my smile bright and big. "Peachy."

"Teale."

Kane always had a knack for telling when I was hiding something. But I refused to go there. Not right now, not until I had my head and heart straightened out. "I'm good. Have fun watching Indiana. He's a classic."

"You were going to vote for him, weren't you?"

I winked. "You'll never know."

I walked into the bedroom and took a deep breath. Before I could get a word out, someone shouted from downstairs, "I'm going to be a father!"

What in the world? Was that Hollis?

We scrambled down the stairs to see Devney standing with Hollis, huge smiles on their faces. When he saw everyone, he looked around. "Oh, that was probably a little over the top. But yeah, I'm going to be a dad."

Everyone went ballistic with cheers of congratulations. I hung out off to the side and took in the situation. I hadn't met Devney yet. She was adorable. From what I'd heard, she was the part-time music teacher at the school, but also worked at the clinic as a receptionist. She reached out her hand. "You must be Teale. I'm Devney, Hollis's girlfriend. I mean, fiancée."

Fiancée? I thought they were just dating. *Is this their way of announcing it?*

There was another rush of congratulations. So the engagement *was* news. Hollis stood beside her, beaming. "Well, as it turns out, I greeted Devney with a proposal when she landed, and she greeted me with news of a baby."

"Congratulations," I chimed in. "Children are such wonderful blessings."

Somehow, I managed to keep it together. But it was a knife to the heart knowing I would never be part of this family. It shouldn't have hurt. I shouldn't have fallen for Kane.

There were more cheers, and Amie said, "I think this calls for a celebration. Let's cut into the chocolate cake Teale and I made today!"

Great. Just freaking great.

There was no hiding out upstairs. Of course I was happy

for them, thrilled actually. Marriage and a baby were the best news. But I felt like I was in a glass case of emotions with nowhere to go. It was suffocating. I needed space—somewhere to think and somehow to process everything so I could keep it together.

We moved to the dining room, where Kane stood behind me. His hand sat possessively on my hip. The touch sent tingles racing down my leg and made me love him even more. I'd never felt this way. With Kane, I loved feeling like I was his. It was heady. Yet, I wasn't his because when spring came, he would let me go and move on with his life.

Champagne glasses were filled and passed around. Drake and Alexa shared a look. Drake stepped forward holding his champagne glass. "I have an announcement to add to the celebration." The room grew silent. "Alexa and I are pregnant. Looks like little baby Foster is going to have a best friend."

Amie burst into tears of excitement. Ike looked so proud, hearing the news of his family expanding. The room was ecstatic. Of course, I was happy, but my heart shattered a little more. When it was my turn, I hugged Alexa. "So many congratulations. You are going to make the best parents. This is one lucky baby."

"Thank you."

Ike held up his champagne flute. "To the next generation!"

I echoed the cheer and tried to stay engaged, but it was hard. Kane hugged Devney and Alexa. I could tell he was excited to become an uncle. My attitude was all wrong. I needed to sort myself out.

Kane whispered in my ear, "You sure you're okay?"

I set my glass down and looked at my phone as if I had a

message. "That's my mom. I'm going to see what's going on in case it's my dad."

I shouldn't have lied. I knew it, but I needed to get away. And I needed Kane to give me some privacy.

Hs watched me closely. "You want me to come?"

I put my hand on his chest. "No, stay here and celebrate with your family. These are happy times. I won't be long."

"Okay, I'll be up in a bit."

"Take your time. This is amazing news, and I think Mom has some business stuff to discuss."

Well, that was true in a sense. Kane kissed my cheek. I wasn't sure if he realized now how much he showed me affection in front of people. It was nothing for him to kiss me goodbye when he left, hold my hand in front of his family, or treat me as if I was more.

I went upstairs, leaving behind the joyful laughter. It was still daylight. Maybe I could get a skate in. Skating always helped clear my head and get my emotions in check. The physical activity would help, too. There had been a few times this week I'd skated with Kory. Hayden had come with us. I would let Amie know where I was going. It was safe and close to the house. I changed and headed back downstairs with my skates. The sound of voices in the hallway caught my attention, and I was surprised when my name came up. It was Kane and his mom.

"Is Teale okay?"

Great, everyone thought something was wrong. I definitely needed to get out of the house.

He took a deep breath. "I don't know. She seems off."

"Did you end things with her?"

I gasped and put my hand over my mouth, hoping no one

heard me. Why does Amie think we were dating? I had been clear that Kane wasn't in love with me.

There was a long pause before he spoke. "What do you mean *end*?"

"I'm sorry, I just—we all just thought you were dating."

I was humiliated. Everyone had seen, and they'd been talking about me. I felt like a pathetic charity case.

There was another long pause. "Mom, we're not dating. She's a friend. That's it. That's all it will ever be. I don't have feelings like that for Teale. After this winter, she'll be leaving and that's that. There's nothing else and never will be."

And with his words, my heart officially broke into a million pieces.

CHAPTER
Thirty-One

Kane

I hadn't been prepared for Mom to ask me about Teale. *Have I been that obvious about us?* There were times I touched Teale, but they knew why. I'd explained we were friends and I wanted her safe. Teale obviously meant something to me, but *girlfriend?* My heart felt like it might beat its way out of my chest at the thought of committing to someone.

After Janine, I conditioned myself to not want to be in a relationship. I wasn't meant for one. And I didn't want to be the cause of someone getting hurt.

Yeah, things had changed between Teale and me, but it wasn't permanent. It could never be permanent. Even if I wanted more… I wouldn't let it happen.

Maybe we had gotten too comfortable.

I looked up the stairs, needing to see her. But I needed a second first. I walked back into Dad's office and started cleaning my gun. *Girlfriend?* A headache began to form, and I took a break. Maybe I should go see her. *In a minute.* I needed more time, so I turned my chair to the wall of evidence I'd created. I could focus on the case for a bit, and then I would go see Teale.

The FBI had found the abandoned car, but the snow had covered up the tracks. I imagined that had been part of the killer's plan. The bastard was taunting me. I looked at the pictures of the vehicle. There hadn't been any fingerprints—the car had been completely wiped down.

My phone vibrated with an email from Agent Gathcart. I sat at the computer to open it. It was a report from the coroner's office.

Sand was found underneath the victim's nails and embedded in the cuts.

Sand.

I kept reading.

A few gold flakes were found on the surface of the skin under the clothes.

Gold.

I knew where the son of a bitch had been. The sand and gold had to be purposely added with the amount of snow. He was sending me a clue on where to find him. I stood, and the chair shot out from underneath me. Mariah's ears perked up. "We need to go, girl. I know where he is."

Almost two hours had passed. It was almost five, and this mess could be behind us tonight. I'd call the FBI on my way over to where he was. In the hallway, I found Mom.

"Have you seen Teale? I was looking for her. She wanted to learn how to make homemade spaghetti sauce. I thought that would be a good celebration dinner."

"She was going up to my room."

Mom's face fell. "Your room's empty, Kane."

"Teale?" I yelled. I walked through the house. "Teale?" I climbed the stairs two at a time to my room. "Teale, where are you?"

I heard more people calling her name through the house. "Damn it, Teale, answer me."

There was no answer.

I had never felt panic like this before in my life. I raced around the house, frantic to find her. "Teale, answer me!"

Something was wrong.

Bad.

Wrong.

I peered out the window. Under the spotlight, all our vehicles were accounted for. And I would have heard a truck crank. I searched our bedroom and noticed her ice-skating bag was open and her skates were gone.

"*Fuck!*"

I tore through the house at a dead sprint, people calling my name as I rushed by. There wasn't time. I needed to get to the pond. At the door, I yelled, "Mariah, come!"

I was out the back door and to the pond behind the shop in record time. *What the hell was she thinking coming out here on her own?* "Mariah, look for Teale."

Voices were still calling behind me. I made it to the bank and saw her skates laying off to the side. No Teale. "TEALE! TEALE!"

Desperation hit me as I searched for any sign of her.

But only silence greeted me. If something happened to her... if he touched her... I couldn't finish those thoughts.

Drake was the first to make it to me. "What's going on?"

"He has her. He fucking has her!" I yelled into the woods.

"Come on, motherfucker! I'm here! Come get me! TEALE!" I hit a nearby tree. "DAMMIT ALL TO HELL!"

Drake put his hand my shoulder. "Kane, you need to calm down. If he has her, you'll need a level head to find him."

My breaths heaved out of my body. Mom ran up with my coat, but I shook my head. I checked my watch. He most likely took her before sunset. Teale wouldn't have been out here past dark. So, he had more than a two-hour head start.

"Dad, I need to borrow a couple of your guns. Mine are taken apart right now."

Mom stepped forward, out of breath. "Kane, maybe we should get the FBI involved," Mom said.

The blood pumped faster through my veins as the rage built. Before I could respond, Dad put his arm around Mom. "Sure, son. I'll get them. Amie, we need to get back in the house. Come on, girls."

Drake, Hayden, and Hollis remained by the pond. Drake was first. "What do you need from us?"

"Stay here. Text if you hear anything." I looked at Hollis as the bile rose in my throat. "I need you to be on standby."

That was all I could say, but Hollis knew what I meant. Teale might be hurt. "I will. I'll be waiting for the call. I have my medical bag in my truck, so as soon as you find her, call me and we can determine if I need to come to you or meet you at the clinic."

I nodded.

Hayden asked, "What are you going to do?"

"Kill the motherfucker."

CHAPTER
Thirty-Two

Teale

My head hurt so bad.

It was hard to open my eyes.

I was sore all over.

Something was off. I felt like I was stuck in some sort of fog, unable to move or think.

What happened?

Where's Kane?

Did I fall asleep?

I tried to focus, but nothing made sense.

I tried to move my hands, but nothing happened.

What's wrong with me?

I tried again, and something bit into my wrist.

Why are my hands bound?

Panicking, I jerked, and my eyes shot open as adrenaline surged through my veins. I was tied to a metal pole, and my feet were bound, too.

What happened to me? The panic grew, and I tried to scream for Kane.

My mouth was taped closed. I struggled to remove the tape, forgetting that my hands were bound.

Someone had taken me.

"Good, you're awake."

Whose voice was that? He remained in the dark. I continued to struggle, ignoring the pain and hoping to break free. I tried to scream again, but the tape muffled it.

"Calm down, or I'll knock you out again. Then you won't be awake for the fun. And it's about to get fun." His voice was menacing and deep, and it sent shivers down my spine. I stilled immediately.

He had to be the killer. The man who had it out for Kane. And now he had me. Things were beginning to make sense. He'd wanted me, and he'd found me. Pieces of the afternoon came back. I'd needed to escape the house and had grabbed my skates. When I'd heard Kane tell his mother we would only ever be friends, nothing mattered but getting out. The grief had overwhelmed me. And because of it, I'd been abducted.

When I had gone out to skate, it was still light. Now it was pitch black. *How much time has passed?* If this was the lumberjack killer, I knew what his intentions were. He would brutalize me before killing me. I needed to be awake in order to escape. I remained still, trying not to shake with fear.

From across the fire, a man leaned forward. I shrank back against the pole as the flames showcased a jagged scar across his face. "Good girl."

I said nothing as his eyes roamed the length of my body. My stomach rolled at the thought of what he wanted to do to me. I would never let him touch me like that. *Never.*

"I would ungag you, but you'll scream like they all did. I can't have that. Not with Foster most likely close by. When he gets here, I'm going to let him watch me take you over and over again."

I choked back a sob as hot tears ran down my cheek. This man planned to rape and kill me in front of Kane. But I wasn't going without a fight. I'd fight with everything I had before I let him touch me. I would die first.

"You see, Foster and I have a long history. A very long history. He took what was mine, and now I'm going to take what is his. I've waited a very long time for this moment. Luck finally went my way when the FBI got him involved."

None of this made sense. I wasn't Kane's.

"Oh, you don't know, do you? You weren't his first love."

Janine.

I tried to tell this pyscho that Kane wasn't in love with me. He'd never been in love with me. But, of course, the tape across my mouth stopped me.

"I'm surprised I got you so easily. I couldn't believe my luck to find you just sitting there, putting on your skates. It was a sign that my quest is nearly over, and now I wait for Kane to end this."

I had been so stupid. After I'd heard Kane talking to his mom, my head wasn't on straight. And all I'd been able to think about was getting on the ice. When I'd gotten to the bank of the pond, I'd sat and cried, feeling sorry for myself. The next thing I remembered was waking up here.

Stupid. Stupid. Stupid.

He threw another log on the fire, and I was grateful because my shaking was not only from fear but from the cold, as well. "Don't worry, I have a tent for later. It's going to be the best night of your life as Kane watches."

That thought made my stomach turn. I was going to be sick. I closed my eyes for a moment to focus on my breathing and regain control.

He ran the knife down his cheek, inhaling deeply as if savoring something. "It's going to be so sweet; I can smell your blood from here. And what you don't realize is how much you're going to love it."

He stood and walked around the fire to kneel in front of me. The stench coming from him was enough to make me nauseous all over again. He leaned over and ran his finger down my chin. I tried to scream and backed as far away from him as I could. With one swift motion, he pulled his hand back and struck me. "Do not back away from me. You understand?"

I refused to concede.

He wrapped his hands around my neck. "Do you understand?"

I closed my eyes, refusing to give him the satisfaction. "Open your eyes!"

In the next second, his hands were gone from around my throat. I opened my eyes to find a knife at my throat. "Do you understand?"

I nodded. Being incapacitated now wouldn't help me escape.

Snap.

There was a noise out in the distance, and I jumped. He threw something on the fire, which made more smoke. "Don't go anywhere. Looks like we have company and he wants me to know he's here. Kane's just in time."

Kane? Kane is here? He won't let this man touch me.

I made as much noise as possible, hoping he'd hear me. The smoke made it hard to see. Something ran up to me, and I screamed behind the tape. A familiar husky licked my face, and I cried in relief. Kane was here. He'd come for me. He was going to save me.

Kane appeared just beyond the flames and jumped over the fire. In one swift move, my hands were free, and I ripped the tape off my face.

"Stay, Mariah. I'm going to end this. Take this." He handed me a gun. "If he gets near you, shoot like I taught you. Understand?"

"Y-y-yes." I should have said more, but I was shaking. Kane roughly kissed my forehead before cutting through the rope that held my feet together. "Remember what I said. The safety is off."

"I will."

From across the fire, an eerie voice chanted, "Come out and play, Foster! I don't mind if you watch us."

Kane stood, danger emanating from him. He pulled out another gun from a holster. The killer had one, as well. My heart sped up as they pointed their guns at each other. The killer gave a smile and kept his gun steady. "I've waited a long time for this."

"Can't say the same, motherfucker."

The killer tsk-tsked. "What would you say to putting down the guns. I've always preferred the blade over the bullet. It always makes the kill last a little longer."

I held the gun firmly.

Kane said nothing and held his gun steady.

The killer laughed. "Fine by me. I'll be sure to graze the girl and the dog in the crossfire. And if they run, I'll just shoot them, too. I'll get one bullet off before you kill me. That way I still win. Which one you want me to shoot?"

I swallowed hard, terrified.

Kane bit out. "Have it your way."

Most likely Kane still had another gun on him somewhere. In unison they laid their guns down. Kane pulled out a knife from his waist. The blade reflected the light of the fire. He readied his stance, turning his head slowly from side to side. The other man walked around mirroring Kane's movements. The smoke grew worse, making it harder to see clearly, and I coughed. Kane moved the knife to his other hand. "Mariah, stay with Teale. Protect."

I held the gun the way Kane had taught me, but my hands were shaking. Mariah stood protectively in front of me, a low growl coming from her throat.

"Who the fuck *are* you?"

The killer cackled. "Like you don't know." Kane remained still and didn't respond. The man shook his head. "You stole Janine from me. She was meant for me."

Kane said nothing. and the man waved his knife, even more agitated. "You took what belonged to me!"

"Janine never mentioned you."

"Fuck you!" he spat. "I dated her for months and she never slept with me. Said I was like her brother. You dated her for a week. A WEEK!"

I stood and took a step back, readying my gun in case the killer came for me. The killer swung his head in my direction. "Don't go anywhere, sweetheart. Foster is going to watch while I fuck you... repeatedly."

"Over my dead body," Kane spat.

"That'll happen, of course. After I'm done taking my

sweet time with her. Maybe I'll keep her with me and let her have my baby."

A baby. With him. Never.

Kane switched the knife back and forth in his hands. "Let's end this, motherfucker."

"I'm going to mess you up so bad."

"Not happening."

My heart drummed in my ears, but I held the gun, ready to shoot but with the smoke and them moving, I was afraid I would hit Kane. My aim was still terrible unless the target was really close.

The man lurched and Kane bobbed left. They moved out of the light of the fire, the smoke obscuring them. I tried to make out where Kane was in the fight. He had to be okay. Mariah shifted her body to stay between me and where the men had disappeared. I focused on the sounds of fighting—blows connecting and grunts of pain—since I couldn't see what was going on.

The two men came into view. The killer swung and made contact with Kane's jaw. My heart stopped. I winced, holding the gun more firmly. *Please be safe, Kane. Please be safe.* The next second, they were gone again. There was a sickening wheeze and a final guttural grunt. I held my breath, waiting for the next sound. But all I heard was the pounding of my own heart.

Then there was silence.

I waited until a figure appeared through the smoke, the gun raised.

"It's me, angel."

With relief, I dropped my arm and let out a breath. "Kane? Is it over?"

"Yeah, it's over."

That meant the killer was dead.

He was dead.

It was over.

Finally.

I dropped to the ground and sobbed as my adrenaline ran out. A gentle hand took the gun I'd been holding, and he swept me up into his arms. I wrapped my legs around Kane's waist as he cradled me against his chest and I held on with everything I had.

I was in Kane's arms. The killer hadn't touched me. I squeezed him tighter, holding on to the man I loved with my whole heart.

Kane somehow managed to get his phone. "Dad. Yeah, I've got her. We're out at the end of the Sanderson property. I need Hollis at the clinic to check Teale out. Call Gathcart and let him know where he can find the body. I'll call him as soon as Teale is checked out."

Kane ended the call, and I pulled him tighter. "You came for me."

"Always, angel. Always."

CHAPTER
Thirty-Three

Kane

I paced the floor of the clinic while Hollis checked over Teale. My family was seated all around me but hadn't said a word. I could feel their eyes on me. I was strung so tight I could snap at any moment. Things had gone to hell in a handbasket.

That sick fuck had planned to harm *my* Teale.

Agent Gathcart was up my ass.

My family wanted answers.

But I wasn't dealing with *anyone* until I was sure Teale was okay. She hadn't said a word on the way to the clinic. She'd only curled into my side and silently cried. It broke my heart, and there was nothing I could do.

I hope I wasn't too late.

If he had touched her, I would never forgive myself.

Alexa came to stand at my side. "Kane, you're bleeding. Let me look at it."

"After Teale." It was all I could manage without snapping. But at least she dropped it and returned to her seat next to Drake.

The examination room door opened, and Hollis stepped out. "She's asking to see you, Kane."

I walked to the door, but Hollis stepped in front of me and put his hand on my shoulder. "There's a bruise on her face from where he hit her. You need to keep it together. Can you do that? She's holding on by a thread, and I don't need you making it worse."

"Yeah, I can do that."

He looked at me, assessing if I had it together. I raised my eyebrow, daring him to stop me.

"Kane, your fists are clenched. You need to get it together."

I hadn't realized it. I relaxed my hands and took a deep breath, waiting for Hollis to give me the go-ahead to see her. I had to play by his rules, or he'd have my brothers wrestle me out of here.

Fuck. I have to calm down.

After a couple of minutes, he nodded. "Yes. Just like that. Teale is going to be watching you to see how you're handling this."

"I got it."

When I entered the examination room, Teale was sitting on the table, playing with her hands.

"Hey, angel."

She raised her head and gave me a sad smile. I hated seeing her spark gone. It fucking slayed me. At first, she didn't quite meet my eyes. But when our eyes connected, her smile grew. "Hey, you."

She was okay. She was alive. I would figure everything else out in due time. I rushed up to her and kissed her hard. She kissed me back, and I fucking savored the moment. For a second, I'd been worried I might never feel her in my arms again.

I put my forehead against hers. "Teale, if something had happened to you…"

Her hand came up to my cheek. "It didn't. He just scared me. You saved me, Kane. He never touched me."

Thank fuck.

"I knew you would come for me."

"Always, angel."

Our voices were soft and quiet, and it was one of the most intimate moments of my life. She looked up into my eyes. "Can things change between us? Do we have a chance?"

I froze like a deer in headlights. If I said yes and then broke her heart, I would never forgive myself. Things could stay as they were for now. Then I would see if I could change. The thought of putting her at risk after what just happened… I needed time to sort out my head. But I couldn't lie to her and give her false hope. "Teale, I…"

I let the words hang out there, unable to finish them, not knowing *how* to finish them.

She gave me a kiss and looked away. "I know. I understand."

This woman understood me in a way no one else ever had. She focused on the blood on my shirt. "You're bleeding. Are you okay?"

"It's nothing. I wouldn't let them look at it until I knew you were okay." It was a small scratch where the killer's knife had grazed my arm. It looked worse than it was.

She got off the table. "Let's get you checked out. Then, I want to go home."

For three days, I was up to my eyeballs in interviews.

Three. Long. Days.

I had to walk the FBI through everything. Agent Gathcart hadn't stopped riding my ass about withholding information and threatened to charge me with obstruction of justice. *What the fuck ever. The killer's dead.* As it turned out, his name was Ivan Thornberry and he lived in Ketchikan while I had been there. Ivan and Janine had been kids together in the juvenile detention center. Those records had been sealed, which explained why I had never found the information in my searches.

Ivan had been killing for years. For some reason, in the last year, he'd escalated to wanting someone to know he was killing. Without him alive to question, there was a lot of speculation flying around.

Regardless, if I hadn't done things my way, I might have lost Teale. All the red tape would have just slowed me down. It wasn't a risk I was willing to take, so I'd deal with whatever consequences they gave me.

From what the FBI psychologist said in her behavioral assessment, the killer wanted me to find him so he could take Teale from me while I watched. Janine's death had been ruled a suicide, so I'd been unaware of his role.

Honestly, who knows the real truth? Pieces of what Ivan had said fit with what the psychologist believed. But the bottom line was the sick fuck was dead.

A huge fucking boulder had been lifted from my shoulders with the knowledge that Janine hadn't committed suicide after losing her virginity to me.

Teale had been interviewed multiple times, but the FBI had gone through the formalities quickly. At my request, they'd come to my parents' house. I wanted her as comfortable as possible. It had still taken a toll on her, though. Man, she was strong.

I pushed through the front doors of the police station, glad this was over. Agent Douchebag came out with his arms folded across his chest. *Shit. I'm so over this.* "You should have contacted us, Kane. It's created a mess."

"And risk her life? Sorry." *Not sorry.* "I wasn't willing to gamble with that. I'll deal with the fallout. But remember, a serial killer has been stopped. Take all the credit; I want no involvement."

For a second, the agent stared at me with his mirrored sunglasses and slicked-back hair. "Well, in my report, I stated that you acted on our behalf. You shouldn't get any more grief."

That was what I'd assumed. It took everything I had not to roll my eyes and flip him the bird. *Maybe I'm maturing.* "Thanks."

It was over. Finally.

Since the incident, we'd been staying with my parents. Hollis suggested Teale stay put and take it easy since I'd be in town, dealing with the FBI. And I wasn't comfortable leaving her at the cabin by herself. I missed feeling her, holding her, and wanted to get her back to my place as soon as possible. There seemed to be some sort of wall between us now. I hated that I hadn't been able to find her sooner. Maybe tonight we could just hang—just the two of us.

I hadn't had a chance to really think about what Teale asked me in the clinic. Time was what I needed. More time.

I drove out to my parents' as fast as I could, needing to see Teale and just hold her for a bit. I walked in the door, and all was quiet. Normally she greeted me, but there was no one around. "Teale?"

"Kane, can you come in here for a second?" Mom called from the living room.

I found her sitting on the couch. Her face was drawn and she looked sad.

"Is Teale okay?'

"Yeah, she's fine. But we need to talk."

Since Teale disappeared, I had an instinctive need to see her on an hourly basis. I was on edge. "Can I find Teale first?"

I was already heading for the stairs when Mom said, "She's gone, Kane. She went back home."

I froze. *Gone? She's gone?* Slowly, I turned back to Mom. "What do you mean she went back home?"

"Will you sit down?"

Numbly, I sat across from her. "What happened? Did something happen?"

"Let me finish before you say a word and stomp out of here. Promise me."

I hated it because that meant I wasn't going to like it. I only nodded.

"Teale asked Hayden to fly her to Vancouver. She's going home to Montana. She heard you and I talking the night she was abducted, Kane. That's why she went to skate—to clear her head."

None of this made sense. "Why would she need to clear her head?"

"Because she's in love with you."

I stood and backed up, nearly stumbling. "No, you're wrong. She isn't. Not love. She's not in love. Maybe she wants more, but not love."

I'd *told* her. I needed more time. This wasn't something I could just change like that.

Mom looked upset and swallowed hard before she continued. "Kane, she did. She told me herself."

I said nothing. There was nothing to say.

Mom shook her head and sighed. "I knew you were stubborn. But I'm shocked you won't acknowledge how you really feel. And that means you could lose Teale forever. She'll heal from this in time, and she'll find someone to spend her life with."

I gritted my teeth. "Are we done?"

"If you need this to be, then yes. She asked me to let you know she left something for you at your house."

Stiffly, I nodded. "I need to go."

"I understand, Kane. I'm here if you need to talk. We all are."

I gave her a quick hug and drove out to my place. Teale was gone. She'd fallen in love with me. I was pissed that she'd skipped out of town without talking to me about it, but what would I have said? Telling her I loved her wasn't an option.

I thought I had more time.

When I pulled up to the cabin, I turned off my truck and looked at my place.

Fuck. She's not in there.

Mariah sniffed everywhere, looking for Teale. She had become such a constant in our lives. I waited for her happy voice to greet me. Instead, all I got was a cold silence. The place was spotless. The cabin felt colder, starker, without Teale's stuff everywhere. In Teale's room, everything was as it had been the day she arrived. All her shit was off my trophies. On my bed was a wrapped present with an envelope on top.

I opened the letter.

Kane,

As I'm sure your mom has told you, I've gone home to Montana. I'm sorry I didn't say good-bye, but I had to leave. You see, I broke my promise and fell in love with you. I never expected it, nor did I want it. But I guess the heart loves who it wants to love.

I know you don't feel the same way. I don't expect that from you. That is the one promise I'm able to keep.

Please don't be mad at Hayden. He only did as I requested. In fact, he wanted me to talk to you, but hearing the rejection face to face... I don't think I could bear it. You're an amazing man, Kane. Someday, when you decide to open your heart, that woman will be the luckiest woman alive.

Thank you for everything.

All my love,
Teale

I sat dumbfounded as I read the letter over again. She wasn't supposed to fall in love. It wasn't supposed to happen this way. My hand itched to call her, but I wasn't able to give her the one thing she needed. Love. I was ready to give her more than what we had been... just not love.

I put the letter on the bed and picked up the package. On top was her yodeling pickle with a note.

In case you decide you want to use mind bullets on pickles to make them yodel, you'll already have a yodeling pickle.

Xoxo,

Teale

Why does it feel like someone just ripped the heart out of my chest?

I pushed back more of the tissue paper and found her next gift. Inside was a black T-shirt. On the front, the words *Mr. Grumpy Pants* were printed in white letters.

Fuck my life.

I had just lost the best thing that ever happened to me.

CHAPTER
Thirty-Four

Kane

I hung the last light fixture in Hollis's cabin, and it was done. From the hallway off to the left, Hollis appeared, wearing red suspenders and his so-called Paul Bunyan hat. *What is this world coming to?* Thank fuck winter had come to an end. I'd burned that hat while drinking a beer. It had been the only good thing that had happened since Teale left.

"I worry about you sometimes," I said.

Hollis patted my shoulder. "I'm just embracing my inner Alaskan. If you want to borrow one of my extra hats or suspenders, you're more than welcome to. I mean, since you burned the last one."

I laughed. "Pass, man. But thanks."

Drake and Hayden put the last of the tools in the bed of the truck. I wiped my brow and stepped back to take a look around. It was a nice place. It was a four-bedroom, four-bathroom cabin with a true rustic feel. It was a place I could live, I figured. From what I'd gathered, Hollis and Devney were going to use it as their primary residence and keep the apartment above the clinic for bad weather or when Hollis needed to stay at a patient's side. They were still deciding what to do with Devney's house in town.

I put the screwdriver in my tool belt and wondered what I would do to occupy my time now. As soon as the temperature got above freezing this past March, I funneled all my energy into helping build Hollis's cabin and taking out hunting expeditions. I started before sunup and finished long after sunset. Now it was the beginning of May, and we were nearly six weeks ahead of schedule. Hollis had brought in a crew to help speed things along. That had to have cost him a fortune, but they'd done as I directed when I wasn't able to be there.

I closed up my toolbox, my thoughts turning to Teale. Regardless of what I did, she was never far from my mind. Sometimes I wondered if I had dreamed her up. I planned on increasing my hunts that summer just to keep me away from everything that reminded me of her. I had enough requests in my inbox from hunters waiting for a spot to open. That would keep me occupied.

What's Teale doing?

What has she been up to?

So many times, I wanted to reach out to her, but knowing I couldn't tell her I loved her stopped me.

Mariah perked up when I whistled to go. She'd been moping around since Teale left, but she'd come around in time. We all would. Or that was what I kept telling myself. At least I knew Teale was safe. I didn't tell my family that I'd checked on her a few times. I worried about how she was handling things after what happened. My contact had agreed not to mention it to Teale but would only assure me that she was okay. It was better than no information at all.

I headed down the stairs. Hollis called after me, "Kane?"

"Yeah?"

"Thanks for everything. I appreciate all you did. Means a lot."

When we'd first started, the man couldn't hammer a nail to save his life. He wasn't going to be building anything on his own anytime soon, but the doc could now put nails in a board.

I grabbed my other toolbox. "Anytime. And now I want to know how you cheated at fishing with Hayden."

Hollis gave me a wink. "Special bait. I'll give you some to try."

I knew it. "What kind of bait?"

"A fisherman never tells his secrets."

I shook my head and chuckled. "Fair enough."

I threw my free hand up to wave good-bye as I walked down the stairs. Outside, Drake stopped at the front of his truck. "You coming out to Mom and Dad's for dinner?"

"Nah, not this time. I have some work to catch up on. Tell everyone I said hi."

I had only been to one family dinner since Teale left. Sure, I saw my parents, but I just couldn't be there with all my family. It felt empty without Teale. Dad had tried multiple times to talk to me, but I somehow found a way to get out of those conversations. At some point, I would need to apologize for the ass I'd been.

Drake's brows creased. "Next time. Sure."

"Yeah, next time."

We knew that there wasn't going to be a next time for a while.

Drake looked back at Hollis. "You coming?"

Hollis put his hand on one of the posts. "I'll be there shortly. This getup is getting a bit warm. It's not quite how I pictured it."

From the passenger side window, Hayden called out, "It'll be cold soon enough."

"True." Hollis nodded to himself. "I think I need a dog."

It was hard not to chuckle at the image of Hollis chasing the dog around the yard speaking in some fancy-schmancy language as he tried to potty train.

That poor dog.

My brothers drove away, and Hollis took a few steps down the stairs. "If Mariah ever has puppies, I want one. Seriously."

"If she does, one is yours."

We said good-bye, and I hopped in my truck. The last thing I ever needed to deal with was puppies. The thought gave me a headache.

I was almost to town when I noticed Drake's wallet in the passenger seat. *Shit, I bet he did that on purpose.* There was no way he just happened to drop it in my truck when there'd been no reason for him to be there. He was trying to force me over there, hoping I'd stay. *Nice try, asshole.* I'd toss it in his truck and leave.

I pulled up to my parents' house and walked over to his truck. *Locked.* Now I knew he'd done it on purpose. Drake never locked his truck, especially out here. The only time he did was during the tourist season at the Red Onion. I should've just taken it with me to teach him a lesson. But with my luck, the *entire* family would come out to the cabin to get the wallet. It was best just to get it over with and head home.

The front door had been left open with the screen door in place. There was a lot of laughter coming from inside. When I pulled open the door, I heard her voice and froze.

"Aww, you guys look so cute preggers. I ordered you some stuff. It should be there any time. But you know how slow the mail is in Alaska."

"Thank you. It's hard to believe I'm five months already," Alexa said.

Devney added, "I think I'm beginning to waddle. Trust me, it's not cute."

There was more laughter, and I stood frozen as I waited to hear her voice again.

"I can't believe you guys are both waiting to see what you're having. I'm dying to know if it's girls or boys or one of each. But I've got my vote. And let's just say I haven't been wrong in guessing."

"The family name is on the line, Teale. If he doesn't have a boy, there'll be hell to pay from me and Ka—" Hayden abruptly stopped, and an awkward silence fell over the group at the mention of my name.

Teale cleared her throat. "Oh, come on, no need to ignore the huge elephant in the room. It's okay to say his name. Promise." There was more silence, and then it sounded like she clapped. "I'm sealing my votes and mailing them to Amie. Will you safeguard them until the babies come?"

Mom answered, "Of course. I can't wait to have little grandbabies in this house."

Teale laughed, and I closed my eyes. I had missed her laugh.

Kory asked, "How's the show coming?"
Show? What show?

I felt like some damn lurker, hanging out in the hallway. I wanted to see her, but I stayed in place. The moment I showed my face, the fun would all end and she'd stop talking. I swallowed hard and dropped my head against the wall.

"Good. Really good, actually. We'll be airing tomorrow. I'm so excited."

"Well, Hollis is very thankful. He's been talking about it nonstop. Next week, he's hoping to share his plans with the town," Devney said.

Plans? How long has Teale been talking to my family?

It sounded like this was a regular thing. No one had told me about it or even *mentioned* it. I was a little pissed they'd kept this from me. *Teale's mine.* I stopped at that thought. She had been mine, but I let her go.

Fuck.

Teale responded, "Oh, good. I can't wait to hear. It's been nice to have something to channel everything into." There was a pause. "Oh, I've got to go. I am meeting this cute little boy, Judson, and his mother for lunch. He's obsessed with all things Alaska. I met him at the hospital. He's absolutely adorable. Let's do this again soon. All my love to the babies."

"Bye!"

The call ended, and I rounded the corner to confront my family. "How long has this been going on?"

Yep, that's me. Accusatory and angry.

Every damn one of them looked like they'd been caught red-handed except one brother. Drake had done this on purpose. I knew it.

He stood and stepped toward me. "I can see you're pissed, man. Everyone has been walking on eggshells around you when it comes to Teale. But I'm done. If you want to be miserable and keep acting like this, that's your choice."

I scoffed. "Act like what?"

"Like you've got a stick up your ass. Like you can't be bothered with your family. Just because you don't want Teale doesn't mean we all have to stop being friends with her."

I took a step toward my brother, seething, my hands balled into fists. "I never said I didn't want her."

"You never said you did. And most importantly, you never told her. There's a reason she left, Kane."

That was a low blow, and I said nothing in response. They had no idea what the full story was. *What am I supposed to say? He's right.* I threw my hands up. "I'm done with this."

My dad's voice made me stop. "Son, you have no one to blame but yourself when you lose her."

"I know." I turned and stormed out of the house. Later, I'd sort it out with my parents and apologize. Right now, anything I said would only end up causing more issues. My brother followed me, but I ignored him. I made it to my truck and reached for the door when Drake's hand shot out to keep it closed. Dad stood behind him.

I clenched my teeth. "Man, you need to step away."

He refused to move. "I'm going to tell you this, although it goes against my better judgment after the dick you've been."

"What?"

"She has a date."

I reared back as if he'd punched me in the face. *Another man thought he was going out with my woman?* I looked at Dad, who said nothing, silently confirming Drake's statement. "Who is the fucker?"

"I don't know. And why do *you* care? She's trying to move forward. If you don't want her, drive back to your place and be a lonely, miserable asshole. But if you do want her, you better not wait much longer, Kane. I'm going to tell you the same thing I told Hayden. It's worth it. Love is worth everything. Stop being a dick."

The weight of the world seemed to crash down on me. "She'll never take me back."

"Then live your life knowing she's with another man. I never figured you to be a pussy and not fight for what you wanted. You're okay with another man touching her, kissing her... making love to her?"

I wanted to spit nails. I pushed past Drake. No way was another man going to touch Teale. She was mine. And I would fight like hell to make sure she understood that.

Dad stood in front of the porch with the rest of the family. I looked at my other brother. "Hayden, can you take me to Montana?"

"It's about fucking time!" Hayden yelled.

The girls clapped and did their happy, squealing shit. I pointed at each of them. "Don't say a word. Surprise is the only thing I've got on my side after the dick I've been."

Mom looked at Hayden, then me. "Just so you're aware, I'm letting this language slide this once because it has to do with Teale." Then, she walked up to me. "Go win her back, Kane. And remember that you deserve this. We'll watch Mariah for you."

"Thanks. I'm going to try."

On the drive to the airport, I took out my phone.

Me: *Hope, it's Kane. I need your help. I want to try and win your daughter back. I don't deserve her, but she's it for me.*

193

CHAPTER
Thirty-Five

Teale

"Miss Teale, do you miss Alaska?" Judson asked as we sat on the front porch of my parents' house, bundled up and sipping hot chocolate.

Judson was a little boy I'd met at the hospital where I volunteered after I came back from Alaska. At first, volunteering had been a way to fill the time while making a difference. And it helped keep my thoughts from drifting to Kane. Through it all, I had met this amazing boy and his mother, Lori. We connected almost instantly.

"Yes, I do miss it. I miss it a lot."

When I'd come to the hospital that first day to volunteer, Judson had handed me a book all about Alaska and asked me to read it to him. It was like fate had brought this boy into my life. Since he was little, Judson's dream had been to visit Alaska. Every day, after reading to him, I would tell him a little more about my adventures in Skagway. He especially loved stories about Mariah and the Twiner sisters.

He took a sip of his hot chocolate as I adjusted his blanket to make sure he was warm enough. "Are you going back when Miss Devney and Miss Alexa have their babies?"

"I plan to. We'll video chat while I'm there, so you can see everyone." It was hard to keep the sadness out of my voice. I missed them so much. I missed *him* so much.

Judson nodded to himself. "I'm going to go there some day. I want to track animals through the woods and be tough like Mister Kane."

The mention of his name formed a knot in my throat. After all this time, it was still hard. At first, I'd left Kane out of the stories I told Judson, but Kane was Alaska in so many ways. Judson ate up every tidbit I had about Kane.

Lori and I had grown close over the last couple of months. As a single mother, she was fighting the battle with Judson's leukemia alone. The last doctor reports we had seen weren't promising. When Lori told me the news, my heart shattered.

I smiled, fighting back tears. Life was so precious and delicate. "You're already tough like Mister Kane."

Judson turned to me with a huge smile. "You really think so?"

"I do. And I know he would think so, too."

He rocked a little more, his chest puffed out. "I want to meet Mister Kane someday."

I said nothing in response, afraid to make any false promises.

After a few minutes, Judson's brows drew in, and he looked at me. "Will you make me a promise, Miss Teale?"

I would give this boy the world if I could. "What's that,

buddy?"

"Will you take care of my momma if the leukemia doesn't get better? I hear her crying at night. I know she's sad because the doc said it wasn't getting better."

A tear trickled down my cheek. His prognosis wasn't good. The options left for treatment had limited success rates. Judson had asked Lori if he could stop the treatments—he just wanted to enjoy his life and not be sick all the time. After much discussion, Lori had agreed.

I grabbed his hand. "I promise you. But I want to focus on you. They're still running more tests."

He let out a big sigh as if the weight of the world had been lifted from his shoulders. "I know. It helps knowing my momma will have you to help her smile."

He was incredibly mature for his young age. But I'd noticed this among so many of the terminal children I'd met. The battles they fought against the diseases that plagued them caused them to be wise beyond their years. While I stayed with Judson, Lori was at the hospital meeting with his doctors to see if there was anything that could be done that would help but wouldn't cause him to be sick. I had so much admiration for her.

I reassured him. "Don't worry about your mom. I promise I will look after her. You just focus on feeling better and having fun."

He gave me a big grin. "I will. You scared about talking to the news people tonight?"

Over lunch, Judson had pinky swore with me when I'd told him my secret about retiring. "No, I'm glad. It gives me more time to be with the people I love."

"Like me."

"Like you." I knew my voice was a little shaky. "I am so thankful I met you."

He gave me a big smile. "Me, too, Miss Teale."

Judson put his hot chocolate on the table and climbed up in my lap. We rocked in silence, and I'd figured Judson had fallen asleep when his body relaxed and his head lolled to the side.

Please give us a miracle. Please. This little boy is so precious to me.

I would give anything to save this boy.

He snuggled in closer and whispered in his sleep, "Love you."

I squeezed him. "Love you, too."

I closed my eyes as I continued to pray for a miracle, savoring each precious moment I had with this boy.

CHAPTER
Thirty-Six

Teale

What a day.

Everything had been a blur since the day before, between making final arrangements for the interview that day. It was nice to be consumed by something. It allowed me to stay focused and kept my mind off other things. I drank a bottle of water while I waited for the show to start.

The anticipation was palpable. The energy fed me. But there was still a piece of me missing.

When I'd returned to Montana brokenhearted, I decided professional skating was over for me. However, I needed something to focus my energy on. After talking with my parents, I decided to announce my retirement right before doing something positive. It had taken me a week or two, but I finally decided to start a nonprofit organization. Judson had been the inspiration. With the help of my parents, we lined up national sponsors, and then we contacted different skaters to see if they wanted to be a part of it. The response had been overwhelming. The money raised that night would go to help the children's hospital here and help Hollis start a new clinic in another rural Alaskan town. Whatever I raised, Hollis agreed to match for Alaska. Hollis was beyond wealthy. In fact, he funded the clinic in Skagway completely on his own. That was impressive.

I had fallen in love with the wilderness of Alaska and wanted to do my part. After my ordeal with the lumberjack killer, I understood how necessary it was to have a doctor in town.

I peeked behind the curtains to see families getting to their seats. There was popcorn and candy and everyone wore a smile. The kids from the hospital had the prime seats. Seeing this made it all worth it.

As we searched for venues, we'd decided to turn my ice rink in Montana into a place we could have a show. One, it was cheaper. And two, the children from the local hospital could attend. The limited number of seats had sold out in record time. The response—including the sponsorships—had been incredible. An event organizer from the network airing the show had donated her time, as well. Judson came up to me. "Momma says it's time to take my seat."

I leaned down to hug him. "Thanks for all your help." Earlier that morning, Judson had helped make the bags of popcorn for the kids.

Lori approached me, clipboard in hand. "Everything is set."

"You two go enjoy the show." I knelt down in front of Judson. "Come find me after. I want to know what you think."

"I will, Miss Teale."

Judson grabbed his mother's hand, and they took their seats.

When I'd asked the kids what they wanted us to skate to, they'd picked *The Greatest Showman*. It was the most talked-about movie in the children's ward. The kids loved watching it.

So far, we had raised over four million dollars, which exceeded the initial goal by a million dollars. That meant each recipient would get at least two million dollars. That was a lot of money. Hopefully, more donations would come in when the show was televised nationally. Information on how to donate would scroll at the bottom of the screen as the show progressed. The sponsors had come together to pay for the TV spot. It still seemed surreal that the pieces had fallen into place like they had.

Hopefully everything went smoothly. As soon as I'd announced my plans, skaters I'd known all my life had asked to be part of the show. I was beyond touched.

The rink dimmed; the excitement was palpable. My breath caught as I waited. Leaning out, I saw the footage of my interview on a screen that lowered from the ceiling. My announcement would be coming any second, and soon the entire world would know. I wondered how my news would be received.

The reporter, Mel, who had been one of my favorites through the years, had come to my house yesterday. We'd kept the interview casual, sharing tea and sitting on the couch.

I watched the screen as she introduced us and began the interview. "So, Teale, you've definitely gained a lot of interest in this event. People have flown in from all over the US."

"Yes, I'm so very humbled by the response. It's been an amazing ride."

"You sound as if it's the end of the road." She tipped her head to one side.

On the screen, I tucked a stray hair behind my ear and said, "This will be my last skate before I enter retirement."

There was a long pause on the screen, and gasps could be heard all around the rink. I hadn't told the reporter prior to the interview.

"Wh-why are you retiring?" she asked.

I smiled, knowing I had made the right decision, as I waited to hear my response. "Every journey runs its course. I'll always skate in some fashion. But professionally, I'm done. It was why I took some time off this winter... to decide what my future looked like."

"You were in Alaska, right?"

My thoughts shifted back to the Fosters. I missed them so. Hopefully soon, I'd find the courage to go up there again when the babies came. I just wasn't sure when my heart would be ready to see Kane.

"Yes, it's a beautiful state."

"If I'm not mistaken, you have two benefactors tonight— the children's ward of the hospital and a clinic in Alaska."

"Yes, that's correct. I've been volunteering at the local children's hospital. They have an amazing staff. In Skagway, Dr. Hollis Fritz runs a clinic that he has personally funded. He's one of the most generous human beings I've ever met. He is currently looking to open another clinic in another isolated part of Alaska. With the funds we've raised so far, we can support both facilities, and each and every person who's donated has helped saved lives. In some places, access to a local doctor just isn't an option. In the case of serious accidents or injuries, patients must be airlifted, which is expensive and reliant on the weather."

Mel shifted in her seat. "So, where did this idea come from?"

"Another wonderful person I'm fortunate to call a dear friend, Alexa Foster. A couple of years ago, she lost her father to a logging accident. There was no local doctor or clinic, and bad weather prohibited airlifting him somewhere he could receive treatment. Car or ferry weren't options because of the distance. If there had been a local facility, he might have survived. While studying nursing in New York, she met Dr. Fritz, who wanted to make a difference. Now the two of them run the clinic."

"That's an incredible story. It sounds like you love Alaska."

Tears gathered in my eyes as I thought about Kane. I still wasn't over him—not by a long shot. I wiped them away, recognizing the same emotion I saw on the screen. I had somehow managed to keep the tears away during the interview.

I responded to Mel, "Alaska will always be a part of me and hold a piece of my heart. Always."

In more ways than one.

"Will you ever go back to professional skating?"

I'd paused as I thought that through. "I think that chapter of my life is over."

"Do you have anyone you want to thank?"

I'd taken a deep breath and looked at the camera. "Thank you to the family who helped me in more ways than you'll ever know. You are incredible. Though I can't be with you, I send all my love."

The images on the screen dimmed and then went dark. People in the audience clapped and cheered.

Mom stood behind me and squeezed my shoulders. My dad held flowers. "We're so proud of you, sweetheart."

I was hit with emotion all over again. Before every skate, Dad had brought me flowers. "Thank you, Daddy."

"We love you, Teale."

This was the right decision, and with my parents' help, I would figure out what the next chapter of my life looked like. I hugged them as the announcer took the ice. "Thank you for everything."

It was time.

The music started. On cue, I took the ice as the lights danced with color behind me and skated my heart out. One song blended into another, and everything I had I left on the ice. Pyrotechnics went off as we skated, adding the dramatic effect.

The songs blended perfectly. The skaters hit their marks with grace and strength. Energy coursed through me. We'd done it. The tireless rehearsals and planning had been worth it. As we came to the end of the performance, I had a hard time believing it was over. As the skaters took the ice to take their bows, I waited just a minute and closed my eyes to savor the cheers.

My name was announced over the PA system, and I skated out as the cheers became deafening. I threw kisses out to the crowd, skating around the roses that were thrown onto the ice. It was one of the most magical moments of my career next to taking home gold at the Winter Olympics.

When it was time for us to leave the ice, one of my fellow skaters, Rosa, stopped me. "Stay on the ice. There's a surprise."

"What?"

This was a live, televised event and a surprise wasn't part of the program. Another video of me thanking everyone was supposed to come up on the screen. I looked at my mom, who nodded, indicating that I should stay put.

So, she knows what's going on.

I waited to see what was going on.

"Teale, I was an ass."

Kane.

My heart lurched, and I looked around the rink, trying to locate him.

"That's a naughty word."

"Bad word."

"Uh oh."

Those phrases morphed into a deafening buzz as kids began to giggle and yell. I kept looking around for Kane. He was here. He came.

Why is he here? I've missed him so much.

Kane spoke again. "Kids, don't say that word. My mom will be really mad if she finds out. Let's hope she's not watching."

The show was being televised live, and I knew Amie was watching. She had texted me a good luck message earlier that morning. She was going to be livid her son cussed on live television. I bit my bottom lip to keep from laughing. The spotlight hit Kane where he stood in the bleachers, and I felt my lip quiver as I struggled not to cry. It had been so long, and he looked so good. He had on his standard jeans and T-shirt. Actually, he looked better than I remembered. His beard was a little fuller, his muscles a little more angular.

"Teale, I was a…" There was another long pause. Surely, he wasn't going to cuss again. "Meaniehead."

Meaniehead? Where in the world did he get that?

I giggled and covered my mouth. Kane was closer now that I could see him. He gave me his crooked grin, and my heart leapt from my chest. He took a few more steps to the opening onto the ice. Our eyes stayed connected. I wanted to skate to him, but I was rooted in place. If Kane wanted me, he had to take the steps to get me. I had to know he wanted this without a doubt. For a second, he looked around the rink and blew out a big breath. "Shi—I mean, man, there are a lot of people here." There were even more giggles at his almost-slipup. "My mother is going to kill me for sure if those cameras are broadcasting live." The crowd erupted in laughter and he stepped onto the ice, his focus back on me. "Teale, I need you and the world to know… I'm sorry. I'm sorry for everything. I'm not good with this stuff, but I don't want to lose you."

This was it. This was the moment I had dreamed of happening. I closed my eyes and took a calming breath. When I opened them, Kane was standing in front of me.

He turned off the mic. Softly, he said, "Hey, you really can skate."

"I really can," I said with a huge smile.

His dark eyes were like a stormy sea as they searched mine. "I'm here."

"It took you long enough," I quipped back sassily, filled with happiness.

He grabbed my hand, and I trembled at his touch. "Yeah,

it did. I'm so sorry, Teale." He touched his forehead to mine. "I want more. I'm ready for more."

I closed my eyes for the briefest of seconds. When I opened them, he was a little blurry from the tears. He reached up and wiped them away. "I missed you, angel."

His soft words spoke volumes. From the anguish in his eyes, it was obvious that our being apart had been just as painful for him. By coming here and making himself vulnerable, he *showed* me the words he wasn't able to say.

"I missed you, too."

His eyes searched mine. "Am I too late?"

"No." My feelings for Kane hadn't changed. In fact, they had only grown stronger during the time without him.

"So, what do I do now?"

It had to be incredibly awkward for Kane to do this in front of so many people. It showed how serious he was. "I think you should kiss me."

Without hesitation, Kane kissed me, claiming me in front of the world. I wanted more. Just as the kiss was about to deepen, he pulled back and put his forehead to mine. "Now everyone knows you're mine."

CHAPTER
Thirty-Seven

Kane

As soon as we stepped off the ice, chaos ensued. Our perfect moment erupted into madness. Everyone wanted to talk to Teale. People wanted to meet me. It was a clusterfuck, and I wanted to go back to it just being us. There was so much left to talk about.

After Teale was pulled away, I found an out-of-the-way spot to hide out with Hayden. I leaned up against the wall and watched her.

People loved her. And she loved them. She thrived around people. I knew this from our time in Skagway, but I hadn't realized just how much. In the spotlight, she was more reserved and not so damn argumentative. I needed to remember that for the future. But she was amazing, and I couldn't keep my eyes off her. And I was ready for this to be over with so we could talk.

"You must be Kane."

I straightened, recognizing the voice of Teale's mom.

"I'm Hope."

I turned and extended my hand. "It's a pleasure to meet you in person, ma'am." I'd had a hell of a time convincing Hope to help me. "I couldn't have done it without you, so thank you."

At first, I had tried to arrange to see Teale before the event, so we'd have more time to talk. But Hope had said the event deserved all of Teale's time and focus, and I'd agreed. Hope offered to help change the end of the event if I was serious about my feelings. She said her daughter deserved to have the world hear how I felt about her if I was serious. After how I'd acted, I wanted Teale and her parents to know I was serious about us. *Us.* The concept was going to take some getting used to.

Hope was an older version of Teale, with the same dark hair and petite frame. "Thank you for making our little girl happy." She turned to the man standing next to her. "This is Teale's father, Everett."

"Nice to meet you, sir."

He eyed me for a second. "After breakfast tomorrow, you and I are going to go for a little walk."

Fuck. That sounded like I might be going to meet my maker at the end of that walk. But I had to agree. "Yes, sir." Teale's dad wasn't a small guy and looked like he was in pretty good shape. I ran my hand through my hair and added, "Hopefully, I'll come back in one piece."

"If you give me the answers I'm looking for, you will." He pinned me down with a stare. This guy was hard to read.

Double fuck. "Sounds good."

Hope batted away her husband. "Don't mind him. You'll

be fine. We'll see you guys tomorrow for breakfast. We had the guesthouse prepared for you and your brother to stay in."

"Thanks."

On the way to Montana, Hayden had said he could only stay for one day, so I wasn't sure where anything stood. I glanced at him, and he nodded—he could stay another night. Teale's dad slapped me hard on the back. "Get a good night's sleep. You're gonna need it." He was probably going to put my balls in a vice.

As they walked away, I could hear Hope saying, "Everett, be nice to the poor boy."

I let out a breath. My head was all over the place, but finally things felt right. I'd be lying if I said I wasn't scared shitless. Putting myself out there to be in a relationship was a big deal. Teale and I still had a lot to work out, and I was nervous what that outcome would bring. At least now Teale knew how I felt. But I was anxious to get her alone.

She lived in Montana.

I lived in Alaska.

This was a potential problem.

My damn phone wouldn't stop vibrating. My family had started with the group texting, and I was sure they were off on some tangent.

"Feels pretty good, doesn't it." Hayden bumped my shoulder and gave me one of those annoying grins.

I raised my eyebrow. "Just because I came for Teale doesn't mean I'm going to get all mushy and shit with my brothers."

Someone pulled on my pants leg, and I turned to find a little boy wearing a huge baseball hat. "Hi, Mister. I'm Judson. I know Miss Teale, too."

I smiled. "You do?"

"Yeah, she tells me stories about Alaska and her adventures with Mariah, Kane, the Twiner sisters, and Ol' Man Rooster. She also tells me about the Foster family."

Teale had been talking about me. I was speechless for a second. "I'm Kane."

Judson's eyes grew round. "You're *Kane*?"

"I am."

For a second Judson only stared at me. "Did you bring Mariah?"

"No, my mom is watching her for me."

He leaned in. "Do you really think she's going to be mad at you for cussing?"

Shit.

"Yes, she's probably going to want to wash my mouth out with soap."

Fuck. I had cussed around all those kids.

He leaned in and whispered, "My momma always says that if I put batteries in my filter, it will help. Maybe your batteries were dead."

I chuckled. "I think I forgot to charge mine last night. Thanks for reminding me."

"Judson, come here for a second. I want you to meet someone."

I turned to see a woman calling for him.

He gave me a huge hug. "Gotta go. My momma is never going to believe I met *the* Kane," he said before taking off toward his mother.

Hayden leaned toward me. "You're going to need something more than a new battery for your filter. Maybe you should zip it and throw away the key. I don't know how long you can go without cussing."

My hand shot up to give him the finger, and he chuckled. Instead of flipping him off, I pointed my index finger in the air. "And you're number one."

"I always knew that. So glad you finally admitted it."

Asshole.

An older woman with a clipboard approached us. "Teale has asked if Kane Foster can join her. The kids want to meet him."

Hayden laughed. "I've got to see this. Let's see how many times you swear."

As we followed, I muttered, "Shut up, dickhead."

"That's considered cursing to kids, by the way," Hayden retorted.

I swore some days I wanted to choke the life out of my brother. "I know that, asswipe."

Hayden pulled something out of his pocket and handed it to me. Turned out to be nothing but air. "Here's my filter; you can borrow it. It's fully charged."

I sighed. *Do not give him the satisfaction.*

The crowd parted, and I saw Teale sitting on a bench. Our eyes connected, and in that moment, I knew all this was worth it. Every single bit. Teale smiled, and it lit up my world. Hell, maybe I had become that mushy guy, but I would never let my brothers know.

When I was close, Teale said, "Well, kids, this is Kane."

"Is he the one from Alaska?" a little girl in pigtails asked.

Teale patted her head. "He sure is."

They all know about me? Teale had been talking about me, which helped ease my nerves. I hadn't been far from her thoughts just as she hadn't been far from each of mine. I noticed some kids had bandanas covering their bald heads, there were bandages at the bends of their arms, and some were in wheelchairs. Hope had mentioned that some of these kids had terminal diseases. I couldn't imagine what that was like.

I squatted down to be eye level with them. "It's nice to meet you guys."

A little girl raised her hand. "Mister, are you going to take Teale away?"

"Well… I…"

Teale saved me. "Do you think I'd let him take me away?"

Damn. Does that mean she's staying? My heart sank.

The kids yelled, "No!"

Teale covered her heart. "Remember how we talked the other day? Wherever people end up, they're still always connected by their love. Just because you aren't close doesn't mean the person isn't always close in their thoughts."

So, she's considering coming back to Alaska?

Hell, I needed to stop thinking so much.

Another girl looked me over. "You're big."

"He's like Superman," a little boy added.

Another boy said, "Or maybe Spiderman."

"Definitely a superhero."

I couldn't keep up with who was saying what. The boy from earlier tugged on my pants leg again. "Mister, did you eat your spinach to get so big?"

"Well—"

Teale cut me off. "Oh, Judson, I was wondering where you were. I wanted to make sure you met Kane. He eats lots of spinach and veggies so he can be super strong."

That was the farthest thing from the truth, but I went with

it. Now that I looked a little closer, I saw how frail Judson was. "I eat so many veggies because they're so good for you."

Lies. Lies. Lies.

At least that part about eating them.

Hayden chuckled to the side, knowing I never ate them.

Judson patted the bench. I sat, and he hopped up on my lap. I wasn't sure what to do, so I just went with it.

"My mom says if I eat my veggies, it'll help me feel better." The little boy took off his baseball cap to reveal a bald head. "What does Alaska look like? Miss Teale told me a lot. I keep asking her questions. She says there's a lot of woods and animals. She also says there's snow and two ladies who report all the news. I love Mariah. Miss Teale says she's the best dog there ever was."

"Yeah, that's right, she is. It sounds like Miss Teale has told you all about Alaska. It gets real cold there in the winter."

Judson put his hat back on. "What do you do, mister?"

Teale jumped in. "Kane does tours in the woods with people to show them the wildlife in Alaska."

Oh yeah, fuck. They might be upset if they knew I was a hunting guide *and* a hunter. *Shit, I'm terrible at this.*

The kids hit me with a million questions that I did my best to answer. After a bit, I relaxed more. And my filter had stayed in place. Soon, some of the kids left with their parents. At one point, only Judson remained. I could tell he and Teale were close. He'd begged his mom for five more minutes with Teale and me.

"I want to see Alaska one day. Can I come see you in Alaska? You could take me on a hike. I want to spot a deer like a real guide. And I want to meet Mariah. I want to see it all." Something about this little boy's curiosity and courage touched me the way nothing had before.

"Yeah, buddy, I like that idea."

His mom came to get him. "Judson, we have to go this time."

His shoulders slumped. "But I don't wanna go back to the hospital. I want to go to Alaska. Momma, I don't want to do any more treatments. I thought you said that was okay."

The mother swallowed hard. "Yes, sweetheart. They just want to check you out. We're going home tonight." The mom's lower lip quivered, and she pressed her mouth into a firm line.

I stood. "Give me just a second, bud. Will you keep my girl company?"

"Yep."

I tapped his cap. "I appreciate it."

His mother and I stepped away. "Can he travel?"

She shrugged. "I don't know. He has leukemia. And the prognosis isn't good. But I'm keeping up hope for a miracle."

Fuck. This little boy was going to see Alaska if I had anything to do with it. "If it's safe for him to travel, I'll pay for him to come to Alaska. My brother can fly you both. We have a doctor in town who can organize details with your doctor."

I glanced over ay Hayden, and he nodded. So he was on board with this plan. I knew Hollis would be, too.

"Why are you doing this?"

I shifted my weight. "Because everyone deserves to have their dreams come true. Here's my number." I handed her one of my business cards. "If you're okay with it, we can start working out the details."

Judson's mom clutched the card to her chest. "He's asked to stop treatment. Judson wants to be a regular little boy and do as much as possible. The doctors don't know how long he'll have. But yes, he would love it. He's dreamed of going to Alaska for as long as I can remember. I think that's why he latched on to Teale so fast."

So it was bad. Really bad.

"Can we tell him?"

"Yes."

She walked over and knelt in front of Judson. I could hear her sniffle before she spoke. "Kane wants to bring us all to Alaska. We'll work with your doctors. Judson, you're going to get to go."

Teale looked at me, her eyes bright with unshed tears.

The little boy ran to me and hugged my leg. "I'm going to eat all my veggies so I can be strong like you when I get to Alaska."

"Your mom has my number. You call me anytime you want to talk and ask me questions about Alaska."

Judson took his mom's hand and looked back over his shoulder. "I will. Promise." Taking a few steps, he pulled his mother's arm. "Let's go to the hospital, Mom. I want to see how fast I can go to Alaska."

I stared at mother and son as they walked out of the rink. When I turned back to Teale, she was nearly sobbing. "What's wrong?"

"You are the most amazing man."

I cradled her face, wiping the tears away. "Angel, don't cry."

"You have no idea what that means to him... to me. Judson has been counting down the days to this event—he's been such a big help. It's all he's talked about. The doctors don't know how he's doing so well. They've told Lori it's simply a matter of time. She was afraid that after the show today, he might go downhill."

He was so young. Too young. Only eight or nine years old.

"Why is he stopping treatment? Can't something be done?" There had to be something.

Teale shook her head. "The last round of treatments didn't work. He's asked his mom if they could stop. He just wants to be a normal little boy for as long as he can. I was there the day they found out that there weren't really any viable options. He's such a brave boy. And Lori's a single mom. Judson's dad walked out on them when Judson was a little boy."

"What a piece of garbage." I couldn't imagine what Lori faced as a parent. Life was fragile. Seeing these children face these terminal cases was awful. It brought my thoughts full circle. And my guilt from having left her grew. It had taken me almost four months to come after Teale. If something had happened to her, I would have never forgiven myself. And now I would do anything to keep Teale in my life, even if that meant moving to Montana.

CHAPTER
Thirty-Eight

Kane

Later—much, much later—we were still at the rink. Teale had a few more things to take care of. I knew I would be in the way, so I helped the crew break down the bleachers. We were nearing the end as I loaded up one of the last beams from the lighting used into the trailer.

Hayden came over to me. "I think that's it."

"Me, too."

"I'm going to go on up to the guesthouse. I assume you're waiting for Teale?"

Teale was near the ice rink, talking to some people, probably doing another interview. She'd changed into jeans and a T-shirt. Hopefully she would be done soon so we could talk. "Yeah, I'll just hang here until she's done."

"All right. Night, Kane. Good luck."

"Thanks, I'm going to need it."

I found a spot out of the way while Teale finished up. My

phone vibrated again, and I pulled it out.

Two hundred and eighty-seven text messages. *What the fuck?*

What in the world required that many text messages? It was the group message... with the whole family. I knew it was a mistake, but I opened it anyway. I only read the texts at the end.

Hayden: *I think the vote is unanimous, Kane's nickname is now princess. He's waiting for her to be done. It's cute.*

Drake: *For sure. Maybe even precious...*

Hollis: *Starbucks on me when Teale and Kane get back. We'll have a celebratory toast complete with a puppuccino for Mariah.*

Devney: *Oh, I love the salted caramel cake pops.*

Alexa: *Yes! I've been craving caramel. We'll get a dozen to get us through the workday.*

Devney: *Yes!*

Kory: *Oh my! Movie night is now going to be tied.*

Drake: *In four months the men will outnumber you again.*

Alexa: *Unless Devney and I have girls. Oh, I hope you are ready to watch chick flicks.*

Hayden: *Well, I think the title of princess might revert back to Drake if he has a girl.*

Drake: *Oh, it'll be stuck with Kane.*

Mom: *It takes a true man to raise a girl.*

Dad: *That might be so, but I'm glad we had boys. Made it a hell of a lot easier.*

Alexa: *Do you know when Kane and Teale are coming home, Hayden? Even when Kane opens this, he'll probably ignore us. Haha! I bet he's mentally cussing at the number of text messages.*

Mom: *Kane, if you're reading this... we're going to be talking about those slips on NATIONAL TELEVISION.*

Drake: *Oh, someone is in trouble.*

Hayden: *Oh, he slipped more than on national television. Said the "s-word" in front of a little boy. That little boy offered his batteries for Kane's filter. Funniest moment of my life... ever.*

Mom: *Oh, dear. Please tell me that did not happen.*

Hayden: *I'm sorry, Mom. Not all of us can be perfect like me.*

Drake: *Or me.*

Alexa: *Hayden... focus. When are they coming home? We need a girls' night.*

Hayden: *As soon as I know, I'll get you more details. Since the show ended, it's been crazy. But I believe our dear brother is smitten as a kitten.*

Hollis: *I think Kane "swooned" us all on television.*

Devney: *You stole my line, Hollis!*

Hollis: *Finders keepers.*

Devney: *I'm engaged to a child.*

Hollis: *A rugged Alaskan child.*

Devney: *True... but back to Kane. Seeing him go after Teale nearly made swoon.*

Alexa: *I sure swooned.*

Kory: *Me, too.*

Hayden: *Okay, I'll admit it... Kane did good.*

Drake: *Agreed.*

Mom: *I was proud...*

Devney: *For sure!*

Alexa: *Do you have any other news to report, Hayden?*

Hayden: *Well, Kane's going for a walk with Teale's dad tomorrow. If he doesn't come back...*

Alexa: *Oh, no! He's going to give him The Talk.*

Drake: *Oh, I remember The Talk.*

Dad: *Your mother's father had me fearin' for my life.*

Mom: *He did not! He just wanted to make sure your wild days were over, Ike Foster. You had quite the reputation.*

Drake: *And this is where I bail on the conversation.*

Hayden: *Me, too.*

I closed out of the messenger, not even slightly interested in seeing any more about my parents. My phone vibrated again, and I muted the conversation. They were going to drive me crazy.

Teale gave someone a hug and waved good-bye, calling, "Thanks again for all your help." She took a deep breath and turned my way. Her smile lit up the room as she walked over to me. When she was just a couple of inches away, she stopped. I reached out to her, needing to touch her again. I was tired of the crowds and wanted someplace that was just for the two of us.

"Can we go somewhere?"

"Yeah, I'd like that."

In silence, Teale led me out the back of the rink. Security she'd hired was around, making sure no one came into restricted areas on the property, which included the main house about a five-minute walk from the rink, and supervising parking and transportation. There was limited parking available next to the skating rink, so attendees had been shuttled from a municipal parking lot about ten minutes away. The city had even donated the transportation for the event. I was relieved to hear that the security team would be sticking around for a while to ensure everyone's safety.

As we made our way up toward the main house and guesthouse, we said nothing. I imagined that was because there was a lot on our minds. I had no idea what to expect.

It was dark, so I couldn't make out much, but I remembered plenty from the quick tour Hope and Everett had given us this afternoon.

What's she thinking? Where's her head at? What if she changes her mind about giving me a second chance? I had been a dick of epic proportions, and she was supposed to be going on a date with someone. I hadn't thought much about that until now.

Shit.

We arrived at a small cottage with the porch light on. "This is where I stay when I'm here. There's also a guest-house, where you and Hayden are staying. My parents live in the main house."

So, I would not be staying with Teale tonight. That probably wasn't the best sign.

Teale hit a code and the door unlocked. As we walked in, she flipped a few lights. It was bright and colorful with lots of sparkles and trinkets. It looked like a studio apartment with a loft. The kitchen, living room, and dining area were all the same room, like my cabin.

"So I see you don't have any victims on these walls."

She laughed. "No, no, I don't have any... I thought we were calling them *trophies*?"

We smiled at each other. I remembered walking into my cabin that first time and seeing my animals dressed up. I hadn't realized then, but that was the first time I had actually begun to live in a long time.

Teale walked into the kitchen and grabbed a bottle of water. "Want a beer?"

"That'd be good."

Things were awkward yet felt familiar. It was odd. I wanted to hold her hand, but I needed to let Teale set the tone. I took a drink, then dove in headfirst. "I'm so fucking sorry, Teale."

"I am, too." I followed her to the living room where she sat on the couch with her feet curled underneath her. It was a cozy place. Teale picked up a remote and hit a button. "*Voilà*, let there be fake fire with no heat."

The pink flames came to life in a fireplace in the wall. Then they turned purple. I remembered finding Teale in Butch's cabin, and she'd mentioned a remote control. Now it all made sense. I chuckled and took a sip of beer. "Is there a button for heat?"

"Yes, it's this button right here. I can also add a crackling sound, so it sounds like a fire without any mess."

I took the remote and looked it over. "Thank goodness for fireplace remotes. If not, you might not have pestered me to death to come to Butch's place and fix the heat."

Again, she laughed. I missed that sound. "True. But I also remember you being upset when I commandeered your truck."

"I was a stupid ass. I should have seen what I had before I pushed you away."

We lapsed into silence again, and I wasn't sure what else to say.

Teale stared at me, and I waited patiently for her to respond. "I'm glad you're here."

"I'm here for you, angel."

She closed her eyes for a brief second before opening them again. They glistened with unshed tears. "I'm sorry I left the way I did. I just couldn't force you into something you didn't want. It wasn't fair. And I was scared of having my heart broken more than it was."

I scooted to the edge of my seat. "I think it needed to happen for me to realize what I'd lost. Please tell me I'm not too late. Just don't go on a date with the asshole."

I had no idea who this guy was, but if he wanted my girl, well, that made him an asshole.

Teale's eyebrows pinched in confusion. "Date? What are you talking about? I don't have a date."

"Drake said you were trying to move forward. That you had a date."

Teale shook her head. "He must have lied to you. You're not that easy to get over, Kane Foster."

Later, after I punched him in the face, I would have to thank Drake. "I'm glad you think so. Teale, I'm sorry for being such a dick. I just—"

She grabbed my hand. "Don't. Kane, you never lied to me. You told me from the get-go. But things changed, and that wasn't fair to you."

"I treated you like a girlfriend in front of my family. That was a mindfuck, Teale. And I nearly got you killed."

She shuddered for a second. "That wasn't your fault. That was the killer's fault."

I swallowed hard. "How are you doing?"

"Good. Really good. I saw a therapist for a while to work through it. Well, I worked through a lot of it. There are still times that I have nightmares. I'm not a fan of being isolated by myself. Staying here, with my parents in the main house, is about my limit."

I rubbed the back of my neck, feeling the tension there. I wanted to kill that asshole all over again for the pain he'd caused Teale. It was an anger I wasn't able to soothe. *Is this normal?* "I'll never forgive myself for what happened to you. I even checked up on you to make sure you were okay."

Teale gasped, "What?"

Shit. I knew I had to tell her the truth. Otherwise, I sounded like stalker. "I… uh… I texted your mom and asked her not to say anything. With how muddled everything got, I didn't want to hurt you again."

Teale smiled. "That was why Mom told me not to lose faith."

"Please don't be mad."

She shook her head. "I'm not. I'm glad she didn't tell me. Knowing probably would have made it all harder."

Her words killed me. "I'm so fucking sorry."

"What you did tonight means a lot to me. It was perfect. And you don't have to keep saying you're sorry. I forgive you, Kane."

"Where does this leave us?"

For a second, Teale watched me. Her voice was soft when she answered. "Where do you want it to lead, Kane?"

"Us together."

"Well, what would you think to starting off slow?"

Thank fuck. She was giving me a shot. "I like the sound of that."

Then the smile that captured my heart emerged. "We can practice wooing each other."

Man, she was going to give me a run for my money. "Wooing?"

"You know, make mixtapes for each other, make each other's favorite dinner, give each other back rubs. That kind of stuff." Teale giggled.

What the fuck is a mixtape? I was in over my head. I had no idea how to do half this shit or how to pull off a *woo.* I laid it on the line like I always did with her. "I've never done this before. I'm going to fuck up."

She grabbed my hand. "All I need is your heart, Kane. I'm just playing with you. I wasn't trying to scare you."

Hell, I was scared shitless just thinking about messing up. "Teale, I mean it. I have no idea about this relationship sh—

stuff. Like, none. I'll give you anything I can, but I've never done this."

She moved to lie against me, her hand resting on my chest. Finally, I had her in my arms again, and I felt some of the tension ease. I relaxed. "This, right here, is what I need. This is it. I want what we had in Alaska. It's the reason I fell in love with you. It wasn't because of all the fancy stuff. Just me and you... like this."

"This I can do."

I held her tighter, and she gave a contented sigh. We stayed like that, lost in our thoughts, until Teale said, "So, I want to propose something to you."

"Okay..." I answered hesitantly.

"Well, we have a location issue."

That was something that bothered me, but I refused to let a couple thousand miles keep us apart. "Yeah, we do. But, we'll figure it out."

She grabbed my hand. "What do you want to do?"

"I haven't thought that far out, honestly. There's a lot of moving pieces."

Teale chewed on her lip for a second, clearly nervous. "What if we fly back with Hayden day after tomorrow? We could spend the summer in Alaska—since I know you have hunts scheduled—while we figure out what we're going to do next."

I'd thought for sure I'd be down here for a bit. "We can stay longer with your parents if you want."

She snuggled closer to me. "I know, but I want them to come visit me in Alaska. I miss Alaska. I miss our life in Alaska."

I sagged with relief. Leaving Alaska hadn't really occurred to me. Honestly, I couldn't imagine living anywhere else in the world. But for her, I would do absolutely anything. I already knew I loved Teale, but I was afraid to say anything just yet because she wanted to take things slow.

"I like that. I miss having you in Alaska." Things were falling into place. "You going to stay with me at my cabin?"

I felt her stiffen. *Uh-oh.* I wasn't going to like this answer.

"I know you are going to be gone some with hunts." Teale shivered and pulled back to look at me. "I don't think I can stay out there by myself. After being taken... and knowing he'd been there, watching me... I'm not sure if I can do it. Maybe in time. I just..."

Her lip began to tremble. I brushed my thumb along it. "Then we'll find another solution."

"I'm sorry, Kane. So sorry. I know you want me out there and I want to be out there, it's just..."

That inner rage flared again, and I wanted to hurt the son of a bitch all over again. I cradled Teale's face. "Do not worry about that. We will figure it out."

She hugged me tighter. "Thank you for coming for me. Thank you for giving us a chance."

Having her in my arms just felt right. Whatever came our way, we would figure it out.

CHAPTER
Thirty-Nine

Kane

It was one hell of a morning. I never thought I'd say another man made me nervous, but Teale's father had my stomach tied in knots. He knew I'd let his daughter go, and it had taken me nearly five damn months to come get her. I deserved whatever he dished out. And probably more.

At six in the morning, he'd pounded on the guesthouse door, saying it was time for our walk. It was nonnegotiable. From the expression on his face when I opened the door, he seemed surprised to see I was already up. Hayden was still snoozing like a teenage girl.

For the last twenty minutes, he'd said little except telling me to follow him. Finally, Everett stopped on a ridge that overlooked acres and acres of land. It was beautiful here. More open than Alaska, but beautiful nonetheless. A gentle breeze rustled the fields of grass. I liked Montana and could see spending some time there.

"I've heard a lot of wonderful things about you, son."

That wasn't how I expected this to start. I had expected some sort of lashing for being an ass and leaving his daughter. Or maybe a shove off the ridge. I turned to face him. "I probably don't deserve that after the way I treated Teale."

"Maybe. Maybe not. But my daughter loves you. And from what she tells me, you never lied to her. Teale says you saved her life."

I nodded. Everett stuck out his hand. "Thank you." Before I could respond, he clapped me on the shoulder. "You know, I was scared of committing once upon a time, too."

Everett reminded me of my father in a lot of ways. He was one of those men you wanted to be like when you grew older—wise, thoughtful, and respected. Hearing that I wasn't the only one helped ease some of my nerves. "You were?"

Once my brothers found their wives, they'd been ready for marriage. From what I understood, the same had happened to Dad. It was just me who wasn't ready to jump in feet first and see what happened. It had taken Teale's leaving to wake me the hell up.

I was still coming to terms with having a relationship with a girl I loved. Asking my family any questions seemed pointless since they had no idea what it was like to fear commitment. Knowing I hadn't caused Janine's death helped, as had being the person to save Teale from meeting the same fate. I balled my fist as I was assaulted by memories of the killer taking her. *Get yourself under control.* I took a shallow breath and refocused on Everett.

He casually leaned against a tree. He smiled. "Son, you're going to be okay. I promise. Hope made me a better man. It took me nearly ten months to realize I had made a mistake by letting her go. So maybe that makes you twice as smart as me since it only took you five."

I chuckled. "I doubt that. I need you to know I didn't mean to hurt Teale. I don't ever want to hurt her again."

"And keeping that in mind will help you. Once I realized I wanted Hope, I never ran again. Of course, there were times I messed up, but we sorted it out."

That was my biggest fear—doing some kind of irreversible harm. "Any advice?"

"Be honest with Teale. No matter what you're feeling or if you have no clue what you're doing, tell her."

"I will."

He nodded. "That's good."

Is it really that simple? I guess time would tell.

We fell into an easy silence. I had a feeling Everett and I would get along well. He wasn't a man who needed to fill every quiet moment with words.

Pushing himself off the tree, he said, "Let's head back to the house. Hope made us a nice breakfast, and Teale made me promise to bring you back alive."

"I'm glad you're able to oblige."

"Me, too."

As we walked, Everett kept talking. "I want you to know I was pretty pissed when Hope told me you were coming. But my wife has a way of calming me down and helping me to see reason. You see, I've only got one baby girl. But after I heard what you did for Judson yesterday, I understood what Teale saw in you and why she was determined to give you a second chance. And, of course, Hope reminded me of what I'd been like when I wasn't much older than you."

"I promise I'll do everything in my power to take care of Teale."

"I know you will, son." We stopped again, and Everett turned to face me. "Judson's mother called Hope, crying with joy yesterday. Lori hadn't seen her son that excited in a very long time. You have just given a child with no hope a reason to believe dreams do come true. You're a good man, Kane Foster. I look forward to getting to know you better."

I was stunned. I cleared my throat, feeling a little overwhelmed. "Me, too, sir." I took a deep breath, putting myself out there. I wanted Everett to know my intentions. "I want you to know I do love your daughter and I plan to ask her to marry me when the time is right. I'm just not there yet."

The corner of Everett's mouth turned up. "You asking my permission to marry my daughter?"

My palms were sweating. *Hell, am I?* This morning, I hadn't planned on saying anything. But when Teale went back to Alaska with me, I wanted him to know I was serious. "It's important you know my intentions. I don't know how long it'll be before I'm ready for that step, but I want you to know I'll be coming down to visit you again at some point, Mr. Delaney."

Everett turned to face me. "First thing, son: call me Everett. Second thing: a phone call will do just fine. No need to waste time and money coming to see me in person."

Someday, I hoped to become part of this family. "I appreciate that."

"Promise me one thing, Kane."

"What's that?" Hopefully I was able to keep that promise.

"Promise me that you won't rush this until you're ready. It's important that you do this because you *want* to, not be-

231

cause you think you *have* to—for your *and* Teale's sakes."

That made sense. "I promise."

"I believe you. You don't seem one to throw stuff around."

I nodded. "I take that sh—stuff pretty serious."

"Me, too. Now, let's pick up the pace. I'm hungry."

Now that it was over, I realized I could really use something to eat. It had been important for Teale's parents to approve of us. Normally I couldn't give two shits what people thought. But I wanted them to know I had Teale's best interests at heart. It just took me a bit to realize how much I cared for her.

CHAPTER
Forty

Kane

Hope pulled me into the millionth hug of the morning. I thought my mom hugged a lot, but I was wrong. Dead wrong.

"Now you take care of my baby girl. And if you don't know what to do, sometimes 'yes, dear' is the best answer. I can FaceTime if you need help."

The woman hadn't taken a breath, and that's when I knew Teale had come by it honestly. But I liked Hope. I swore between Teale and her mom, neither Everett nor I had been able to get a word in edgewise.

I looked forward to Teale's parents visiting Alaska. After working with Lori yesterday, we were hoping she and Judson could make the trip at the same time. They were coordinating with Hollis to make sure the trip went as smoothly as possible. The doctors wanted to run one more series of tests before they committed to a date.

Everett hugged Teale, whispering something in her ear.

"I'll miss you, too, daddy."

We boarded the plane, and I took the seat next to Teale. Hayden called from the pilot's seat. "We'll be taking off in about ten minutes. The weather should give us a calm ride. You guys need anything?"

I scratched my chin. "I could use a beer. Maybe a burger?"

As he turned to face forward, he flipped me the bird. "Dickhead. It's not too late, Teale. I can reopen the door."

She giggled, and I raised my eyebrow. Quietly, I said, "Don't think about it. You're not leaving."

Instead of giving me any sass, Teale snuggled into my side. Finally, things felt a little more settled. The caution Teale had been acting with over the last couple of days appeared to have eased, which put me less on edge. Being back on familiar ground would be good for us.

I cleared my throat. "So, I talked to Hollis and I want to run something by you."

"What's that?"

"Devney's house is vacant. They aren't sure what they want to do with it. I asked if we could rent it, but I wanted to get your thoughts about it first. It's close in town, so when I'm gone hunting…"

Teale pulled back, a sad frown on her face. It slayed my heart. "I hate that I can't stay at your place by myself. I'm so sorry."

"We'll stay out there when I'm in town. And if you want, stay at Devney's when I'm gone. That way we can still have our own place."

"I like that… a lot. Thank you."

I kissed the top of her head, thankful I had her back in my arms. "Anything for you."

Neither of us said much as the plane took off. I wanted to make Teale feel special. I thought of some of the dumb shit Drake had done for Alexa over the years since they'd started dating when she was in high school.

He took her flowers.

One night he did some sort of picnic. Well, Mom cooked the food and packed it.

He made her a tape of songs she liked. Oh, hell, he'd made a mixtape.

Fuck. I'm in over my head.

Teale hugged me. "What are you thinking about?"

Tell her the truth.

"I want to make things special for you."

She kissed my cheek. "Just be yourself. That's all I want."

Those few words were the reassurance I needed.

The lightness she brought to my heart made me the happiest man on earth. And now I sounded like a pussy. Man, I hoped I did right by Teale. She deserved the best.

Not long after we took off, she fell asleep, and I tried to come up with a plan to show her how much she meant to me. Doing the ordinary stuff like flowers seemed too mundane for Teale. She had so much life it felt like my plan needed to be over the top.

As I pieced together the endless hours she'd worked on the show, I realized how tired she must have been. I shifted and tried to make her as comfortable as possible so she could sleep the whole flight. We'd gone by the hospital the day before for her to say good-bye to the kids. They loved her. And she promised to video call them every day. Before I knew it,

Skagway came into view, and Hayden prepared to land the plane.

It was good to be home. Mariah was going to be glad to see Teale again. She'd been moping around as much as I had been.

The wheels touched down, and Teale stirred, opening her eyes and tucking her dark hair behind her ear. "Oh my, I slept the entire flight."

"And you snored."

For a second, Teale looked horrified before she hit me on the shoulder. "I did not."

"And drooled."

"Now I know you're lying."

She was too damn cute. I shrugged. "Maybe."

Hayden opened the door, and we grabbed our stuff. Of course, I had one small bag. Teale had packed everything she owned in the world and then some. If it was possible, she had more shit than the last time she'd been to visit. As we exited the plane, my entire family ran out of Hayden's office, yelling, "Surprise!"

Well, at least the girls yelled surprise. They were holding balloons and a banner that said welcome home. Good grief, they were going to try and steal her. I closed my eyes. It was going to be a fight getting to spend time with Teale.

"Oh my! This is amazing!" Teale squealed beside me. All I wanted was to take her to my place for some alone time.

Teale skipped over to the girls, where they hugged and gushed. Mariah sat patiently until Teale kneeled in front of her to give her love.

"Oh, I missed you, sweet girl. I missed you so much."

Teale was where she was supposed to be... with us. It

was like the piece that was missing in my life had finally fallen into place.

Then she stood and touched Alexa's and Devney's stomachs. "Oh, you guys are so adorable with your little tummies. Hello, baby Foster and baby Fritz. This is your Auntie Teale. I've got stuff in my suitcases just for you guys."

Mom came up and hugged me. "Glad you're back and things worked out."

"Me, too." I needed to get out of there before I got in trouble for my slips on television.

She pulled back and pinned me with a stare. "You are in so much trouble, Kane Foster."

Shit.

I raised my hand. "Does it not count that I brought Teale back? That should count."

Before Mom could respond, I heard Kory say, "We should do a girls' night."

Oh no. That was my cue. *Not tonight.* "Gotta go, Mom, before they take Teale. We'll chat later, but just think about the positive results and not so much what I said."

Mom laughed. "Good luck. They were thinking of having a 'spend the night' party, I think."

Nope.

No way.

No how.

I walked over to the girls. Drake had one of those shit-eating grins on his face. Yeah, the taunting was coming, but not today. I pointed in his face. "Don't even think about it."

Drake held up his hands. "Whatever you say, princess."

I should have never ever called him that. It would haunt me until the day I died. I discreetly shot him the bird so Mom wouldn't see—I was in enough trouble. Of course, Drake's obnoxious laughter probably gave me away. If I got pulled into an argument, the girls would drag Teale off to some sleepover shit. *Let him win.*

I walked over to my sisters-in-law and Devney. When Teale looked my way, I said, "Time to go."

"I—"

Before she could say anything, I hoisted her over my shoulder. I wasn't giving her a chance to use those puppy-dog eyes on me. "Bye, family. Teale won't be available for quite some time. Call me to schedule anything. Mariah, come."

The girls started calling my name, but I kept walking.

Teale was laughing. "Put me down, Kane. You're man-handling me."

"Nope."

"Kane."

I continued to move without responding to her.

"Mariah, bite him."

With a chuckle, I kept going. "That still wouldn't stop me. And last time I checked, hauling you out of the Red Onion worked pretty well for us."

Laughing, Teale lifted her head up. "Rain check, guys. It appears Mr. Grumpy Pants doesn't want to socialize."

The girls all laughed, and I caught the word princess from my brothers. *Do not engage.* If I flipped them off, I'd get a lecture from Mom, which meant I would have to put Teale down. So, I kept walking.

I deposited Teale in the front seat. We smiled at each other like goons. "Now that you've kidnapped me, what are you plans?"

"Well, first I'm going to drive over to the plane and load

your million bags. Or we could send them to Lost and Found and call the airport for delivery." Hayden would kill me, but it might be worth it.

She clapped. "You'll have more luggage miles added to your account."

Luggage miles. I forgot about those damn things. "I need to know what I can trade my points in for."

Shit on a stick, I already sound like a moron. This was why my brothers acted stupid all the time.

Get a girlfriend, act like a buffoon.

But it was worth it. Teale was worth everything.

CHAPTER
Forty-One

Kane

I swore the world was against me and Teale spending any time together. The entire fucking world. Now I knew what Drake and Hayden felt like after they'd gotten their girls back. I swore this was karma coming to bite me in the ass.

This morning, Dad had called asking for help from me and my brothers. One of his employees was out of town and the other had a sick wife. He had a big shipment to get over to the port and not a lot of time.

After helping Dad, Butch called, needing help with the heater, and then Drake's security feed broke, and I'd had to fix it. The whole day had been a mess. Butch was going to put his house up for sale and move farther into the woods. He was more antisocial than I'd ever been. He had a place in mind, and there were only a few months out of the year where traveling to it was possible.

I knew Kory and Hayden were interested in purchasing

more rental properties. They were currently renting out Alexa's dad's cabin along with Hayden's cabin when they needed the space. Apparently, they had bookings for the rental properties as far as eight months out. It was a great extra income for them and Drake and Alexa. Another cabin would help, and those were hard to come by. It was rare a place went up for sale.

I'd given them the heads-up about Butch's cabin. Of course, I'd had to get involved in that, too. I'd thought the discussion would never end, but Butch appreciated it. He'd been a good friend to me.

I pulled up to Devney's house and smiled when I caught sight of Teale as she sat in the big rocking chair with her feet tucked under her, sipping a mug of what I assumed was her afternoon tea. *She's mine.* Thank goodness I'd had the balls to go after her. Until I got her back, a major part had been missing in my life. I wondered how my family had put up with me. I'd been hell on wheels after she left. I owed them an apology.

Last night I had slept just holding her. In Montana, Teale wanted to take it slow so I was trying my best. But I wanted her... craved her.

Movement caught my eyes. *Fuck me.* The Twiner sisters were there with Teale. We'd be in another newsletter today for sure. And they had those gold digger uniforms on again. They loved to educate the tourists who came in on the cruise ships. This was literally the day that wouldn't end.

They waved to me, pencils and paper ready at their sides. I was wrong, the day was going to get worse. All I wanted was to spend time with Teale.

I'd tried to think of some of that romantic shit for tonight. She deserved the best, but nothing I'd come up with felt right.

It had me worried I wasn't going to be enough for her.

As I got out of the vehicle, Teale rose and turned to Elvira and Sylvia. "Ladies, it's been a pleasure, but my ride is here."

Elvira made a note. "Oh, dear, he's so sweet. I never thought I'd see the day when Kane Foster was smitten. I'm so glad you gave him a second chance. We were heartbroken when you left. We're counting on you to join our force."

Oh, hell no. Teale glanced my way and giggled. "If I see anything newsworthy, you'll be the first to know. I got your backs."

It was Teale's loving nature that drew people to her. She had a way of making herself part of the group and being real at the same time.

Sylvia put away her notebook. "Well, we appreciate the tip for the dating site we want to get together."

"Anytime, ladies. You can finish your tea if you want. The cups are yours. I ordered a bunch from a deal I found online."

I smiled at Teale as she came my way. "You ready to go?"

Opening the truck door, I helped Teale in the passenger side. "I owe you big."

"Yes, you do."

The plan was to stay at Devney's for the first few nights to get situated, then my place over the weekend.

Turning to the Twiner sisters, I threw my hand up in the air in acknowledgement. "Night, ladies."

"Night," they said in unison.

I got in the truck and started to drive. "What was that about?"

"I figured you probably weren't in the mood for having

tea with Sylvia and Elvira."

I turned left at the end of the street. "Is there anyplace you want to go? It's been a long day and nothing has gone as planned." Instead of avoiding the question, I used Everett's advice. "I figured I'd buy you flowers, but the store was sold out. Then I was going to make you dinner or something. I wasn't sure. I was hoping I would know exactly what to do, but damn it, this is hard."

Teale looked at me. "Aww, that would have been sweet, but doesn't sound very Kane-like."

"Kane-like?"

I glanced her way, and she grinned but said nothing. I prompted her to continue. "So what is Kane-like?"

"Well, what sounds fun to you?"

"Honestly, just a walk through the woods. Me and you away from everyone. Or just watching a movie together. I don't know."

"I think that sounds more perfect than flowers or dinner. You don't have to change who you are just because we're dating, Kane."

I'm going to fuck this up for sure. I know it. How in the hell am I going to come up with stuff? A walk in the woods was only going to go so far.

"Kane, pull over."

Oh shit. Is she pissed now?

I pulled the truck over, unsure what else to say. Teale grabbed my hand and squeezed it. I waited for her to say something.

"You are so tense." She squeezed it again. "I fell in love with *you*. Not a different version of you. *Just you.* I don't need you walking around on eggshells. I don't need you to change

243

who you are."

"But I want to earn your love, Teale. I know that sounds sappy and shit, but I want to be the man you deserve."

She waited until I looked at her. "You are; don't you see that?"

This was so damn confusing. "But you left because I was *me*. I don't want you to leave again."

Teale sighed. "No, I left because I thought it wasn't fair to you to change what we'd agreed to. I should have stayed and talked to you. From now on, if there is a problem, I will talk it out with you."

That all seemed straightforward enough. "So, what did you do today?"

"Oh, let's see. I saw the girls for lunch at the Red Onion. I think I might have made a love match with Ol' Man Rooster's granddaughter and Crete. Oh, and I met Morgan, the loan officer. She's really nice. The quilting circle invited me to learn how to quilt. I'm not sure how patient I'm going to be at that, but this winter it'll be fun, I guess. Oh, and then the Twiner sisters stopped by and had tea, looking for the scoop on Crete. So instead, I gave them tips on what to do on their dating website as a distraction from Crete."

"Hell, woman, did you take a breath? I think you saw the entire damn town."

She laughed. "Pretty much. Oh… Elvira and Sylvia wanted me to join them in the new dance club they're starting. They want us to join."

I whipped my head around to look at her. Surely, she wouldn't. She tapped her finger to her chin. "Oh, I can see your wheels spinning, Mr. Foster. It might be fun to do the fox-trot together."

"Teale."

She shrugged, but I could see the mischievous glint in her eyes. "It could be fun. I mean, think about it, we could waltz at the Christmas Jubilee this year."

I pulled out my phone and switched on the flashlight. Then I focused it on Teale. Desperate times called for desperate measures.

"Why are you shining that at me? I'm not lost." She laughed and batted my arm away, but I kept it steady.

"Because when you were in the spotlight on the ice, you never argued. I figured it might work now. I'm saying no to the dancing. And you can agree."

Teale's mouth dropped open before she started giggling. "Point to you."

I guessed that meant it was working. I continued to shine the light on her. "So, no dancing with the Twiner sisters?"

"You win this round, Mr. Foster."

That was too damn easy. There was no way a flashlight would make her give up that easily... unless it wasn't in the plans to begin with. "You already told them no, didn't you?"

"I'll never tell."

She'd told them no. I turned off the flashlight and drove toward the cabin, smiling like a fool the entire time.

"So, I read some of those self-help books while I was home. Guess what I learned."

"I'm afraid to ask."

She gave another giggle. I fucking loved the sound of it. Mariah had her head on Teale's shoulder. We had missed her terribly. "Well, I'll tell you anyway. I'm spaghetti, and you're a waffle."

I chuckled. "What the hell?"

Teale nodded to herself, affirming the statement. "It's true. Men compartmentalize everything. Each thing has a square it fits into—like the waffle. Women just jumble it all together like spaghetti noodles. Or so they say. I know that's not the case for everyone, but studies show this to be a factor."

"I have some swampland to sell you, as well."

She smirked. "It's true. Think about it. I mean there are exceptions, and that doesn't fit everyone, but it for sure fits us."

"I'm not a waffle."

"Oh, you are certainly a multigrain waffle with burnt ends at times. And I'm very often a compilation of multicolored noodles."

The corner of my lips tugged up. "Angel, if you slather butter and syrup all over it, it's just as messy as spaghetti."

"You're a dry waffle."

"Man, I missed you."

Teale squeezed my hand. "So, you agree?"

"Yes, dear."

Teale slapped my shoulder playfully as I used the advice her mom had given me.

When we pulled up, I turned off the truck. She looked around, surprisingly at ease. "It's so peaceful out here. I'd really only seen it covered in snow. But your house takes my breath away."

I swallowed hard. "It can be your house, too."

She grabbed my hand. "Our house."

CHAPTER
Forty-Two

Teale

Three days later, it was still hard to believe. Things were the same, yet different. We hadn't made love, but there had been lots of kissing and touching. Each time it got a little heavy, Kane pulled back and I followed his lead. He was doing as I requested… taking things slow. It was about to drive me crazy, but I didn't want to push. Things were going well, but I was in serious need of an orgasm that wasn't provided by a dildo.

Now, I was in town visiting the girls. Actually, Kane had suggested it since he needed to help his dad. But time had gotten away from us girls and now it was late. Since it was summer, it was still light outside even past eight in the evening.

While I was with them, I'd also finalized the plans for Judson to come to town. We had to move up the timetable after his latest medical report. It didn't look good, and my heart was breaking. Kane knew how serious it was, but he didn't really acknowledge it when we talked. It was rare for Kane to let anyone in so fast, so I imagined Judson's terminal illness made it more complicated for Kane to process.

My phone rang with Kane's ringtone. *Double crap*. I had forgotten to text him on my way home like I promised because I'd been talking to my mom. "Hey, I'm about twenty minutes away. Each time I tried to leave, something came up. I really did mean to be home earlier. I'm so sorry. I got to talking to Mom once I got in the car and forgot to let you know."

Kane worried with me being out on the road so late. It was sweet. "Good. Be careful, angel. You hungry?"

"Starving. The girls just had little appetizer stuff. I require real food three times a day."

He laughed. "Protein shakes are not real food."

"Are so."

Something ran out onto the road, and I screamed as I slammed on the brakes. My life flashed before my eyes. I waited for the impact, but it never happened. My heart pounded in my chest as I stared into the eyes of an animal not two feet from my bumper.

"Teale? *Teale!* What the fuck is going on?" Kane was starting to sound panicked.

I tried to find my voice. "I—"

"Teale, where are you? What happened?"

The moose took a step forward, and I leaned back in the seat. "Moo-moose. It's not leaving the road."

My hands were shaking, and my heart was beating like I'd run a marathon.

"Teale, damn it. Are you okay?"

"Y-yes." I took a deep breath as the shock began to lessen. "I'm fine. It just scared me. He came out of nowhere. And it won't leave the road. It's huffing at me. Like it looks really mad, Kane. Do I honk my horn to get him to move? He's just staring at me."

"Stay right there. Don't do anything."

I locked the doors. I knew it was stupid since moose couldn't open car doors, but it made me feel safer. From the whooshing sound in the background of the call, it sounded like Kane was driving. "Are you in your truck?"

"Yes, I'm headed your way." His truck came around the bend, and the moose took off.

The truck skidded to a stop, and Kane jumped out of the truck and opened my door. "Are you okay?"

His hands searched for injuries as he stared at me.

"I am. I promise. It just really scared me. He came out of nowhere."

Kane pulled me to him and held me close. "You scared the shit out of me. I thought something had happened to you."

"I'm sorry. We have wildlife in Montana, but with the rink there at the house and people always coming by, I don't drive a lot at night."

"It's not your fault, angel. I'm just glad you're okay." He kissed the top of my forehead and held me. I could feel the tension coming off of him in waves. "You ready to go home?"

"I am. I'll follow you."

Kane got in his truck and whipped it around. I put my car in gear and followed. Hayden was letting me borrow one of his spare vehicles he used at the airport until I could get a car. The fact that Kane had dropped everything and come for me was something I hadn't expected. This man was it for me.

I followed the taillights until we pulled up to the cabin. He came over and opened my door. He seemed a little more fidgety than normal. My heart rate still hadn't slowed down. "You okay?"

Kane nodded stiffly. "I will be in about three minutes. Hopefully. Maybe. *Fuck*."

Three minutes. That was awfully precise. He was starting to worry me. "What's wrong?"

Before I could ask any more questions, Kane grabbed my hand. "I'll explain inside. Just trust me."

"Okay." Kane walked fast. It felt like a sprint by the time we entered the cabin. And then he stopped abruptly. I nearly fell into him before he steadied me. I peered up into his eyes; there was something else there. Kane was nervous. Really nervous. This wasn't like him. Even at the ice rink in Montana when he'd come for me, Kane hadn't been like this. "What's going…"

My voice trailed off at the sight of the rose petals on the floor. There was food on the table. I put my hand over my mouth as I walked a little closer. "Kane."

"I'm not good at this romantic shit. Honestly, I got the idea from Mom. But I wanted this to be a special night. Alexa, Kory, and Devney kept you busy until I was ready."

I turned around and threw my arms around his neck. "Oh, Kane, this is amazing. I can't believe you cooked for me. What did you make?"

"Go and see."

I walked over to the table and began to laugh. There was a plate of waffles and another of spaghetti. This was beyond perfect. I whispered to myself, "Waffles and spaghetti—I think that just became my new favorite meal."

It got really quiet behind me, so I turned around. Kane was on one knee, holding out a black velvet box. "Please say yes."

He's proposing. My breath caught as the man I loved with all my heart was telling me he was ready for the next step. I bit my lip and took a step forward. "What am I saying yes to?"

"You're going to make this difficult, aren't you?" he asked with a huge grin on his face. That told me that Kane was happy about this. Being together was what he wanted.

I took another step until I was nearly in front of him. "Of course. When have I not?"

He touched a button on a remote he was holding, and from the ceiling, a spotlight shone on me. I nearly fell over laughing. I calmed down pretty quickly, pretending that the light had tamed me. Mr. Foster would win this round again.

Kane nodded. "Better."

I giggled but remained silent. It was hard to believe this was happening.

He sighed, serious again. "I don't want to wait. I feel like I've waited my entire life for you. I have your dad's blessing. I want you to say yes… to us, to being it for each other."

For not being the romantic type, when Kane spoke from the heart, it sent goose bumps along my skin. I took another step forward, still not saying anything but soaking in the love I saw on his face. I'd wanted him to love me for so long, and now he was openly declaring it. My hands trembled, and tears formed in my eyes.

"I love you, Teale. I'll love you beyond my last breath. You're it for me. Please say yes to becoming my wife."

I threw my arms around his neck. "Yes! Yes! Yes! A million times, yes!"

He slipped the ring on my finger. "This was my dad's mother's. I can get you a new one if you don't like it. But I thought it fit us."

It was a beautiful sapphire stone surrounded by diamonds. "I love this. Oh, Kane, it's perfect. I don't want a new one. I want this one."

Kane stood and kissed me. "Never in my life did I imagine being this happy."

"Neither did I. I never imagined I could be this happy." I looked up to him. "Will you make love to me? No condoms. Just the two of us. I'm still on birth control."

Taking my hand, he led me to the bedroom. Slowly he stripped me down and laid me on the bed. "I'm the luckiest man alive."

The way his eyes devoured me sent goose bumps along my skin. He trailed kisses up my leg. The moment his tongue made contact with my clit, I arched off the bed. I had missed his mouth on me. The warmth nearly sent me off the edge. When I was on the verge of orgasm, Kane slid his finger inside me, and I felt the euphoric feeling. Finally.

Kane moved on top of me. "I can't wait, angel."

"Please don't."

Slowly he pushed in, and I could see the veins protruding in his neck as he held back and went slow. "Fuck me. You feel amazing."

It was the most incredible feeling in the world. As Kane slipped all the way in, the last of the puzzle pieces fell into place.

CHAPTER
Forty-Three

Teale

I woke up the next morning and stared at my ring.

I'm engaged. I'm going to marry Kane. He's going to be my forever.

It was still hard to believe how far we'd come in what seemed like a lifetime, but relatively speaking, it hadn't been that long. Kane lay beside me, looking peaceful as he slept. The dark circles he'd had beneath his eyes when I'd first met him were gone.

Last night, I'd finally felt like the missing piece of me had slid into place. Kane made me whole.

I shifted, and Kane pulled me closer to him. I was so incredibly lucky to have him. "What are you thinking about, angel?"

"Just how perfect everything is. Who would have thought we would end up together when you pulled up to Butch's cabin? And to think you were so mean to your future wife."

253

He pulled back to look at me. "I wasn't mean. You commandeered my truck, dressed up my trophies, and had the town convinced I was your boyfriend all within days of us meeting."

I gave him a kiss on the lips. "Aren't you so lucky?"

Pulling me tighter, he nuzzled my neck. "I am."

"When were you thinking about getting married?"

Kane rolled onto his back and watched me while I wrote what would be my new last name on his chest. "Whenever you want to. I just want to know it's going to happen. When, where, how... it's all the same to me as long as you say yes."

I raised my eyebrow. "So if I said tomorrow..."

"I'd say, 'Tell me what time.'"

No part of his body tensed. Kane remained absolutely calm and okay.

"It doesn't scare you?"

Kane shook his head. "Being tied to you forever? No, that doesn't scare me. Fucking up what we have? That terrifies me. And I know what it's like not to have you, so I more than want this life with you."

I melted inside. "Me, too." I treasured the knowledge that no one saw this side of Kane but me. He had finally let me all the way into his gooey marshmallow center. I laid my head on his chest, wanting to know more details. "What made you decide to propose?"

"I wanted to tell you I loved you when I proposed. I knew I loved you in Montana. I told your dad of my intentions when I was there. I even offered to fly back down to formally ask him, but he told me a phone call would do. So, I asked him yesterday morning."

That explained why Mom had been hinting all around about Kane and me. Good thing he asked me last night, or she might have spilled the beans before he had a chance to ask. Something else occurred to me. "You know, in total, we've dated less than a month."

Kane shrugged. "When it's right, it's right."

That was true. "So, what's on the agenda for today?"

"I want to show you something. See what you think."

That sounded a little mysterious. "When?"

He chuckled. "Now, if you want to go. It can be whenever."

I sat up, taking the sheet with me. "Can we go to Starbucks after? I know Mariah wants another puppuccino, and I could use a latte. Pretty, pretty, pretty please."

Kane said nothing, so I took matters into my own hands before he could reach for his phone and shine the light on me again. I said, "The right answer is..." I moved his lips and lowered my voice to sound guyish. "Yes, dear."

"Yes, dear," he said with a smile.

"You are the best husband-to-be. I'll get you a venti café Americano in a white cup and black dot."

He groaned. "Just call it what it is. No need to fancy that shit up. And this is a one-time thing. Don't expect this regularly. I have my dignity."

Oh, he would go for me. I loved pushing his buttons. I gave him a chaste kiss. "I love you. Give me thirty minutes, and I'll be ready."

I streaked across the room and ran to the shower. Before I could close the door, Kane was there and backing me against the wall. "I need to give you a proper kiss first. And then I need to make love to my fiancée."

We went for a walk in the woods. It was beautiful—so different from when I'd been here over the winter. So green. I wondered where Kane was taking me. When we first entered the forest. I'd felt a little apprehension thinking about the lumberjack killer, but I knew Kane would never let anything happen to me. In some ways, it felt therapeutic. Kane stopped at an area that looked like it had been cleared within the last day or so. I looked around the clearing but saw nothing but trees. Nothing looked familiar. "Where are we?"

Kane put his hands behind his neck and stretched out his elbows. He was nervous about whatever he had to tell me. "Well, I met with my parents and brothers yesterday while you were with the girls."

I knew he'd been having lunch at his parents' house. I hadn't given it much thought or sensed anything serious was going on. Unsure what to say, I answered, "Okay. I knew you had plans yesterday."

"Well, you may or may not know that my parents own a lot of acreage. Five years ago, they went ahead and deeded some of it to us kids."

I nodded. "I wasn't sure of all the details, but I figured some of it."

"Yeah, it'll all get divided up at some point. None of us is in any hurry. The piece of land we're standing on was supposed to go to Hayden at some point."

"Okay, so what does that have to do with you?" I wasn't following where this was going.

Kane brought his hands down from his neck. "Well after looking at the current division, there were a few things that didn't make a lot of sense. After talking with them, Hayden and I swapped some things so our land ties into the cabins we already own. The entire family agreed."

This seemed a little odd to be discussing this in the middle of the woods. "That was nice of him."

Kane pointed through the tree line. "It's about a three-minute walk to my parents'. Only about fifteen to twenty minutes from town. If you like this piece of land, I want to build us a place here. It'll keep you closer to town, so I won't have to worry about you driving at night as much. But it also gives me a little isolation. A compromise for what we each need."

A compromise. I smiled, so happy I thought I might burst. I stood on my tiptoes and wrapped my arms around Kane's neck. "You're going to build me a house. Like *build*, build it."

I could tell he remembered one of our first conversations. "Yeah, like *build* it, build it. I'll use a hammer, nails, and some other shit."

He's building our house. I grinned. "So what are you thinking?"

Kane walked around while he talked, no longer nervous. "I know we won't spend all our time here, but I'm hoping we'll live in Alaska some and Montana some. We can work around my guiding schedule and I can move things around for when we go to Montana. All I know is I need you safe and near family. When I'm on an overnight hunt, I don't want you at our cabin, so far from everyone."

And that wasn't something I was ready for, either.

Kane waited for me to respond. This was going to be perfect. I jumped and wrapped my legs around Kane's waist. "I love this. I love you."

He kissed me hard and set me down. "We'll need to break ground soon if we have any hope of finishing the important stuff before winter. I'm hoping we can be in by September or October. We'll get the outside of the house done and all the supplies ordered, and I can finish up the inside of the house."

"What about your job?"

"I've scaled back, charged more, and will make more. I'll still take some jobs to keep my name out there. But I want to get this done before winter hits. And I made a hell of a lot of money while I had my head up my ass. I doubled my work-load."

Maybe this was the perfect time to tell him my thoughts, as well. "I wanted to talk to you about something."

"Okay." Kane remained at ease as we walked, moving a limb out of the way so it didn't smack us in the face as we passed. I loved to watch his muscles flex in his short-sleeved shirt.

"Well, I want to buy Devney's house. She and Hollis have practically offered it to me for nothing. I want to make Alaska my primary home—that is, if my parents are willing to come up here for at least part of the time. They can live at Devney's. It's in town, close to everything, and perfect for them."

Kane scratched his head. "Where does that leave Montana?"

"I plan to keep the house there for now, and we'll just see how things go. I would like Alaska to be our primary home, but I can't leave my parents, either. They're getting older. I think they'll like it here. If they do, I was thinking about making the Montana house into some sort of ice-skating camp. I'll have to see. I've got options, but I don't want to commit yet."

Kane took a few steps toward me. "I'd never ask you to leave them."

"I know you wouldn't. I love Alaska. If they move here, it will make things easier. But I want to keep the place in Montana just in case they want to go back. At least for a year or so. Then we'll know where life is going to lead us." I shrugged. "And I can still skate on the ponds here in the winter."

Cradling my face, Kane started at me. "We'll build you an ice rink here, angel. It just may have to wait until next summer."

I blinked, shocked. "You're going to build me an ice rink?"

"Well, yeah. Don't you want one?"

"Umm… yes, of course. A rink built by my future husband. Well, you'll be my husband by then. So that will make it uber sexy."

That cocky smile I loved came out. "Uber sexy?"

"Like, you're going to get so much sex, you won't know what to do with yourself." He grabbed my hands, and I snickered. "Where are you taking me?"

"To my parents' to get the plans going. Then I'm going to take you home to make love to my fiancée."

I held Kane's hand, hardly believing this was happening. "Maybe we could have a quickie on the way home and then sauna time."

"Done."

Kane picked up the pace. I never imagined I could be this happy in all my life.

CHAPTER
Forty-Four

Kane

Dad stood and raised his glass. "To Teale and Kane. We're so happy to be adding another beautiful daughter to our family."

I was ready to get the hell out of Dodge, but we'd come over to look at plans. The next thing I knew, we'd been invaded and were currently having a family dinner. I held my glass and toasted. Teale gave me a playful smirk and leaned over to whisper, "Play nice and I'll make sure it's worth your while."

"My price is really steep."

"I'll even throw in some luggage miles."

Shit, this woman had me by the balls, and I wouldn't have it any other way.

We'd spent some time with the building plans, and after seeing what Teale liked, I suggested we aim for around three thousand square feet. My cabin was too small for a long-term solution. Teale had been adamant about having a normal-sized place that wasn't so big we'd never see each other. We'd actually used my parents' place as inspiration. She loved the vibe of their house. The new house was being designed to allow for additions, if necessary.

Teale leaned against me, and I felt at peace. Life was good.

Kory looked at us. "If you need any help with the wedding, let me know."

"Oh, I'm counting on it," Teale said. It was so easy and natural with her around.

Mom leaned forward. "Where were you thinking about having it?"

Teale and I had talked about it a little, but on the way to my parents', she'd decided what she wanted to do. "Well, I want to get married in our new house. Before we ever stay there, I want to be married. So it depends on when we can get it finished."

"It'll be done before winter," I said.

My brothers nodded. "Yeah, we can get it done by then."

Hollis looked at us. "I'll bring in some contractors. It'll give you the manpower like we had at my place. My gift to you."

For a second, I wanted to refuse, but I looked at Hollis and considered his words. We had become close over the last couple of months. He truly wanted to help. This was his way of saying thank you for helping with his cabin. "I appreciate it. Thank you."

"Thank you. Because of Teale, donations for the new clinic continue to pour in. I believe we're going to have enough to fund two clinics."

The response had been amazing. The story of the New

York doctor who'd opened a clinic in Skagway had gone viral.

Alexa changed the topic. "So, for the wedding... What are your colors going to be? Is it going to be big or small?"

All these details would be the death of me. Teale looked at me, but I shook my head. "That's all your call. You know how I feel."

"I'm thinking family only." All eyes swung to Teale, including mine. That wasn't the answer I'd been expecting. "I know you guys expected me to say 'Invite the world,' but I always pictured my wedding as a small, intimate thing. But if Kane insists on inviting the world, I can do that."

I held up my hands. "Fu—fudge that."

Mom pointed her finger at me. "If you curse on your wedding day, I'm going to break out the paddle from when you and your brothers were younger."

"Mom, let's talk about this." I held up my hands. "Teale has loaned me her curse word allotment. I'm sure I can get some other people to lend me theirs, too. Then it'll be like I'm not even cussing."

She shook her head. "Nope, that's exactly what I'm going to do. No cussing on your wedding day."

Drake leaned forward. "Please tell me you're going to cuss."

I raised my eyebrow. "You're not helping."

"I can get a paddle engraved with their wedding date. Then if Teale needs it later, she'll have it as a memento," Hayden added.

My hand nearly shot up with the bird, but I pointed my index finger, instead. "Thanks to my brothers for always being number one."

Dickheads.

Mom tilted her head with a smile. "Now, that's more like it."

"Mom, he's just flipping us off incognito," Hayden snitched.

I held up my hands. "Mom, I would never do that. I'm trying to turn over a new leaf."

For a second Mom looked at us and then turned to my dad. "This is all your fault, Ike."

"Mine? How?" Dad looked totally perplexed. He'd been sipping his coffee in peace, minding his own business.

Mom got up from the table and went into the kitchen. "If you boys all have super prissy girls, that will be payback enough."

My brother Drake paled, and I shrugged at him. "If Alexa has a girl, you've got the princess title for life."

"No, that's not how it works," Drake retorted.

Bingo. This was my ticket to shed the title. I looked over at Hayden, who scratched his chin, waiting for his vote. In the Foster family, two votes carried the motion. "Yeah, I think it should work that way."

The girls started to smack us on the arms. "Girls are not that bad."

"Angel, we need to keep our numbers."

Alexa laughed and patted her stomach. "Well, we shall see who ends up with the numbers. And if we have a girl, I expect her daddy and uncles to play princess and let her paint their toenails."

I grinned. "Drake would look awfully pretty in pink glitter."

"Yeah, he would," Hayden added. "Maybe even some feathers."

Drake muttered, "Assholes."

From the kitchen, Mom called, "Drake, I'll paddle you, too."

Life was good. Perfect, actually.

CHAPTER
Forty-Five

Teale

"**M**omma, can I please go exploring with Kane. *Please*? I want to see the woods like a real Alaskan."

Lori looked worried but put on a brave face like she had for the last three days. "Just take it slow. And if you start feeling bad, tell Mr. Kane so you can rest."

Judson leaned over and kissed his mom's cheek. "I will, Momma. Don't worry. I'll be just fine. I had my vegetables this morning in the shake Miss Teale made me."

I pulled him close for a hug. "You keep Kane safe, okay?"

"I will. We don't want your mister hurt for the wedding." When Judson had heard about the wedding, he'd been so excited. Every day we video-called him. After I talked to Judson, I would talk with the children at the hospital.

"No, we don't."

Judson patted his legs. "Come, Mariah."

Mom and Dad had traveled with Lori to help her. They had grown to love Judson like a grandson. They smiled, watching him pet Mariah.

It worried me that I could tell Judson had lost weight since the last time we'd seen him. That little boy was so brave. I watched Kane nod to Mariah to obey Judson. She ran over to him. Since he'd arrived, she'd been his shadow the entire time.

Judson had met everyone in town and was featured in the Twiner Tellings. He and Ol' Man Rooster shared a cup of hot chocolate from Starbucks. And he got to experience a huge Foster family dinner at Ike and Amie's.

The door closed, and Lori let out a heavy sigh. "This trip has taken a toll on him. But he's so happy. I feel so helpless." Lori looked out the window as Kane and Judson disappeared in the tree line. When she turned back to us, she began to sob.

Mom and I sat by her side. In that soothing tone all mothers have, Mom said, "Now, now, dear. Let it out. We're here."

Dad nodded to me and headed out the front door to give us some space.

The worst part was that nothing could be done. The doctors said it wouldn't be long, but they couldn't give any sort of time estimate. It could be days or weeks or months. This little boy had come into our lives and wrapped us around his finger in such a short amount of time. He meant so much to me, and I knew Kane felt the same way. Each day we prayed for a miracle. I brushed away a stray tear as I said, "You are such a brave mom."

"With no job and a dying son. I just... I don't know what to do. I know he's getting worse. I can see it."

In addition to the weight loss, there were other physical

changes in Judson. Dark circles were permanent features underneath his eyes. He seemed so frail, but Lori had told us he had a new sort of energy about him from the moment he'd arrived in Alaska and had seen Kane. I felt like we were clinging to a false hope.

Since Judson arrived, my stomach had been in knots at the possibility that all this additional exertion was hurting him. But Lori had remained firm that this was Judson's life to live no matter how short it might be.

Once Judson was off on his walk with Kane, it was time to present my plan to Lori. Maybe it would ease some of her worry. I had talked to my parents and Kane, and they supported it. In some ways, things were working out better than I'd imagined, but it was all happening while a little boy lost his fight with a terminal illness. Life really was cruel sometimes.

"Lori, I have an idea I hope will help." She looked up at me. "I want to offer you a job. You don't have to start now... just when you're ready. I don't want it to take any time away from Judson."

"What kind of job?"

I took a deep breath. "I'm going to start an ice-skating camp, and for now, I want to do a yearly show. I need a right-hand person in Montana I can count on. The guesthouse is included, rent free."

Lori looked from me to my mom and back to me. "Why are you doing this?"

"Because your son has touched my heart. And one day over the summer when he was at my place, he asked me to make sure his mother was okay. The amount of work you did for the show was inspiring. I just want you to know you won't have to worry about things."

She stood and hugged me tight. "Thank you. I won't let you down."

"Focus on Judson now. We'll work out the details later. I'm going to make Alaska my primary residence, and my parents are going to go between Alaska and Montana for now as they start the process of retiring here. It'll help to know I have someone there to watch over them when I'm here."

"For sure. Oh, Teale, I cannot thank you enough."

"Thank you for raising such a loving, precious boy." My throat grew thick. "I wish there was more I could do. I'd move heaven and earth to heal him if I could."

She hugged me again. "I know you would." Lori pulled back and said, "The first day you walked out of Judson's room, he told me you were his guardian angel. I believe him. Thank you."

I was too choked up to talk.

Mom looked out the window. "They're coming back. Let's dry those eyes, girls. We don't want Judson to think you're upset."

Furiously we started to wipe our eyes and then watched out the window as Kane kneeled with Judson to show him something. Judson nodded, paying attention to everything Kane said. Kane pointed at something else, and Judson jumped up and threw his arms around Kane. I never would have imagined Kane so at ease with a child before, but with Judson, he seemed like a natural. They shared a very sweet bond. It made me think of my future as the mother of Kane's children and watching him blossom as a father.

After a few moments, they stood and continued toward the house.

We all sat at the table, pretending to *not* watch them and

trying to not lose it all over again.

The back door opened, and they came inside. "Momma, we saw a deer. It was the last thing I wanted to see in Alaska. Kane is the bestest tracker I've ever seen. He's like a superhero."

I looked up and smiled at Kane. He squatted down to Judson's height. "You're a quick study, little man. You found those tracks and were able to follow the trail in the woods."

"Yeah, I'm just like you." Judson took a few shallow breaths. He looked exhausted. Weakly, he flexed his muscles. "It's because I ate my veggies. Lots and lots of veggies so I'd be strong enough for the trip."

"That's good. Real good, Judson. You keep eating those veggies. Tomorrow, I'll ask Teale to make us both another one of those fancy shakes with veggies and protein."

Judson nodded and beamed at Kane. "I'd like that."

Lori looked at Judson, obviously worried. He seemed to be getting paler. "Hey, buddy, why don't we go take a nap together?"

Kane pointed toward the guest room. "Go ahead. The guest room is right through there."

Judson swayed on his feet. "I'm awfully tired, Momma." Then he dropped like a sack of potatoes.

"Judson!" Lori cried out.

Kane picked him up. "In the truck. We're going to the clinic."

Sprinting to the door, he called behind him. "Hope and Everett, meet us there."

"We're on our way!" Mom called from the kitchen.

In seconds, we were in the truck and headed toward Hollis's clinic. Kane had the phone to his ear. "We're coming.

He's collapsed. Yes." He ended the call, handed me the phone, and gunned the gas pedal.

Lori sat in the back seat holding Judson. "It's okay, my sweet boy. Just rest. We're heading to the doctor. It'll be fine."

"It's okay, Momma. I'm not scared."

I faced forward and watched the road as the tears streamed down my face. This little boy deserved to live, yet he was losing his battle with leukemia. I wanted to scream in frustration. I glanced over at Kane and could see the worry on his face. He looked at me and took a deep breath before he said, "Hang in there, buddy. We're almost to the doc's."

"I'm going to be brave like you, Mr. Kane."

"You're braver than I could ever be, buddy."

Judson's voice was getting weaker. "Did you hear that, Momma?"

"I sure did, my brave, sweet son." In that moment, Lori was showing unbelievable strength and grace.

Kane pulled up and parked the truck. Hollis met us outside. "Bring him to room one. I want to get oxygen on him."

There was a flurry of movement. Hollis attached something to Judson's finger and then listened to his chest with a stethoscope. "His pulse is high and oxygen levels are low. I can hear a rattle in his chest."

"Turning up the oxygen to a six." Alexa turned the dial as she spoke.

On the monitors, Judson's heart was racing. As the oxygen increased, his heart rate slowed some, but Hollis's face was tight with worry. On the next breath, there was an audible rattle. "Were there any problems this morning?" Hollis asked.

Kane shook his head. "No, we were walking and talking. For a while, it seemed like he wasn't even sick. When I asked if he wanted to rest, he said he wanted to keep going."

After checking a few more things, Hollis patted Judson's shoulder. "Hey, Judson. It's Dr. Fritz. I'm going to talk to your mom for a second. Can Teale stay with you?"

He nodded, and my eyes teared up. *How in the world is this happening to one of the most precious boys in the world?* Kane followed Lori out of the room.

Judson looked at me. "Will you lie down with me? Like you used to?"

"Of course." I climbed up on the bed, making sure I wasn't putting pressure on him at all. "Did you have fun with Kane?"

"Yeah. I wish I had a dad like him."

I closed my eyes to try and rein my emotions in. "Well, I bet he wishes he has a son like you someday."

"Miss Teale?"

"Yeah?"

The heart-rate monitor began to slow a little more. That seemed like a good thing. "You gonna keep the promise you made?"

"Yes, I am. I'm going to keep my promise and make sure your mom's okay. I have a place for you and your mom when you get back to Montana. She's not going to have any worries and will be able to focus on you."

The door opened, and the grim looks on their faces told me it wasn't good. Lori had red-rimmed eyes. This was worse than I expected. I got out of the bed so Lori could lie beside her son. She stroked his face as he curled up against her. Kane wouldn't look me in the eye, which concerned me, but I let him be.

Lori kissed Judson's cheek. "Hey, sweet boy."

"My body is just gettin' tired. It's about time, Momma."

The tears brimmed in Lori's eyes. The rattle in his chest was getting worse. It was going fast, too fast. *Isn't this supposed to be slower? We need more time.*

Judson turned his eyes to Kane. "You gonna take good care of Miss Teale?"

Kane knelt beside the bed. "Always."

"I'm getting awful tired. Don't forget me."

"Never, buddy."

He turned back to his mom. "You're the bestest mom. Miss Teale is gonna make sure you're okay."

"Oh, Judson, please don't leave me. I love you so much. I'm not ready to let you go."

Her pain was almost too much for me to take.

"I love you, Momma. But I'm so tired. I need to sleep now."

"Okay, sweet boy, you rest. Your momma is going to be right here. I'll never leave you."

I barely heard what he said next as his voice grew fainter. "We always have our dreams."

"Yes, we do. I'll meet you in my dreams every single night."

Tears streamed down my face. It was like the dam had broken. Judson closed his eyes, and I grabbed his hand. His heart rate slowed further, and Lori kept whispering how much she loved him over and over again. She looked at me. "I'm not ready to let him go. I don't know how I'm going to do this."

I had no answers. *How did this happen so fast?* We weren't ready.

As the minutes ticked by, Hollis monitored Judson as his heart rate slowed even further. Lori finally took a deep breath.

"I love you, Judson. It's okay to let go. You're going to be in heaven where you can run and play and make all sorts of friends. Don't worry about me. I'm going to be okay."

And with one more breath, Judson sighed and passed away from this world.

CHAPTER
Forty-Six

Kane

At the cemetery, I was alone. We'd buried Judson earlier, and now Lori was resting in the guest house back at Teale's parents' place. Teale thought it would be best to stay there with her.

I think she'd sensed the restlessness growing within me, and she'd given me some space to sort out my head.

The guilt.

Fuck, the guilt was going to consume me. If I hadn't taken Judson for that hike, he'd probably still be alive. It had been too much for him. I should have known. But for a short time, it had felt like I was hiking in the woods with a normal, healthy boy, talking and laughing as he noticed something new.

Lori had clung to me and cried, thanking me for making the last of her little boy's dreams come true. This feeling helpless wasn't something I was good at. When Janine died, I'd shut down that part of me because I didn't want to be open to that kind of hurt again. *And now this.*

Fuck.

There was a fresh mound of dirt on the ground where the casket had been hours earlier. I sat on the ground and just stared at it. Life wasn't fair. It had happened so fast. I thought we would have had more time at the end. But in a blink of an eye, Judson was gone.

I replayed every moment in my mind over and over again. I pulled out the picture Teale had taken of me and Judson at the Red Onion when he first arrived in Alaska. He'd had a huge smile on his face and had been wearing the *Real Alaskan* T-shirt Teale had gotten for him.

I cracked my neck, trying to hold back the emotions that swelled within and wanted to break free. I beat them back with my big-ass stick, determined to keep them locked away. Everyone else was dealing with so much. I could handle this on my own.

A raindrop fell on the mound of fresh dirt, and I watched as it was absorbed into the ground. Over my head, the storm clouds were growing darker—it was the perfect weather for my mood.

Another raindrop fell. Then another. If I stayed here too long, I was going to be soaked through, which would cause Teale to worry, so I got up. "I meant what I said. I hope one day I'm lucky enough to have a son as brave as you were. Thank you, Judson, for more than you'll ever know. I promise I'll never forget you."

With that, I turned and walked away. This was why I didn't want to put my heart out there. *How can I ever have kids knowing this is what can happen?* All I knew was I needed a drink—a stiff one to numb the pain.

CHAPTER
Forty-Seven

Teale

I t was late, and Kane wasn't home yet. Since we'd returned from the funeral four days before, it was clear something was bothering him. Well, honestly, it had been clear six days ago when he came back the night of the funeral. My dad had gone to pick him up, which was unusual, and when he'd arrived, I could smell the alcohol. I'd asked if everything was okay, but all I'd received was a simple "Yep" each time I asked.

We were all heartbroken. But it felt like Kane was wrestling demons he hadn't dealt with since Janine had died in what he thought was a suicide. I had hoped with time he would confide in me, but so far, he hadn't.

Judson's death had left us all a little adrift. He'd touched our lives, and he would never be forgotten. We were setting up a Judson Wright Memorial for the yearly show I planned to put on. There would be a fund set aside to make dreams come true for terminally ill children.

Lights shone through the window as Kane's truck pulled into the driveway of our cabin. Since we'd arrived back to Skagway, I'd been staying with Ike and Amie. I hadn't wanted to be alone and Kane had suggested it for the time being while he worked on the cabin. I suspected there was more to it. Kane came by for breakfast, but after that, he'd give some excuse why he wasn't able to stay there for various reasons. He barely touched his food, and all his responses were limited to two or three words. Then he would give me a chaste kiss good-bye and go to work on our future home. Each time I brought him lunch, he told me he'd eat it later and kept working. When dinnertime came, I'd receive some sort of excuse why he wasn't able to come.

I stared at the text he'd sent about forty-five minutes before.

Kane: *Headed home to get some tools for tomorrow. See you at breakfast. Love you.*

Me: *Love you, too.*

When he blew me off again for lunch the next day, I was determined to get to the bottom of this. Six days was too long and had given Kane a chance to rebuild his walls. Ike had brought me out to the cabin earlier that afternoon. The place had been a mess. It had taken me a good part of the day to get it straightened up.

And in some ways, it had been therapeutic for me to be out there by myself. I wasn't ready to stay the night anytime soon without Kane, but during the day was a possibility.

I worried I had waited too long to talk to Kane.

I sat in the dark as I waited for Kane to come through the door. I knew Mariah wouldn't bark because I was a fixture in this house now. I heard footsteps on the front porch before the door opened. They were heavy and slow. He had to be running on fumes. From what his brothers had said, Kane barely spoke as they worked and only took a bite or two of his food after I left.

My stomach churned with worry that Kane might shut me out forever. When he opened the door, he looked tired. His shoulders sagged as if he carried the weight of the world. The fact that he hadn't sensed my presence yet told me volumes about where his head was. Kane noticed when the smallest thing was out of place.

He flipped on the lights as he walked in. When he was halfway across the living room, he stopped, finally noticing I was there. "How'd you get out here?"

His tone was almost accusatory, which wasn't going to fly. I tilted my head and deadpanned, "Teleportation."

The corner of his mouth lifted ever so slightly. So, this was how I was going to get through to him. It had always been how I got through to him—by making him smile. That afternoon, I hadn't been certain what I would do to get his attention.

As quickly as the smile appeared, it was gone, and the distance came back to his face. "Why are you here?"

I knew if I came out and said the real reason why, Kane would probably walk out the door again. *Shit.* I had to think fast.

"I had the urge to hear my yodeling pickle. I was sitting at your parents' house, using my mind bullets to try and teach their jar of pickles to yodel. Then I realized I had the perfect tool for that."

The corner of his mouth lifted again before it fell. But he had no comeback. No smart-ass remarks. Good grief, he'd retreated inside himself more than I'd realized.

He continued on to the kitchen where I could hear him opening the cabinets. A few minutes later, he returned with a full glass of bourbon.

"Have you had dinner?" I asked.

He held up the glass. "I have now."

I had two options—get aggravated or continue on the course I'd already set. Kane had been closed off emotionally to everyone but his family for years. So, I sat in my chair while he took a sip, watching me, testing me. Kane wasn't the type to play games, but he was definitely trying to push my buttons.

Finally, Kane's eyes darted to the table. "What is this shit?"

"Pictures," I stated. I had been going through them for the wedding after Kory had asked if I wanted some sort of display for pictures of us growing up. I thought it was a fun idea.

He pinched the bridge of his nose. "Teale, I'm too damn tired to do this."

"To do what? I'm just sitting here waiting for you to tell me where my yodeling pickle is. And you asked what this *shit* was, so I answered."

"Top dresser drawer, on the left."

I gasped in horror and stood, hand over my heart. "That poor pickle! He's been in the dark all these months?"

"Yep." Kane was trying to keep his mouth tight, but the corners rose again.

I got up and went to the bedroom to retrieve my yodeling pickle. When I sat back down, I waited silently for Kane to say something. Thank goodness I had brought my latest finds with me this afternoon.

When he remained quiet, I pulled the bag I brought in front of me. "I got some more stuff this week. There are some real gems, if you ask me. I figured I'd put them in a safe place so I could use them when we move into the new house."

No response.

I pressed on. "I'm going to take your silence to mean you're really dying to see my latest amazing purchases."

No response.

Geez, he's going to be a tough nut to crack. I opened the bag and pulled out the first box. "Well, first up, we are never, ever going to eat tacos the same way again. I've just changed our lives. This triceratops taco holder holds two tacos." I pulled out the green plastic dinosaur. "I ordered twenty for when we have the entire family over. I figured we could celebrate moving into the new house with a taco Tuesday after the wedding."

"What in the world would possess someone to make a dinosaur taco holder?"

That was more than two words. Good, I was getting through to him. "Someone with superb creativity." I set the large bag with all my plastic dinosaurs aside.

I opened the next bag. "Okay, this one backfired on me. Sooo… originally, I thought I would make you dinner one night and leave the can on the counter to create a unique dining experience. And, well, yeah… it didn't turn out like that." I pulled out the colorful tin can. "I thought, 'Oh it'll be so funny to serve Kane unicorn meat since he's are a connoisseur of meat and potatoes.'"

"What the fuck is unicorn meat? Isn't that a mythical creature?" Kane took another sip of his bourbon, but this time set it down and leaned forward. He was now plugged into the conversation.

I looked up at the trophies on the walls. "Must be mythical because you've got everything else mounted with creepy glass eyes."

That response got a chuckle. *Good.* I continued, "Well, I thought it would be like Spam or potted meat. I didn't really read the description because, hello, pretty label." I opened the can. "Well, I noticed it wasn't sealed the way food would be, so I opened it. And inside... well... it's not food."

"What is it?"

I pulled out the little unicorn that was Velcroed together. "Well, it's a unicorn and you pull it apart for the 'meat.' It's like a kid's stuffed animal gone bad. Like, hello, dead unicorn, now I'm going to tear you apart and serve you." I shook my head with a shudder. "Then I figured, wow, this might be a stuffed animal Kane could put on his desk."

I got up, stuffed the animal back inside, and handed him the can. "Here ya go! Do you love it?"

"Umm... Yes?"

Giggling, I sat back down. "I thought you might. Now when you have the urge to hunt and you can't, you can pull that little cute unicorn apart with your bare hands."

He gave another chuckle and opened the can to inspect the poor stuffed animal.

"I have one more gift, and then that's it for the fun stuff. Want to guess?"

"I would have a better shot at the lottery, angel."

Angel. He used my nickname. For the last few days, he'd

only called me Teale. Hopeful, I got the tin can out of the bottom of the bag. "Well, you go into the woods a lot. And I'm sure you only pack the necessities. Hollis told me how when you went fishing with him last year, you sat on a bucket. I mean, that's scraping the bottom of the barrel, don't you think? If we go camping together, just know that I'm going to need a lot more necessities than a bucket. I don't even want to know how you deal with undergarment changes."

"Angel, I don't have undergarment issues. And if I need to, I can go commando."

I flicked my wrist in his direction. "Well, I've solved the issue about having to either go commando or being forced to re-wear your underwear."

His eyebrow rose, and I handed him a bag. "There are fifty pairs in this bag. Each little tin has one disposable pair of underwear compressed into a compact pellet. Just add water, dry them by the fire, and voilà, fresh underpants."

Kane took one of the small tins out of the bag and looked at me. "Fifty pairs?"

"Well, yeah, you do a lot of hunting trips. And they gave me a huge price break for buying in bulk. They're disposable, too. Just toss them into the fire, and no more underpants. Open up a new tin, soak, and repeat."

"I have no words."

Some of the tension eased from his shoulders, and I moved aside the bag so I could sit in his lap. With my hands on his face, I moved his lips as I said, "Thank you, Teale. You're the world's most amazing fiancée. And now I'm going to talk to you about what is really going on inside my head instead of running away from you."

His head jerked back. "Teale."

I placed my hands on either side of his face. "I know you're hurting. We're all hurting, Kane. But this is the time in a relationship when we lean on each other. It's how we survive the hurt." I pointed to the bourbon. "And that is not a proper diet. I know from the amount of empty liquor bottles I cleaned up today that you've been drinking every night. You've got to talk to me, Kane. We have to lean on each other. It doesn't make you a weak man because you're hurting—it makes you human."

His eyes cast downward. "I've been terrible to you."

"No. No, you haven't. Each night, you text me that you love me. Every day, you go and work on our future home. I know you're still in this relationship, but I also know that you've closed yourself off to everyone. And I think it's because you're scared."

His hands snaked around me, and he buried his face in my hair. "If I lost you, I'm not sure I would survive. I'm in deep, angel. Deeper than I realized."

"I know it's hard, but at least we got to know him, to love him, before we lost him. We aren't promised tomorrow, Kane. But we do have today. Judson lived each day to the fullest. It's all we can do."

He took a deep breath. "I'm sorry for being a dick."

"You've got nothing to apologize for, Kane. You're grieving. But I want to be your partner in good times *and* in bad times. It's okay to lean on me."

I grabbed his drink and set it aside. "And I have some homemade potpie in the oven on warm. I made it at your mom's. No more liquid dinners."

"Deal." He took a deep breath, and I could tell more was coming. I waited, giving him time. "What if I caused him to die earlier than he was already going to by taking him on that walk?"

I'd wondered if that was what had been on his mind. "Judson was going to die. He was terminal. Hollis confirmed it to us when Lori gave him access to review his medical records. But for argument's sake, let's say Judson lived for one or two more days if he hadn't taken that hike." I paused, and Kane's eyes shot to mine, concerned about where I was going with this. "What if, for those two days, he begged you to go on a hike and you didn't take him? The guilt at missing that opportunity would be eating you up. Kane, you gave him a chance to see the deer, to see the woods. It was the last thing he wanted to do. His bucket list was complete. Would you have denied him that last wish?"

"No. Never."

I kissed his forehead. "Then let it go. It's time to let go of the guilt. You gave that boy the greatest gift by bringing him to Alaska. You were his hero. You're my hero."

Kane held onto me fiercely. "I'm so sorry, angel."

"We're in this together. Just never let me go."

"Never."

CHAPTER

Forty-Eight

Kane

I sat around the campfire with my brothers and Hollis, thinking about the future. The weather had turned colder, and in two days, I would be married. *Two*. It was hard to believe I'd done a complete one-eighty on relationships, but with Teale, it just felt right. She was in New York with my mom and hers, getting her dress. For a dress she'd wear one time, it seemed a little over the top, but whatever made her happy. And my mom loved being part of it. Our parents seemed to get along great.

There wasn't a day that went by that I didn't think about Judson. But the hurt got easier each day. I would keep my promise and never forget him. Keeping in touch with Lori helped. She was doing better. The foundation gave her something to focus on, and it was doing well.

The support my future wife gave Lori was amazing. I touched my throat, feeling the chain that hung there. Lori had given Judson's favorite medallion—the one he carried every-where—to Teale. It was a coin of Alaska he'd carried for years. Teale had it made into a necklace that I wore every day.

Drake stoked the fire, the crackling of the flames breaking my thoughts. "It's hard to believe you're going to be a married man."

"Yeah, I am. You ready to be a dad?"

It was nice to have some time away from the craziness with my brothers and Hollis. Drake could hardly contain himself. "Yeah, I am."

Hollis was setting up some contraption near the campfire. I asked, "What the hell is that?"

"They're portable camping hammocks. I have three more in the truck. It's got fantastic ratings and is made for the perfect night's sleep while out in the elements."

Fuck my life.

Hayden and Drake stood and started walking to the truck. "Hollis, you are the man."

"A true Alaskan man." Hollis added. Next, he pulled out a blanket. On it was a picture of the certificate Mayor Richards had given him at the town meeting, certifying Hollis as an Alaskan. Everyone knew of his fixation with being a real Alaskan.

I shook my head. "Put that away. We're in the woods. We don't need furry-ass blankets."

Hollis laughed. "It's snuggly. I have one for each of you guys. Consider it a memento from the bachelor party."

My brothers came back with the blankets and portable bed things. "No way we are related. No fucking way."

They grinned. Hayden said, "You're in the same boat, asshole."

"No, I'm sleeping on the ground. Not even close."

Drake leaned down and picked up something from the ground. "Disposable underpants? Just wet, dry, and wear? Who do these things belong to?"

Shit. I thought I'd tossed them all into the woods. Looked like I missed one.

I said nothing. Drake tossed it to me. "Yep, not in the same boat at all. Let me know how those work."

"Teale gave some to Devney. I brought some to share, if anyone needed," Hollis chimed in.

I *knew* I had gotten rid of mine. Hayden looked at me. "Kane, this is a judgement-free zone. If you like disposable undies, that's none of our business."

Assholes.

I wasn't going to dignify what they were saying. Instead, I reached for my phone, which vibrated with a message from Teale.

Teale: *Are you having fun?*

Me: *I'm camping with a bunch of pussies. Portable beds... wtf?*

Teale: *You know I'm going to require a portable bed if we ever go camping.*

Me: *I will treasure our marriage too much to ever take you camping.*

Teale: *I knew there was a reason I wanted to marry you. Love you. Have fun.*

Me: *Night. Love you, too.*

I put away my phone and got more comfortable on the bed of pine needles I'd made. "Night, assholes. I hope your beds collapse."

They chuckled. "I hope you get bit, dickhead," Drake said.

"Good thing we have a doctor here."

Hollis interjected, "I feel like we should sing Kumbaya with all the love I'm hearing."

I groaned and the guys laughed. *Bastards.*

In unison, they all started singing. It was as if I had entered an alternate reality. Three grown men singing some stupid shit. "Are you sure you came to the right party? The bachelorette one was last weekend."

Disposable undie tins were flung at me. Chuckling, I shielded my face. This was the life. And I wouldn't want it any other way.

I stood on the back deck of the new cabin. The decorations were done—Kory and Alexa had done an amazing job. It was exactly the way Teale wanted it. Lights were strung in the open yard. There was an arch decorated with some greenery and tables off to the side. It was small and intimate. To satisfy Elvira and Sylvia, Teale had promised the Twiner sisters exclusive pictures. I'd be in another damn newsletter.

I took a long sip of my coffee, just enjoying the view. This was going to be my new home. It had been a little weird spending last night in the other cabin knowing that it would no longer be home. For years, it had been my place of solitude. And now, I wanted to build this new life with Teale.

It was a miracle we'd gotten the new house finished before winter hit. The extra crew members, thanks to Hollis, had helped get it done in record time. Teale hadn't seen the place finished yet. She wanted it to be a surprise, so our wedding night would be when we would stay in our house for the first time. Instead of a honeymoon she wanted a "staymoon." I liked the idea. It gave us the chance to just be with each other. It seemed like I'd barely had time to just spend with Teale lately.

In a couple of weeks, I had some hunting expeditions that would keep me away for days at a time. And during that time, Teale was going to work on her ice-skating camps.

I checked the time. Only a few more hours. Teale arrived last night from New York, but I wasn't able to see her because of traditions or some shit like that. Which pissed me off. For the last two weeks, there had been a no sex rule. She wanted to make our wedding night special. I thought I was going to go insane not being able to have her.

"I'm going to head out to get the girls. You ready?"

I smiled at Drake. "Never been readier for anything in my entire life."

It was obvious Drake wasn't sure how to respond. Normally, I kept my feelings close to the chest around anyone but Teale. "I'm proud of you, Kane. I know that sounds sappy as shit, but I am."

"Thanks, man. And I appreciate all you did to get this place ready."

"Anytime. That's what family is for, right?" I nodded in agreement. Yeah, through thick and thin, Fosters stuck together. He waved as he walked away. "I'm off."

"Sounds good."

I took a deep breath. In a month, I would be an uncle. And Devney was due any day now. Life was never going to be the same. After working through things, I was able to let go of the blame for Judson's death. And I kept remembering him, just the way he'd wanted.

I heard footsteps from around the corner before Dad joined me.

"Hey, son."

"Dad." I tipped my mug in his direction.

"You got a second?"

"Of course."

That took me a little off guard—I wasn't sure how to read him. We sat in the chairs Dad had made for the back deck. All the furniture had been custom made as Mom and Dad's present to Teale and me for our wedding.

"There have been two other days in my life that I've been this proud. Those were the days of Drake's and Hayden's weddings. And now I have a third day to add to that list. All we've ever wanted for our boys was for them to be happy. And I think you've found that with Teale."

I smiled. "I have."

"I want you to remember there are going to be ups and downs, but you need to lean on each other. If you make sure to lean on each other, you'll find your way."

That was the hard part. I had found that out when Judson died. "What if I fuck it up?"

"Then you get up, admit you're wrong, say you're sorry, and do better the next time."

That sounded easy enough. "Thanks, Dad. For everything."

"Anytime you need to talk, I'm here." Dad stood. "And your mother wanted me to remind you about your language today."

I nodded. "The only words I'm going to say are *I do*. I figure that way I'm safe."

"That's a good plan."

CHAPTER
Forty-Nine

Kane

It was time.

The fancy music played, but I just wanted to see Teale. It had been nearly four fucking days since I'd set eyes on her. I kept waiting for her to appear at the end of the aisle. I was two seconds from going to find her. Right before I took my first step, she appeared.

My angel.

She was stunning in her white dress with her hair done up in some fancy style. The lights hit her dress, and it sparkled against the night sky. Her eyes lit up when she saw me. As she took a step forward, I realized I needed to talk to her. There was something I wanted her to know before we did this. As I walked up the aisle, I heard sounds of protest from my family. *Too bad.* I hadn't seen her in what felt like forever.

She smiled when I reached her and said, "You were supposed to wait at the end of the aisle for me to come."

"I know." I swallowed hard. "Before we do this, I needed you to know how much I love you. You are my world. I will love you always."

Teale's eyes glistened with tears, and I turned to her father. "I promise I'll take care of her. Always."

"I know you will, son. That's the only reason I gave you my blessing. Now, you head back so I can walk my beautiful girl down the aisle before I hand her over to the man who's going to spend the rest of his life looking out for her."

"Yes, sir."

I jogged back down the aisle and winked at my mom as I passed. I mouthed, *"No cuss words yet."*

She raised her eyebrow and mouthed back, *"Keep it that way,"* pointing to a wood thing in her purse.

Shit. She had a paddle. I knew I had better keep my mouth shut. I adjusted the collar of my white shirt as I waited. Teale had decided no tux for me. I was wearing black dress pants with an untucked white shirt. I would have worn the penguin suit for her, but it wouldn't have felt natural.

Slowly Teale made her way down the aisle. I swore I was going to age a few years before she made it to me. Another three steps, and they stopped. *Finally.*

"Who gives this woman away?" Reverend Arnold asked.

Everett proudly said, "Her mother and I."

Teale hugged her dad and whispered something in his ear. Everett placed Teale's hand in mine. She was mine forever and always to protect. It was euphoric. I took Teale by the hand and brought her to me. "You are stunning. Abso-f—lutely stunning."

Shit. I almost dropped an F-bomb. Thank goodness it was a whisper. And hopefully the good reverend wasn't a snitch.

"I missed you," I added.

Teale cupped my jaw. "I missed you, too. Are you ready for forever?"

"I am."

The preacher cleared his throat. "If I may begin."

We nodded, lost in each other's gaze. Thank goodness Teale squeezed my hand when it was time for me to say *I do*.

"I present to you Mr. and Mrs. Kane Foster. You may kiss the bride."

I swooped in and claimed her mouth.

I was married.

Teale was mine to protect and honor.

And I would spend the rest of my life doing just that.

CHAPTER
Fifty

Kane

We'd been married for a week, and I couldn't have been happier. Teale and I had stayed tucked away in a little bubble in our new cabin. After everything we'd gone through, we needed time to just be together.

I heard her walk into my office, where all my trophies were now. That had been our compromise. She'd asked for no taxidermy animals in the main house. Only in my office. I saw her reflection in my monitor as she stood in front of the bear, her head cocked to the side.

She sighed. "Can we at least put sunglasses on them?"

"No." I fought a smile, but I knew she could hear it in my voice. I had no doubt the damn animals would be dressed up soon enough.

She pressed her point. "At Christmas, we could give them wreaths?"

I turned around and raised my eyebrow. "I thought you said I could do what I wanted in the office."

She crossed the office floor to where I sat. "I just didn't think the entire entourage would join us. I was thinking one or two, not the entire zoo."

I chuckled and turned toward her. Before I could say anything, the phone rang. It was Dad.

"Alexa and Devney are in labor."

"*What*? At the same time?"

Teale's eyebrows arched.

Dad continued. "Yeah, Devney is already past her due date, and Alexa is full-term. While Devney was in labor, Alexa's water broke. Apparently, they were doing an exercise video together this morning."

I stood. "Okay, we're on our way." I hung up the phone. "Devney and Alexa are in labor."

"What? At the same time? How is that possible?"

I shrugged, knowing I would never be able to answer any questions Teale had. It was best to go to the hospital where she could get all the details. "I don't know."

"Let me get my shirt. Do you want yours?"

"My shirt?"

Teale flicked her wrist. "Yeah, I ordered you one. I figured we could be that cute married couple who has matching gender-prediction shirts."

Oh, fuck. Teale ran to our bedroom and came back out with a pink shirt. It said in white letters *I'm an uncle to a beautiful niece.*

"How do you know it's a girl?" If this was a ploy to get me in a pink shirt, I wasn't buying it. If my brother had a boy and I wore this, I would never hear the end of it.

Teale put her hand on her hip. "Trust me, it is. I just know these things, remember?"

I grinned. "My brother is having a girl."

"Unless my guessing meter is off, which it never has been."

"What is Hollis having?"

"A girl as well."

Hell yeah. I was going to be rid of that princess shit. I grabbed the shirt. "I will wear this happily."

Teale handed me a sweatshirt. "Put this over it. We don't want to ruin the surprise."

I smiled. Never in my life would I stop loving this woman.

When we arrived at the clinic, Devney was in one room and Alexa was in another. Hollis was dashing from room to room. The excitement was tangible. Mom was helping in Alexa's room, and Kory was helping Devney after she'd delivered a beautiful baby girl about forty-five minutes before. They named her Yvette Marie Hollis and she was beautiful.

Fuck yeah! One down, one to go. So far, Teale's predictions had been right. Next week, Devney's mom was coming up. Last week, we'd gotten news she was in remission. Best news we could have hoped for.

Currently, Teale was helping Hollis as he bounced from room to room. She was his substitute nurse. It sounded like Alexa was ready to push. There was some talk about full moons and spicy food and all sorts of shit to explain why they had gone into labor at the same time. None of it made sense to me.

Hayden looked at me. "Why are you so damn happy?"

I scrubbed a hand down my face, unsure if I should say anything. *Fuck it.* "I'm losing the princess title today."

"Are you serious? It's girl?"

I shrugged. "That's what Teale said. And she had shirts preprinted." I lifted my sweatshirt to show him,

Hayden smirked. "Dude, you are so whipped."

"And proud of it." Yeah, I was. I'd realized it when I'd actually put this pink shirt on.

My dad chuckled. "Whatever the sex of this baby is, we will love it. Remember that, boys."

"Of course," my brother and I said.

A few minutes later, Drake came into the room, beaming. "I'm a dad. Baby Abigail and Lex are doing great."

Fuck yes, a girl. We stood and rushed to congratulate him. My brother was a dad. Drake was so damn happy it was contagious. "Do you want to meet her?"

"Yes," we all said.

The family walked into the room to find Alexa cradling a little baby wrapped up in a blanket. She was beautiful. The next generation of Fosters was here.

A surge or protectiveness came over me. I would love this little girl and be there for Abigail anytime she needed. The same went for Yvette, too.

Everyone cooed over the baby. We all apparently turned into saps around babies.

Teale came up beside me, and I put my arm around her, pulling her close. I whispered in her ear, "That's going to be us some day."

"I can't wait."

And for the first time since Judson died, I knew I would want children with Teale someday.

CHAPTER
Fifty-One

Teale

One year later

I was twenty weeks along, and we were waiting in Hollis's office for the news. After Abigail had been born, something had come over Kane. He wanted children of his own. We'd decided at our six-month anniversary I would go off birth control, and it had taken no time for us to get pregnant.

Today we were finding out the gender of the baby. I was already pretty sure what we were having, but I hadn't told Kane my prediction.

Kane was beside me, holding my hand when Hollis came in.

He turned on the sonogram machine and squirted the cold gel on my stomach. "You two ready to find out?"

"Yes!"

A month ago, Hayden and Kory had found out they were having a girl. The Foster family was now overrun with females, and I loved it. Being an aunt was the most amazing thing. Kane was smitten with his nieces, too. He had turned into a gentle giant. It was hard to believe just a little over a year ago, I had met the man who would change my life forever with his Mr. Grumpy Pants ways.

Kane hovered his hand over my stomach and looked at Hollis. "There's a lot riding on this reading, doc."

"You do realize it was your sperm that decided the sex of this baby, right?" Hollis asked.

I rolled my eyes. These men loved their little girls, but I knew there was still a competition between his brothers. It really didn't make any sense because these Alaskan Foster men turned into complete mush around their nieces and would do anything for them.

Hollis placed the wand on my stomach and moved it around, taking measurements and marking spots on the screen. After what seemed like forever, he turned back to us with a smile. "Congratulations, you two."

I gasped when my suspicions were confirmed.

We went to Ike and Amie's to share the news. My parents were there, as well. Their move to Alaska had gone well. Now that Lori was fully transitioned into her role, my parents would move up here permanently.

The show had been amazing this year. My role, as far as ice skating was concerned, had been limited because I was pregnant. But so far, we'd been able to make twenty-seven kids' dreams come true. The Judson Wright Foundation was growing by leaps and bounds thanks to Lori. She was doing an amazing job. Through all the heartache, Judson had changed our lives in more ways than I'd ever imagined. He would never be forgotten. His name would live on forever.

"Uncem Kan!" Abigail and Yvette toddled to Kane, who picked each one up with an arm.

"How are my favorite nieces?"

They smothered him with sloppy kisses as he squeezed them tighter. I couldn't wait to see how he would be with his own child.

"Play. Play."

He put them down and kneeled at their level. "I'll play in just a bit. We're going to tell everyone about the baby in Aunt Teale's tummy."

A year ago, I never would have imagined this kind of softness coming from Kane. Of course, he still cursed like a sailor.

My mom was the first to jump on his words. "Oh, are you guys going to tell us? The anticipation is killing me!"

I swore Kane was going to burst with pride. He held up his hands, and the room grew silent. I pressed my lips together, trying not to laugh.

Drake shook his head. "Tell me you're a princess."

Abigail waddled to her dad and pulled on his pants leg. "Pwincess."

Leaning down, Drake scooped up his daughter. "Yes, you are Daddy's princess."

All eyes shifted back to Kane. "Looks like I'm going to follow Dad's footsteps."

Drake and Hayden shook their heads, grinning. My mom nearly squealed in excitement. "A boy? Oh my! I'm so excited."

Kane put his hand on my stomach. "In just a few months, we'll be welcoming Judson Delaney Foster to the family."

It was the perfect name to carry on the legacy of a little boy who touched our lives forever. The family cheered. Everything was just as it should be. I never imagined I would be this happy.

Epilogue

Kane

Two years later

I pulled up the covers over Judson's small, sleeping frame. I loved watching him sleep. It was still hard to believe I was a dad. A real fucking dad. I put Judson's bear beside him. A gift from Lori, it had been her son's favorite stuffed animal. And now my kid never went anywhere without it. I watched him for a few minutes. Sometimes the emotions were so strong it was hard to take my eyes off him.

Today had been a big day. Judson and Amelia, Hayden's kid, had tried to keep up with Abigail and Yvette. All our kids were thick as thieves. How my mom had survived all those years with three boys was beyond me. She deserved sainthood.

I snapped a picture of Judson and sent it to my brothers.

Me: *Tuckered out.*

Drake sent a picture of Abigail.

Drake: *She's out.*

Hayden did the same for Amelia.

Hayden: *Gone to the world.*

Hollis sent a picture of Yvette running down the hall, naked.

Hollis: *Mine is still going strong. Last man standing. Must be the Alaskan in her coming out.*

Yvette was a wild one. Hell, every time we watched her, she ran us ragged, and when she went home, I felt like I had never been so exhausted in my life. Taking a bear down in the woods was easier than keeping up with her. But, fuck, she was adorable. They were all amazing kids, and I would do anything for them. But poor Hollis and Devney had their work cut out for them.

I scrolled through my texts, and hell, all we sent each other were pics of our kids. Yeah, we'd definitely come full circle.

Me: *Just going to throw this out there. We've all become pansies.*

Drake: *Pretty much.*

Hayden: *For sure.*

Hollis: *Alaskan pansies.*

I chuckled and put my phone away while it continued to vibrate. They'd text for hours. I walked to our master suite to find Teale asleep already, her hands cradling her stomach. I was going to be a father for a second time in about four and a half weeks. Another boy. We had decided we wanted our kids to be close in age.

Double the trouble was more like it. And in a few years, maybe we'd have another one. Yeah, I wanted a lot of kids, but Teale had kyboshed that idea, so we'd settled at three.

I ran my fingers down her cheek, and she stirred. "Hey, angel."

She stretched and opened her eyes. "Is Judson asleep?"

"Yeah, I went ahead and put him to bed. I knew you were tired."

"Oh, I hate missing bedtime."

I kissed her forehead and got into bed beside her. "He was asleep before his head hit the pillow."

"His cousins wore him out today. Oh, Kory and Alexa are pregnant again. They slipped today at lunch."

I chuckled. "My brothers slipped, too. I don't know why they try to keep things a secret."

"Me, either. It'll be nice to have all the cousins close in age."

"Yeah, it will."

I touched Teale's stomach and felt our son kicking up a storm. "He's active."

"Mm-hmm... he's like his father."

Leaning down, I kissed her stomach. "I can't wait to meet you, little man."

He kicked in response. "I love you, Teale. Thank you for this life."

If it hadn't been for Teale, I wasn't sure I would have ever been saved. She cuddled further into me, and I knew it wouldn't be long before she was asleep again. "I love you, too. There's no one else I'd rather do this with."

She yawned, and I pulled the covers up over us. Our son continued to move, and I savored the moment as I held her to me. "Sleep, angel."

I had been changed by this woman in all the best ways.

Life was perfect.

A Sneak Peek at Kristin Mayer's Next Novel,
Unexpected Love.

Be on the lookout for Spring of 2019

UNEXPECTED LOVE

Prologue

Addilyn

My stomach turned at the sound of a key in the lock on the front door. I sat in the dark, as unsure of how I was going to handle the confrontation I was about to face than I had been four hours ago. I had been betrayed and lied to by the person I trusted the most.

Hear him out. Maybe you misunderstood.

The evidence was too damning. Deep in my gut, I knew what I had found was the truth, which meant my marriage was over.

Fury surged through me. I clung to that emotion—fueled it, even—so I wouldn't let this be explained away. Too many times in the past, I'd let that happen. I dug my fingernails into the palms of my hand to give myself something to focus on while I waited silently for him to come into the house.

The door opened, and moonlight spilled into the house. Braden's silhouette appeared in the doorway and then disappeared into the darkness as he closed the front door and stepped into the foyer.

I took a deep, quiet breath to prepare myself, wondering which parts of my marriage had been a lie and which parts were actually true.

The foyer light flipped on, and he placed his keys in the ceramic bowl we bought on our honeymoon in the Caribbean. Next, he hung his coat in the closet on the third hanger from the left. It was a ritual with Braden.

Everything had a place.

All things were done in the same order.

I considered myself organized, but Braden took it to a whole new level. It had never bothered me because I'd considered it just part of his quirks. He never expected the same of me.

The click of the closet door was loud in the silent house. My muscles tightened as I readied myself for the confrontation.

We were supposed to fly to the Florida Keys to celebrate our first anniversary in two days. The plan was to start a family. Or at least start to try. Sitting there, I cringed at the thought of being connected to Braden for the rest of my life. I felt nauseous and slowed my breathing to get that under control.

Braden put his briefcase under the table, to the far left, where it stayed while not in use. I turned on the lamp beside me, casting a soft glow in the living room. I felt like a stranger in my own home—the home I had made with Braden.

Braden loosened his blue pinstriped tie as he stepped toward me. Blue was a good color. I always loved buying him blue because it matched his eyes. Those eyes traveled down my body. If I hadn't known better, I would have sworn it was love on his face.

"Hello, my darling. I thought you might be in bed. I didn't want to wake you." He gave me a crooked grin and sauntered a few steps closer. I knew that walk. It was the *I-want-to-get-lucky* walk. "Maybe we could get an early start on our family planning."

I want to vomit. I stood and shook my head. "No."

He appeared confused, head cocked to one side as he stared at me. "Okay... obviously you're angry. Do you want to tell me why? Because, darling, I honestly have no idea."

The sound of the pet name was like nails on a chalkboard. I grabbed the card from the table and tossed it at his feet. "Care to explain this."

Slowly, he knelt, and his eyes widened when he saw what the card was. Typically, it took a lot to faze Braden. But at that moment, he rose slowly, as if trying to come up with some sort of explanation. "Where did you find this?"

I scoffed. "Where do you think I found it?"

I waited for him to open the card, but he didn't. Because he knew what it said. It was a handmade card, drawn in crayon, that said *World's Best Dad.* Inside was a picture of Braden and a child about six or seven. And this kid was Braden's mini-me.

I knew the picture was recent because he had been wearing a blue sweater I'd bought him for Christmas less than two months earlier. And unless Braden had a twin brother I'd never heard of, he had a son with a woman who appeared to be very much a part of his life.

"Addilyn, I can explain." He rubbed the back of his neck, his gaze on the card in his hand.

Of course, he would have some sort of explanation. One of Baden's specialties was smooth talking. That was how he got me to agree to date him. Initially, I'd said no. After some time and sweet gestures, I agreed to go on a date with him. From that day, and each day after, Braden had been the definition of attentive, caring, and loving.

Lies.

It hurt so much to think about, so I got to the point. "Are you that child's father?"

Braden's jaw flexed, and his response was stern. "Addilyn."

I balled my fists, and tears stung my eyes. I didn't have any other proof, so I bluffed. "Don't lie to me. I know the truth."

For a second, Braden eyed me. He was of average height, but handsome and well-built. It was hard to believe our marriage had come to this. "I will file for divorce from Bridgette tomorrow. We'll go to marriage counseling. We can work this out."

I froze in shock for the second time that day. That was not what I had expected. An affair? Yes. But married to someone else? *How?*

When I remained silent, Braden continued. "I will end things with Bridgette. I'll get joint custody of my son. I want this life with you. I want the family we were planning to start. I don't want to lose you, Addilyn."

Nothing made any sense. *We* were married. Not he and Bridgette. I blinked a few times before I asked, "You're *married?*"

His eyes widened, and he cursed when he realized I hadn't really known the truth. "Fuck."

There was no apology.

No acknowledgement.

Braden was only aggravated because he'd been caught.

And now he realized I had lied.

There was nothing he could say that would matter. It was over; I'd heard enough.

I pointed to the door. "Get out. Get out of my house. This is over."

Braden took a step forward. "Addilyn, be reasonable. Let's talk about this. It was a mistake."

This was more of a mess than I'd imagined. I was the other woman. I wanted to be sick.

Braden mistook my silence and stepped closer. I backed up, pulling my phone out of my pocket. "Get out or I'll call the cops. So help me, if you don't leave this house, I will call them."

Braden stepped back, holding up his hands. "I'll give you some time to cool off and come back in the morning."

There would be no cooling off. *Just keep it together until he leaves.* I shook my head. "No, do not come back. Anything you need to say you can say to my attorney."

Braden grabbed his briefcase and keys. Ignoring my comment, he said, "I love you, Addilyn. Don't give up on me. We'll talk tomorrow."

The door shut, and the dam that had been holding back my tears burst. I dropped to my knees and cried into my hands as my heart broke into a million pieces.

How did this happen to me?

Chapter One

Addilyn

Three years later

I stared at my computer screen, a picture of Braden's latest wife, Monique, staring back at me. It was like looking in a mirror. His new wife had long, dark hair, chestnut colored eyes, and was slimly built—just like me.

Three years later, my stomach still got tied up in knots just thinking about the battle it had been to divorce him.

One. Year.

It had taken a full year to get everything sorted from my sham of a marriage.

It was twelve months I would never get back. As it turned out, I was the legal wife. Bridgette and Braden had been married in Mexico and had never gotten a US marriage license. It was a mystery to me why Braden had fought the divorce every step of the way. The judge in our case had been crooked—coordinating with Braden's attorneys at every turn. On my limited budget, I hadn't been able to afford the best attorney. Braden had three attorneys, which made mine merely a puppet in the show.

I'd had to go through court-ordered marriage counseling.

He contested everything.

I'd even had to go to meeting with his son, Devin.

It was the worst kind of hell.

In the end, I offered to walk away from the marriage with only my car, my clothes, and the few things from my grammie. He was welcome to the house, the bank accounts, the investments. I didn't want them, anyway. That had been the only way to get out of the marriage. The judge had been forced to rule, although Braden still objected. It had been the best feeling in the world, even when I'd had nearly nothing.

Shortly after the divorce was settled, my Grammie passed away, leaving me a small inheritance, which helped me get back on my feet.

Grammie.

She had been in a nursing home with dementia for a couple of years before I married Braden. Thank goodness, I had been able to keep the divorce from her. During her more lucid moments, it was easier to let her believe I was happy. I hadn't wanted Grammie to stress about me. It was worse when Braden showed up randomly when I was there. He was such a bastard.

I wiped an errant tear that ran down my cheek. Those days had been hard in so many ways. There were times I wished I could give her a hug and she'd tell me everything would be okay.

Everything is okay.

I was free from Braden.

I had a successful career.

I was living my best life.

Yep, everything is okay.

The door to my office opened, and I jumped with a little yelp. Ria cocked her head to the side, her latest weave done in long dark braids, that were piled on top of her head in an artful bun. "You okay, girl? You're awfully jumpy."

I plastered on a fake smile. "I was really focused on my presentation to Carothers Media on Monday."

She flicked her wrist. "You got this. I've gone over your pitch, and it's spot on."

"Fingers crossed." I held up both hands, crossing my fingers in the air. "And maybe cross our eyes, too."

I brought my eyes to the center of my nose, and she laughed. "Go on, get out of here. It's the weekend. Go be wild. Have some fun. Maybe have some hot naked sex with a random guy."

My cheeks heated. I loved my boss, but she was definitely eccentric. "Umm… I think I'll settle for pizza and an old movie."

Ria rolled her eyes. "If I had a body like yours, I would definitely be hitting the clubs."

I giggled, grabbing my laptop and changing the topic to something more appropriate. "What are you doing this weekend?"

"Chuck's family is in town. So, we're *entertaining* for the weekend." Ria held up her perfectly manicured fingers and air quoted. Her in-laws were a bit high maintenance. They needed to have something to do every second of the day. "Let me grab my stuff and we can walk to the subway together."

"Sounds good."

After the year of fighting to get a divorce, it had taken me nearly two more years to rebuild my life. It was hard to believe three years had passed since I found out that Braden had had another life with another *wife*. I wondered if he was still with Bridgette. *Poor Monique.* I had no idea who she was, but my heart went out to her, knowing the heartache that would be coming her way if he hadn't changed. From what I knew, he still lived in our old home, still drove the same car, still had the same job. Made me sick.

Shortly after the divorce, I left Virginia and moved to New York City. I had no living relatives, and Wynter, my best friend from college, lived there. She'd begged me to come and start over. It was the best decision I'd ever made. The city that never sleeps kept me occupied. I also felt safer in a city with so many people. It made it easier to blend in case Braden tried to find me.

After the divorce was final, Braden had become almost stalkerish. He knew enough about the law to stay out of trouble. So I decided the best thing was to remove myself from the situation. I hoped I never saw him again.

I'd come to New York, and Ria have given me a chance. She owned Impact Marketing, a small firm with only four people. I'd worked in sales before, so it seemed a good progression in my career. Ria was brilliant and an amazing mentor.

Life in New York was exactly what I had needed.

The crisp October air hit me as we walked outside. I loved New York City in the fall. As we walked on the busy sidewalk, Ria pulled her scarf a little tighter. "If you need anything this weekend while you prep for the meeting, call me."

"I will."

Before Ria could continue her pep talk, her phone rang, and she launched into a conversation with whoever was on the phone. My boss could talk a mile a minute.

My plan was to spend the weekend pouring over my notes and working on my presentation. Two months ago, I'd found an opportunity online to present a marketing campaign to Carothers Media for their dating app. They were looking to expand their current marketing base and get a fresh perspective. By some miracle, they granted us a meeting. It would be career-changing if I managed to land the job.

The down side was that it was a dating app. I had zero knowledge about these types of apps. So, I created an account on the site in order to learn the program and present the best marketing strategy. I hoped it worked. The experience so far had been interesting, to say the least. I had received more dick pics than I wanted to think about. But if we landed the account, it would be worth it.

As we approached the subway, Ria ended her call, and I said, "Have fun *entertaining*."

She laughed. "I may show up at your place with alcohol if I reach the end of my rope."

We started down the steps, and people rushed past us on both sides. Since it was rush hour on Friday, the subway was a madhouse. "Well, I only have a twin bed, but you're welcome to crash on the loveseat."

"Deal! Have a good weekend, Addilyn. Don't stress too much about the presentation. You're prepared. See you on Monday."

"See you. Thanks for all the help on the sales pitch."

She flicked her wrist in my direction and hustled down the steps to the right. I headed to the left. Our trains went in opposite directions. I lived toward Central park and Ria lived in East village. I hustled with the group of people to the train. Once in the subway, you learned to walk fast or be trampled.

I'd barely made it before the doors closed. As usual, it was standing room only. I found a little spot to stand next to the door and settled in. My phone vibrated with a text from my best friend, Wynter.

Wynter: *What did you think of the article?*

Me: *Creepy. How did you find it?*

Wynter: *I get alerts for any news.*

Me: *Of course you do.*

I smiled at my best friend's tenacity. She was one of the few people who knew what happened between me and Braden.

Wynter: *Will you please come with me tonight? Pretty please. You can literally walk here from your subway stop.*

I wanted to go home, but I needed to support my best friend. Her company was doing a toy drive for a local shelter.

Me: *I'll be there in twenty.*

Wynter: *Good! There are a lot of hot single guys here.*

Oh, good grief.

Chapter Two

Addilyn

The restaurant where the fundraiser was being held was hopping. I dropped my toy off in the bin that was over-flowing with donations. Wynter worked at Hamilton Industries, which was a tech company. She was one of their techies. I honestly had no idea what she did.

She held up her cocktail and motioned to me. "You're here!"

"I'm here." I laughed as I gave her a hug. She was wear-ing the latest fashion, her outfit edgy as always.

She grabbed me a drink from the tray of a passing waiter. "Drink up."

I took a sip of the champagne and saw Wynter's wheels turning. "So, at eleven o'clock we have a hottie. He has been watching you since you came in."

"Wynter, seriously, I don't want to be set up tonight."

"Just look."

Casually, I changed my position and saw the guy. He was good looking. With his glass raised, he nodded our way. My cheeks heated and I gave a quick nod back. I looked more like a stiff robot. I was out of practice.

It felt warmer in here. "His name is Andy. Want to meet?"

Part of me wanted to. "I don't know. Not tonight. I think I'm going to head home. I wanted to stop by and give you support."

Another girl came and tapped Wynter on the shoulder. She looked torn. "Go handle your business. I'm going to go grab dinner."

She hugged me. "Thank you for coming. Wanna do brunch on Sunday?"

"It's a date."

Sunday brunch was our thing. We made it a point to get together at least once a week. I hugged her. "Adios."

"Adios, bitchacho."

I laughed and headed to the door. When I was nearly there, someone bumped into me, and I lost my balance. Before I hit the ground, two strong arms caught me. I righted myself but had to catch my breath when I looked up at the man who had caught me. Tingles erupted along my skin, and I took a step back.

"You okay?"

"Umm... yes... Sorry, someone bumped me, and, well... the rest is history."

Stop babbling.

He chuckled. "Do you work for Hamilton Industries?"

"No, I came to support a friend. You?"

"No. I came to support a friend, too."

I smiled. His eyes were a dark golden brown with flecks of black in them. They were stunning. I blinked to break the connection. "Thank you for saving me from complete humiliation."

"Anytime."

"There you are!" a voice called from behind him.

He whipped his head around and held up a finger, signaling he would be just a minute, before turning back to me. "Would you like a drink?"

I hadn't expected that. He looked up again and his brows pinched.

"I need to get going. But thank you again."

Before he could say anything, I ducked out the door.

Once I was a couple of blocks away, I slowed my pace. On my evening walks home, I enjoyed taking my time and absorbing the environment. But I was tired and not in the mood to cook, so I popped into a little café two blocks from my studio apartment and sat at an empty table.

The waiter, Chris, came over to take my order. "Hey, Addilyn. You want your usual?"

"Please."

I loved the Stromboli here. Chris gave me a sweet smile as he took my order. He was a nice guy around my age. After I'd been coming into the café for a few months, he'd casually hinted about going out together. I'd still been so raw from the divorce at the time, so I'd said no. If he asked again, I might consider going. Though Chris never gave me that toe-curling feeling I hoped for. Neither had Braden, if I was being honest, but I had settled because he'd said all the right things.

No, I wouldn't go out with Chris.

I would never settle again.

The handsome man from the restaurant came to mind. I'd felt those tingles just looking at him. I wanted those types of feelings if I ever chose to date again. I wanted the tingles.

As I waited, I turned to watch the pedestrians as they

passed by the café. The wind was blowing, and on the sidewalk, people pulled their coats around them. Soon Thanksgiving would be here. The Macy's Thanksgiving Day parade was one of my favorites. Then Christmas would be here, which was truly magical time in New York City.

My phone vibrated with a notification, and I smiled. Okay, so I *sort of* met someone on the dating site while I was researching my marketing pitch to Carothers Media.

Mister_Mystery: *So… I took your advice.*

Well, that was intriguing. I bit my lip as I replied.

Me: *On?*

The three little dots appeared, and I waited for his reply.

Mister_Mystery: *I ate at the hot dog stand on the corner of Madison and 55th. You were right.*

He'd actually taken my advice.

I looked up as a plate was placed in front of me. Chris gave me a pleasant smile. "It's good to see you happy."

I put my phone away and gave him a polite smile. "Thanks, it's been a good day." Changing the topic, I gestured to the food. "Looks amazing. Thanks, Chris."

Chris nodded, tucking his blond hair behind his ear. "Let me know if you need anything."

"I will."

He lingered for a second before turning and walking away.

Yeah, it seemed crazy that I would give anyone online the time of day after my experiences with Braden. But there was something about Mister Mystery. It was hard to explain, but it felt honest.

I shrugged; maybe I was crazy.

We didn't know any identifiable details about each other. And we had no plans to meet. Maybe it was just the fact that there was no pressure... ever. We were just two people conversing. It had been nice to tell someone else about Braden's betrayal. Mister Mystery had also gone through a nasty divorce a year ago. We'd both been betrayed by the one person we should have been able to trust more than anything. I made sure that I didn't get enough details of my circumstances that he could find me through an internet search. He'd been similarly vague. The only thing I knew about his location was that he lived in New York City.

I felt my phone vibrate again, but I ignored it as I ate. Later, when I got home, I would check it. Chris was acting a little weird, coming up to my table, asking if I needed more water, and then walking away again. It made no sense; my water glass was clearly full.

After the third time, I decided that maybe I should take a break from eating there for a bit. If he was working up the courage to ask me out, I wasn't interested.

When I dated again, it was going to be for the right reasons. My therapist had helped me break past the thinking that every man who walks the Earth is evil. Over the last two years, I had grown substantially.

After paying my bill, I left the restaurant with only a quick wave good-bye to Chris. As I walked home, someone had a fire burning their fireplace. I loved the smell; it made me think of cozy nights curled up in front of dancing flames. I turned the corner and saw the blue awning of my building.

At first, I'd rented an apartment in a neighborhood in Brooklyn that wasn't the safest. After my first raise, I moved to a studio just west of Central Park, which I loved—all three hundred and sixty-nine square feet of it. The building had a doorman, which was a must for me. It added an additional layer of security knowing someone was there watching who came and went.

I smiled and gave a small wave. "Hey, Clay."

"Ms. DeRoss. Welcome home."

"Thank you. How's your wife?"

He chuckled. "Ready to have that baby. Any day now. The doctor is going to induce if he doesn't come by Monday."

"Aww, I can't wait to see pictures."

He tipped his hat. "I'm sure I'll have plenty."

I climbed the three flights of stairs instead of waiting for the elevator. I entered my apartment and set my stuff on my little table for two just inside the door. I took off my coat and put it on the back of the chair. It always felt good to walk through the door on a Friday.

I was filled with a sense of accomplishment. My apartment was tiny, but it was mine. The kitchen, living room, and bedroom were all one room. I had a small bathroom, which was its own space, thankfully. There were a few closets across from the kitchen. The building had a common laundry area, which was fantastic.

I kicked off my shoes and flopped onto my loveseat. Against the far wall, I had a dresser and a twin bed. Since it was just me, there was no need to waste the space with anything bigger.

I pulled out my phone, wondering what Mister Mystery had sent me. The last message had been about trying the hot dog stand I suggested.

Mister_Mystery: *Curious... how many hot dogs have you consumed to determine which hot dog cart was best?*

I laughed out loud. That would be a random detail he would ask about.

Me: *Sorry, I was eating dinner. I am ashamed to admit it, but let's just say I had to take up walking a few extra blocks every day to stay in my current pants size.*

His response was almost immediate.

Mister_Mystery: *That is impressive. My turn... there's a coffeeshop you should try. It's on 10th Ave. between 56th and 57th called Rex. Best coffee in town.*

That wasn't far from me. I wondered if Mister Mystery lived nearby. It was oddly exciting that we might be in the same place at the same time without ever knowing it.

Me: *I'll give it a go and let you know in the next week or so.*

Mister_Mystery: *Good. I'll be back shortly. Business calls.*

I wondered what he did. There were a lot of times Mister Mystery had business calls at random hours, so I wasn't sure if he would come back or not. Sometimes he'd disappear until the next day.

I typed out a quick response.

Me: *Have a good night.*

That was most likely a "talk to you tomorrow." I closed out of the *Lots of Fish in the Sea* dating app. First, the name had to go. It was terrible, and I had that noted as part of my presentation. The one feature I enjoyed was that the app allowed for platforms to be created. It was more than a dating network which wasn't being capitalized on.

Finally, I turned on the television, found the original, black-and-white version of Casablanca on cable, and settled in for the evening.

Would I ever find the true love?

Other Books by Kristin Mayer

Available Now

The Trust Series
Trust Me
Love Me
Promise Me

Full-length novels in the TRUST series are also available in audio from Tantor Media.

The Effect Series
Ripple Effect
Domino Effect

Timeless Love Series
Untouched Perfection
Flawless Perfection
Tempting Perfection

An Exposed Heart Series
Intoxicated by You
Wrecked for You
Changed by You

Full-length novels in the EXPOSED HEARTS Series are also available in audio from Audible.

The Twisted Fate Series
White Lies
Black Truth

Standalone Novels
Innocence
Bane
Whispered Promises
Predestined Hearts (co-written with Kelly Elliott)

Coming Soon
Unexpected Love – New standalone novel
Play Me – Joint collaboration with Kelly Elliott